KENNER   FOREST PARK PUBLIC LIBRARY

Under m

P9-BZC-684

32026002656780

KENNER   Kenner, Julie.

Under my skin.

SEP - - 2015   32026002656780

$16.00

DATE			

FOREST PARK PUBLIC LIBRARY

BAKER & TAYLOR

BY J. KENNER

THE STARK TRILOGY

Release Me

Claim Me

Complete Me

STARK EVER AFTER NOVELLAS

Take Me

Have Me

Play My Game

STARK INTERNATIONAL NOVELS

Say My Name

On My Knees

Under My Skin

MOST WANTED SERIES

Wanted

Heated

Ignited

under my skin

under my skin

A STARK NOVEL

J. KENNER

BANTAM BOOKS   NEW YORK

FOREST PARK PUBLIC LIBRARY

SEP   2015

FOREST PARK, IL

Under My Skin is a work of fiction. Names, characters, places, and incidents either are the product of the author's imagination or are used fictitiously. Any resemblance to actual persons, living or dead, events, or locales is entirely coincidental.

A Bantam Books Trade Paperback Original

Copyright © 2015 by Julie Kenner
Excerpt of *Dirtiest Secret* copyright © 2015 by Julie Kenner

All rights reserved.

Published in the United States by Bantam Books, an imprint of Random House, a division of Penguin Random House LLC, New York.

BANTAM BOOKS and the HOUSE colophon are registered trademarks of Penguin Random House LLC.

This book contains an excerpt from the forthcoming book *Dirtiest Secret* by J. Kenner. This excerpt has been set for this edition only and may not reflect the final content of the forthcoming edition.

Library of Congress Cataloging-in-Publication Data
Kenner, Julie.
Under my skin: a Stark novel / J. Kenner.
pages cm—(Stark; 6)
ISBN 978-0-553-39523-5
eBook ISBN 978-0-553-39524-2
1. Man-woman relationships—Fiction. 2. Sexual dominance and submission—Fiction. I. Title.
PS3611.E665U53 2015
813'.6—dc23   2015023217

Printed in the United States of America on acid-free paper

randomhousebooks.com

9 8 7 6 5 4 3 2 1

under my skin

one

There is peace in these moments between sleep and wakefulness. In the soft minutes that seem to stretch into hours, warm and comforting like a gift bestowed by a benevolent universe.

This is a world of dreams, and right now it is safe. It is right. And I want to stay here, wrapped tight in the comfort of his arms.

But dreams often turn into nightmares, and as I move through the corridors of sleep, dark fingers of fear reach out to me. My pulse pounds and my breath comes too shallow. I curl toward him, craving his touch, but he is not there, and I sit bolt upright, my skin clammy from a sheen of sweat. My heart pounding so hard I will surely crack a rib.

Jackson.

I'm awake now, alone and disoriented as a wild panic cuts through me. I'm afraid, but I don't remember why.

Too quickly though, it all rushes back, and as the memories return with wakefulness, I long to slide back into oblivion. Because whatever horror my mind would fabricate in dreams couldn't be any worse than the reality that now surrounds me, cold and stark.

A reality in which the world is crumbling down around my ears.

A reality in which the man I love desperately is suspected of murder.

With a sigh, I press a hand to my cheek, my memory sharpening as I shake off the haze of slumber. He'd brushed a kiss over my cheek before slipping out of our warm cocoon and into the chilly morning air. At the time I'd been content to stay behind, snuggled tight in the blankets that still held his scent and radiated the lingering heat from his body.

Now I wish I had roused myself when he did, because I don't want to be alone. Alone is when panic creeps closer.

Alone is when I'm certain that I will lose him.

Alone is what I fear.

And yet even as the thought enters my mind, the solitude is shattered. The bedroom door bursts open, and a dark-haired, blue-eyed bundle of sunshine races toward me, then leaps onto the bed and starts bouncing, her energy so vibrant I laugh despite myself. "Sylvie! Sylvie! I made toast with Uncle Jackson!"

"Toast? Really?" It's work, but I manage to keep my voice perky and upbeat despite the fact that fear still clings to me like cobwebs. I give Ronnie a quick, tight hug, but my attention isn't on her anymore. Instead, I am focused entirely on the man in the doorway.

He stands casually on the threshold, a wooden tray in his hands. His coal black hair is untidy from sleep, and he sports two days of beard stubble. He wears flannel pajama bottoms and a pale gray T-shirt. By every indication, he is a man who has just awakened. A man with nothing on his mind but the morning and breakfast and the bits of news that fill the paper tucked under his arm.

But dear god, he is so much more. He is power and tenderness, strength and control. He is the man who has colored my days and illuminated my nights.

Jackson Steele. The man I love. The man I once foolishly tried to leave. The man who grabbed hold and pulled me back, then slayed my demons, and in doing so claimed my heart.

But it is those very demons that have brought us to this moment.

Because Robert Cabot Reed was one of those demons, and now Reed is dead. Someone entered his Beverly Hills home and bashed his head in with a decorative piece of carved ivory.

And I can't help but fear that the someone was Jackson, and that soon he will have to pay the price.

We arrived in Santa Fe late yesterday afternoon, both of us feeling light and happy and eager. Jackson had intended to spend the weekend with Ronnie and then go to court on Monday in order to set a hearing on his petition to formally claim paternity and establish that he is Ronnie's father in the eyes of the law. That plan, however, was sideswiped when local detectives met our plane, then informed Jackson that he was wanted back in Beverly Hills for questioning in Reed's murder.

The afternoon shifted from a happy, laid-back reunion to a frantic flurry of activity, with calls between New Mexico and California, lawyers squabbling, deals churning.

At the end of it all, Jackson was permitted to stay the weekend, on condition that he go straight to the Beverly Hills Police Department Monday morning. In truth, Jackson could have garnered much more time—unless the police wanted to actually arrest, their leverage was limited—but his attorney wisely advised against it. After all, playing games isn't the way to win either police cooperation or public opinion. And while we don't yet know what physical evidence the police have collected, there's no lack of motive for Jackson to have killed Reed.

Motive.

The word sounds so clean compared to Reed, who was a dirty, horrible man.

Not only had he abused and tormented me when I was a teen, but he'd recently threatened to release some of the vile photographs that he'd taken of me back then if I didn't convince Jackson to stop trying to block a movie that Reed wanted green-lit. A movie that would expose secrets and deceptions—and that would thrust Ronnie, an innocent child, into the middle of a very public, very messy scandal.

Did Jackson want the movie stopped? Hell, yes.

Did he want to protect me from the horror of seeing those pictures flashed across the internet? Damn right.

Did he want to punish Reed for the things he'd done to me so many years ago? Absolutely.

Did Jackson kill Reed?

As for that one—I truly don't know.

More than that, I'm not allowed to ask. According to Charles Maynard, Jackson's attorney, it is very likely that the police will interview me, too. And there is no privilege for girlfriends. Which means Charles wants me to be able to honestly say that Jackson was under strict orders from his attorneys, and that he didn't say anything to me about whether he did or did not kill Reed. Not yes, not no, not maybe. Just nothing.

Nothing.

I know what that means, of course. Nothing is code for probably.

Nothing is code for *that way you can't later incriminate him.*

Nothing is code for *we're trying to forestall the worst.*

Just thinking about it makes me tremble, and I sit up, my back against the headboard and my pillow tight in my arms as I watch the man I love set the tray and the newspaper on the small table tucked in beneath the still-curtained window.

It's a small task, but he performs it with confident precision, just as he does so much else in his life. Jackson is not a man to let circumstance get the better of him, and he is not a man who will let an injury go unavenged. He is a man who protects what he loves, and I know with unwavering certainty that the two things he loves most in this world are his daughter and me.

He would, I'm certain, kill to protect either of us, and that's a thought that sends a little shiver of pleasure through me. But it's tempered by fear and dread. Because Jackson would go even further; he'd sacrifice himself if he thought it would protect us. And I'm horribly afraid that's exactly what he has done.

And, honestly, if Jackson ends up behind bars, I don't know if I'm strong enough to bear the guilt.

He comes over to sit on the edge of the bed and is immediately assaulted by a three-year-old cyclone demanding to be tickled. He smiles and complies, then looks at me. But the smile doesn't quite warm his ice blue eyes.

I reach for him and take his hand in mine. How many times in the hours since we arrived have I searched for the perfect words to soothe him? But there are no perfect words. I can only do my best. I can only just be here.

"Anything about you in there?" I ask with a nod to the paper that he's left on the table.

"No, but since that's the local Santa Fe paper I wouldn't expect there to be."

I frown. "Do you want me to look?" I'm not talking about

the local paper, and he knows it. I'm offering to hop online and scope out the various gossip sites from back home, especially those that focus on Los Angeles, Beverly Hills, and all things murder and celebrity.

He shakes his head, and his response only deepens my frown. He told me yesterday that he didn't want anything to mar this time with Ronnie, and I get that. But we've already got the cloud of a murder hanging over us—and knowing the gossip means being prepared.

I argued as much last night, but I'm willing to make my case again. In fact, I'm opening my mouth to do just that when he presses his finger to my lips. "I looked this morning," he says gently. "There's nothing."

"Really?"

"Really," he confirms. He squeezes my hand, then holds out his free one for Ronnie. "I got on my tablet and looked while this little one was making toast. Didn't I?" he asks, as she scrambles into his lap. "Didn't I?" he repeats, then tickles her until she squeals and says, "Yes! Yes!" even though she clearly has no idea what we're talking about.

"Your witness seems a little tainted to me." I fight a smile. He's such a natural dad, and the ease with which he's slid into the role awes me a bit.

"Maybe. But the testimony is all true." He kisses the top of her head, then pulls her close, the action so full of wild, heartbreaking emotion that it almost shatters me.

"You should go on outside with Grammy," Jackson tells the little girl. "Fred's probably wondering where you are."

At the mention of the puppy, her blue eyes, so like Jackson's, go wide. "You'll come, too?"

"Absolutely," he promises. "Let me talk to Syl while she drinks her coffee and then I'll come find you."

"And eat your toast?" she asks, her earnest question aimed at me.

"I can't wait for the toast," I say. "I bet it's the best toast ever."

"Yup," she confirms, then shoots out of the room like a rocket.

Jackson watches her go, and I watch Jackson. When he turns back, he catches me eyeing him, then smiles sheepishly. "It's hard to believe sometimes," he says. "That she's really mine, I mean."

I think about the little girl's dark hair and blue eyes. Her cleverness coupled with a vibrant personality and fierce determination. "Not hard to believe at all."

I had hoped to coax a smile, but still he just looks sad.

"There was really nothing?"

"I promise." I must look dubious, because he continues. "The police aren't going to release names. Not until an arrest. Or until it drags on so long they feel like they need to get ahead of a leak."

"And you know this because of your vast experience in the criminal underworld?"

"Years of watching television," he corrects. "But you know I'm right."

I nod. It makes sense. Plus, the police don't yet know everything. As far as I'm aware, they know only about Jackson's determination to block the movie. The blackmail and Ronnie's existence remain hidden.

That, however, doesn't lessen my fear. Because if—no, *when*—those come to light, it will look worse for Jackson.

"Are you okay?" I ask. It's a stupid question, and it hangs there, as awkward and inadequate as I feel.

He shakes his head, just a little. "No," he admits. He brushes his fingers lightly over my cheek, his attention on my face, his eyes searching mine. At first, he looks lost, but that soon changes as heat and need build in his eyes. Both are directed at me, and neither is a question. There is no permission to be granted, no request to be made. He simply slides his hand around to cup the back of my neck and pulls me toward him, then captures my mouth with his.

I open to him without hesitation, not just my lips, but my entire body. I am his, wholly and completely, and however he needs me.

He deepens the kiss, his tongue teasing and tasting. His mouth hot and desperate against mine.

We didn't make love last night, too exhausted from both travel and the emotional whirlwind. Too wrapped up in seeing family and spending time with Ronnie.

And that is part of why I now expect more than the wildness of this kiss. I expect the crush of his hands upon my breasts. An explosion of breath as he pushes me back on the mattress, then rises to slam the door shut and flip the latch. The shift of the mattress as he returns, and the sound of ripping cotton as he strips me of my panties.

I anticipate the feel of his body over mine. Of my wrists bound tight by his T-shirt that I wear in lieu of pajamas after he yanks it over my head and uses it to constrain me.

I imagine the tightness in my inner thighs as he roughly spreads my legs, and the quick burn of friction as he enters me hard in one thrust and then loses himself to this wild passion that he needs. That he craves.

I expect all this because I know him. Because his world has spun out of control, and Jackson is a man who not only needs control, but who takes it. He is not a man to be swept up in the tide, battered by the rise and fall of circumstance. He fights back. He wins. He *takes*.

I channeled control into sex.

He'd told me that once. And he's shown me as much many, many times.

And yet he doesn't come to me. He doesn't take. He doesn't claim.

Fear slithers over me as he releases me, then stands. He doesn't meet my eyes, but simply turns and moves from the bed to the window, then drags his fingers through his hair.

"Jackson?"

He doesn't react. He simply stands there, his back to me, his shoulders slumped. And I am certain that he didn't hear me, because how could he? Right then he is miles away, not just a few short feet across the bare wooden floor.

The table is in front of him. My coffee and toast are still there, untouched. He pushes the tray aside and opens the curtains, letting in the morning light.

We are in Betty Wiseman's house, Ronnie's maternal great-grandmother. The family is well-to-do, but this New Mexico home is a small getaway, a "mere" five thousand square feet. Jackson and I are in one of the guest rooms that overlook the back of the property. The view I'd seen yesterday evening was magnificent—the rocky, rising terrain of the mountains, dressed up in their fall colors. The verdant grasses and evergreens. The browns and reds of stones and foliage. And, of course, the vivid blue sky, so wide and resplendent that it seems to slide into and fill your soul.

But from where I still sit on the bed, stiff and awkward and just a little scared, I see only a small section of the covered patio and a view of the side of the house. I'm not at the proper angle to see the beautiful panorama that Jackson is looking at right now. Instead, our perspectives are entirely different, and that small reality eats at me.

I lick my lips, feeling distant and impotent and lost. And, yes, a little bit angry, too. Because, dammit, I don't want to see him in pain, not if I can soothe him.

But that's the heart of it, isn't it? That's really my greatest fear.

Not that I'm unable to soothe Jackson, but that he would rather bear this burden alone.

Screw it.

I toss the covers aside and walk to him, his T-shirt that I slept in brushing my thighs. I slide my arms around his waist from behind so that I am pressed against him, my cheek against his back. I breathe in the scent of him, male and musk and just the tiniest bit of fabric softener. It's clean, maybe even a little bit domestic. But on Jackson, it's also very, very sexy.

My hands are at his waist, and it would be so easy to slide them down. To stroke him and make him hard. To play and coax. To seduce and please.

To make him so hot and so hard that he wants nothing but me, can think of nothing but me. To tease him until he picks me up and throws me onto the bed in a violent explosion that not only consumes us both but destroys the shadows that have crept in between us, banishing them with fire and heat and light.

But even that's not what I want. Not really. What I want— what I need—is for Jackson to come to me. To use me as he has in the past to soothe his wounds and make himself whole.

So instead of sliding my hand down to close around his cock, I simply hold still, clinging to this man who I love and need. And hoping against hope that he is not slipping away from me.

A moment passes, and then another. I hear the dog barking on the back lawn and the high-pitched squeal of Ronnie's laughter followed by the lower tones of her great-grandmother and Stella, the housekeeper-turned-nanny.

Jackson is perfectly still, but then his hands rise to his waist to close over mine, so that as I hug him from behind, he is holding me in place. I close my eyes, relishing the strength of his touch. But then he very gently pulls my hands apart and steps out of the circle of my arms.

I hug myself tight against the loss of his warmth. But it's

no use. I am chilled to the bone. Lost, angry, afraid. And very, very alone.

He goes and sits on the edge of the bed, then scrubs his hands over his face. When he gazes up at me, he looks so tired that all of my anger and insecurity seems to spill out of me, and all I want to do is console him. I go to him, dropping to the ground in front of him and pressing my hands to his knees.

His smile, though tremulous, warms me, and when he gently brushes my cheek with his thumb, I almost weep with relief.

"Oh, hell," he finally says. "I'm a fucking mess."

"A bit," I say, and am rewarded with just a hint of a smile. "But you'll get through this. *We'll* get through it."

"All I wanted was to take my daughter home."

His words seem to twist inside me, as if they are just slightly off-kilter. It takes me a moment to realize why. "Wanted?" I repeat.

"I called Amy first thing this morning." His voice is flat and emotionless, as if he is working very hard to keep it that way.

"Oh." Amy Brantley is his family law attorney in Santa Fe. She's the one who filed his petition to establish paternity and parental rights. And although I have yet to meet her in person, I know that she's the one who will be setting the hearing on that petition as soon as possible. "So what did she say? When are you setting a court date?"

I see a shadow in his eyes. "We're not. We're going to wait."

"Wait? But . . ." I try to gather my thoughts even as I realize that I should have expected this. Because I know what this means. This means he doesn't think he'll be around to take care of her.

"Oh, god, Jackson." I don't mean for it to, but my voice is full of dread and fear.

"No," he says, then repeats it more firmly. "*No.* I'm not giving in. I'm not folding. Not even close. But I'm also not taking risks with my little girl. What if the worst were to happen and I end up in a jail cell? Megan may be her legal guardian right now, but she won't be once my rights are established. Would a California court send Ronnie back to New Mexico? To Megan? A former guardian with a host of mental health issues who's checked herself into a center while she tries to get better? Or to Betty, an elderly great-grandmother? Maybe. But more likely she'll end up in foster care. I can't risk that. I won't risk that."

I want to protest. To point out how much this means to him. To beg him to believe that he'll get through this. But I fear that saying those words will only highlight the extent of his loss. So all I say is, "I'm sorry."

"Me, too."

I want to slide into his embrace and hold him close. I want to lose myself in him. I want to breathe in his scent and let the feel of him erase all my fears.

But he is not reaching for me, and I can't bring myself to move through this dark cloud and into his arms, because what if he pushes me away?

Instead, I do the opposite. I stand, then force a smile. "All right, then. So what's the plan? You have to be in Beverly Hills in the morning, right? So what time are we leaving here?"

He looks almost relieved at the shift in conversation. "This afternoon. I want some face time with Charles and the new attorney before I walk into the lions' den tomorrow," he says, referring to Charles Maynard, his attorney back home, as well as the kick-ass criminal defense attorney that Charles has promised to retain.

"Have you told Grayson and Darryl?" I ask. Grayson Leeds is the head pilot for the Stark International fleet, and when Damien offered Jackson the use of one of the smaller jets, he also offered Grayson's services as pilot, with Darryl, a new hire, coming on as co-pilot. Originally, the men were simply going to make the two-hour flight, drop us in New Mexico, and then return to California. But when the police showed up with the news that Jackson needed to return to Beverly Hills for questioning, Grayson and Darryl stayed. Now, they're holed up in two of the guest rooms after having enjoyed a night of the Wisemans' hospitality.

"I just told them," Jackson says. "They'll be ready when we are. I'm shooting to get out of here right after lunch."

"Then this room isn't where you need to be." I glance toward the window, then offer him my hand and tug him to his feet. "Go spend some time with your daughter, Jackson Steele." I reach up and stroke his cheek, his beard stubble scratchy against my hand. "Just a bit today, but that's okay. You'll be spending a lot more time with her very soon."

For a moment, I think he's going to argue. Then he nods. "Are you coming?"

"I'm going to shower first and get dressed. And," I add, picking up the now-cold toast, "I can't go out there until I've eaten the best toast ever."

He actually laughs a bit, and I'm proud of my rather lame joke.

I watch him go, then shut the door behind him before returning to the window and waiting for him to appear on the lawn. It takes a few minutes, but he finally shows, and as I watch, he calls to Ronnie. Both she and the puppy lope toward him, and he scoops her up and swings her around, his expression glowing.

My heart twists. Because I know that his happiness will be fleeting. And I fear it will get worse before it gets better.

More than that, I fear that it won't get better at all.

My phone starts to ring just as I'm stepping out of the shower. I don't recognize the number, and I almost let it roll to voice mail, but then go ahead and answer it, just in case it's my best friend, Cass, calling from a friend's line, or Charles calling from another attorney's office. Or even my boss, Damien Stark, calling from a hotel with Nikki after a spur-of-the-moment getaway.

Of course it's none of those people.

Instead, the voice on the other end of the line belongs to my father.

"Sylvia. Honey, we need to talk."

I cringe, his use of the endearment grating on me as much as his tone. Like he cares. Like he actually gives a shit about me.

I know better.

I know he's only calling me because Jackson forced my dad to confront a truth that he'd avoided since I was fourteen—that Robert Cabot Reed had sucked the marrow out of me, and my father had handed me to the bastard on a platter and then looked the other way.

"Sylvia," he prompts. "Sylvia, talk to me."

"This isn't a good time." My voice is tight, and I can barely squeeze the words out.

"I've left at least a dozen messages. You haven't called me back."

"And so you thought you would trick me by calling from an unfamiliar number?"

"What choice do I have? I need to talk to you."

"*You* need?" The words hang in the air, dark and twisted. Two simple syllables, and yet they seem to sum up my entire, horrible childhood.

"We need," he corrects immediately. "*We* need to talk. About Reed. About what happened. About those photographs he threatened you with."

"I can't." I'm shaking my head, wishing I could block out everything he is saying. Trying to push back the memories he is invoking. But it's no use. The floor is shifting beneath me, and I reach for the counter to steady myself.

"You can't keep ignoring me."

Yes. I can. But I can't manage the words. Not then. Not with the way my throat is closing up and the room is turning gray and the floor is starting to angle sideways, as if to let those horrible memories roll more easily toward me.

"We have to talk, Sylvia. We have to." His voice sounds miles away, as if it is just a noise and has nothing to do with me. And I don't want to hear it anymore.

I can't. I can't, I can't, I can't.

I'm not sure if I'm actually speaking those words or if I'm just screaming them in my head. Somehow, though, I manage to jam my finger hard against the proper button to end the call before the phone tumbles from my hand. My knees give out, and suddenly I'm on the ground, my legs pulled right up against my chest. I close my eyes and squeeze them tight and rock back and forth as I fight the panic and the memories that are rising fast to consume me.

I hate this—the terror. This sense of being lost. Of being out of control.

Of being thrust back into pain and memories without any warning at all.

If I'd known it was him, I could have prepared. Could have steeled myself.

Could you? Would you? Or would you have just hid from his words? From his voice?

My chest is tight with the weight of the truth. Because I would have hid. If I had my way, I'd hide from my father for the rest of eternity.

I take deep breaths and I tell myself to get a grip. He's gone. It's over. And I can handle this.

More than that, I *have* to handle this.

It hasn't yet been a week since Jackson told my father what Robert Cabot Reed did to me. Not that my dad didn't already have some idea. He was the one who'd set me up with

Reed as a teen, after all. Who'd accepted exorbitant amounts of money from Reed in exchange for my services, supposedly as a model, but that damn sure wasn't the extent of it.

And it was my father who'd ignored my pleas to stop the photo sessions.

So, yeah, my dad knew what went on in Reed's studio, but he'd never really faced it. Not until Jackson forced him to not only acknowledge the past, but to look at the present. A present in which Reed was blackmailing me, threatening to release those horrible, ugly, intimate photos to the press if I didn't convince Jackson to quit blocking his movie.

Since that night, my father has repeatedly called me, and I've repeatedly ignored him. And that's not going to stop now. As far as I'm concerned, that man stopped being my father when he drove me to Reed's studio the first time. And if he's calling to apologize, I really don't give a damn. And if he's calling to ask for forgiveness, that's not something I'm willing to grant.

I shake out my arms, then slap my cheeks lightly as if I'm a trauma victim who needs to be revived. Because when you get right down to it, that's exactly what I am.

I have to get my shit together, because I cannot, cannot, *cannot* let Jackson see me like this. Not because I'm afraid that he won't comfort me, but because I am certain that he will. He might be pushing me away from his problems and fears, but he won't ignore mine. On the contrary, my pain would slide in and mingle with his own, and I can't put this on him. Not now. Not today.

But even though I know that keeping silent about this call is absolutely the right decision, I can't help but feel as if my silence is the first step on a dark path leading me away from Jackson. And if I don't fight to keep him by my side, I'm going to lose him to the shadows.

two

"*Ms. Brooks?*"

Grayson's voice breaks through the cotton that seems to fill my head and I sit bolt upright, my heart pounding in my chest as panic crashes over me. "What?" I demand. "Are we okay? Why are you here? Aren't you supposed to be flying this thing?"

I don't like air travel—it makes me queasy and nervous and unsettled. About the only thing I do like, in fact, is the moment after landing when I realize that I've miraculously survived being hurtled through the air in a giant steel canister. So when Grayson told us that there were storms over New Mexico and Arizona, I'd succumbed to pressure from him and Jackson and taken a couple of motion sickness pills. Normally, that would just make me a little bit sleepy. But at lunch Stella had brought out a pitcher of sangria, and since I was already hot and sweaty from playing in the yard with

Jackson and Ronnie, I'd gulped down more than I should have.

Which meant that I was already drowsy when we'd climbed on board. Once the pills hit my system, I was a goner. And being startled awake only fed my phobia.

"It's okay. Everything is fine." Jackson's voice is soft and soothing, and I force myself to relax. We're in the jet, and I'd been sound asleep. Now Jackson eases me against him, and I gratefully comply, thinking that maybe air travel isn't such a bad thing if it means that Jackson will hold me close and safe, his arm tight around my shoulders.

I sigh, cherishing the comfort that he's offering. I have said nothing to him about the grayness that seems to fill the space between us. Instead, I am clinging like a beggar to each and every subtle connection. Every brush of his fingers against mine. Every press of his hand upon my back as he guides me. Every soft glance, every gentle smile.

It's not enough, though. We have always fit together, Jackson and I, like pieces in a puzzle. But now it feels as if someone has bent the pieces and the fit is awkward and slightly off, and that disconnect is making me crazy. I don't think I can stand it much longer, and soon I'm going to have to confront him. To grab him hard and pull him back, and then demand to know why the hell he's so far away from me—and then hope that he doesn't run even further.

Not now, though. Right now, I just need to know why the pilot is crouched in front of me instead of in the cockpit where he belongs.

"Seriously," I demand as I narrow my eyes at Grayson, "why aren't you at the wheel or the stick or whatever they call it?"

"Darryl has it under control," Grayson assures me. "And I'm sorry to wake you, but there's a satellite call."

"Damien?"

"Trent," Jackson says. "I offered to handle it, but he insisted he needs to speak to you."

That's odd, and I force down the rising worry and tell myself that this isn't necessarily a big deal. After all, I call Damien all the time when he's flying. It's just one more method of communication. He probably needs a contact that Rachel can't find. Or wants me to run interference for him on one of his projects if he ended up double-booked. Something mundane and easily handled.

Something not a crisis. Because honestly, at the moment, my crisis quota is all filled up.

Grayson returns with a headset for me and I put it on, then wait for him to return to the cockpit and patch the call through.

A few seconds later, I hear Trent Leiter come on the line. "You sitting down?"

"I'm in a plane, Trent. What do you think?"

"Sorry. Sorry." His words spill nervously on top of each other. And since Trent isn't easily rattled, that alone is enough to make me stand up and start to pace the length of the cabin.

What? Jackson mouths.

But all I can do is shrug. "Dammit, Trent. What's going on?"

"Oh, hell," he says, and I can practically picture the way his shoulders slump. Trent's not a bad-looking guy, but neither is he the type who commands a room. His asset is a boyish charm that takes clients by surprise. He knows how to work it, too, getting friendly with them in sports bars and at Lakers' games. Reeling them in with a few beers and the latest player stats.

So the fact that I can actually hear the nervous discomfort in his voice lets me know that whatever he has to say is bad. More than that, I'm positive that this is about the resort, and my brief fantasy that he was calling so I could hold some investor's hand during a walk-through in Century City has flown completely out the window.

So, yeah, I stand. *"Trent,"* I demand as I start to pace.

"It's out," he says. "One damn leak, and it's everywhere."

I'm almost to the closed cockpit door, and now I turn back, my eyes immediately meeting Jackson's. He starts to stand, obviously concerned by the look on my face, but I shake my head. "What?" I ask, my voice tense and tight. "What's out?"

"It was an article in *The Business Round-Up,*" he says, referring to a small local paper that serves downtown Los Angeles. "I don't know how they got the story, but it was on their website this morning, and the tabloids picked it up a few hours later, and now it's pretty much everywhere."

"What is?" I repeat. "Come on, Trent, just spit it out." But even as I'm talking, I'm hurrying back to my seat, then rummaging in my bag for my tablet so that I can check out the *Round-Up* myself. I try to get a connection, then remember that we told Grayson not to worry about booting up the wifi—the flight's only a couple of hours, and we'd plummet headfirst into reality soon enough.

"The article says that the investors are worried. They were already antsy because of Lost Tides," he says, referring to a competing resort that is being developed in Santa Barbara, just a few hours away from my resort on Santa Cortez. It's a huge thorn in my side because the developers are keeping the details under wraps in anticipation of a big PR event as they get closer to opening. But I know enough to know that the resort was inspired by my idea for Cortez. And, frankly, that pisses me off.

Trent clears his throat and continues. "Now they're saying that if the Cortez resort's architect is a suspect in a murder, then maybe that's not the kind of project they want to fund."

"*Fuck.*"

I'm not sure when I sat back down, but all I know is that I am seated, and Jackson is leaning forward, his expression concerned.

Tell me, he demands silently.

And this time, I do. "It's out," I whisper. "It's leaked. They know you're a suspect." I increase my volume for Trent. "How did this happen?"

"Best guess is some tenacious reporter has a mole in the Beverly Hills PD. If you're looking to report hot celebrity gossip, that's the place to flash a little cash and see whose pockets need lining."

"Shit." I draw a breath and try to stay calm. Beside me, Jackson looks like he could very easily put his fist through the plane's hull. Since that thought really doesn't jibe well with my fear of flying, I take one of his hands in my own and squeeze. What I want is to get off the phone. To toss this damn headset across the cabin and climb into Jackson's lap. To hold tight to him and let him hold tight to me, and simply breathe.

But even that's not true, because I want so much more. I want his mouth on me. His hands touching me. I want him to make me forget. To erase my fears.

And I want to do the same for him.

But this is not the place for that—a small jet with a thin door between the simple eight-seat cabin and the cockpit.

And, truly, what I fear even more is that Jackson would push me away. Gently, and with a soft touch and a kiss. But effective and painful nonetheless.

Frustrated, I stand again, too antsy to sit still, as Trent says tentatively, "Syl? Are you there? Did I lose you?"

"I'm here. Does Damien know?"

"He knows."

At the mention of his half-brother's name, Jackson rises,

too. He brushes his fingers over my shoulder in a silent gesture of support, then goes to the back of the plane. He's not pacing so much as imploding. As if all of his anger and energy is being sucked into himself. He needs to lash out—I know that he does. And I both fear and welcome the explosion when we finally do get the hell off this plane. He needs to explode, I think. And, dammit, so do I.

"So?" I prompt. "What's Damien's take?"

"He's concerned," Trent says. "He's got reason to be. The investors pull out and you've got a mess on your hands. He's trying to do damage control right now."

"How?"

"Dallas is in town—the *Round-Up* actually contacted him." Dallas Sykes is one of the resort's primary investors. And any story that touches on the bad boy heir to the department store empire is bound to go viral. His dating escapades are constant tabloid fodder, and he's been in the media spotlight since he was a kid. Everything from fights to over-the-top parties to reckless driving, not to mention more than a few times when he disappeared off the planet altogether, presumably holed up with some willing female.

"I should call Damien," I say.

"No need. He's already doing the drink-and-soothe routine. I told him I'd call you."

"Is Aiden around?"

"I'm the one who spotted the article," Trent says testily, and I cringe.

"Sorry. I didn't mean anything." I get why he's touchy. Trent's in charge of projects in the Southern California area. By rights, The Resort at Cortez should be his. But since the idea was mine in the first place, Damien put me in as project manager—and I report to Aiden Ward, the VP of Stark Real Estate Development, jumping over Trent entirely.

"Listen, I really do appreciate the heads-up."

"Yeah, well, I figured you'd want to get ahead of it. The resort's already on shaky ground, and I'd hate for you to lose it because of this. It's bullshit."

Lose the resort.

Lose the resort?

With an unpleasant jolt, I realize that I've had blinders on. I've been so focused on the possibility of Jackson ending up behind bars that it never occurred to me that the resort might slip through my fingers simply because Jackson's a suspect.

A thick, cold dread swirls inside me. I have done everything humanly possible to get Cortez off the ground. I've lived it, breathed it. Risked my heart for it.

I shake my head, vehemently. "No way in hell am I losing the resort. That is not even an option." But even as I say the words, I can't escape a growing terror. Because I can't control the media, and if the investors think Jackson is toxic, then all of my work just blows away, like so much dandelion fuzz.

"I didn't mean—" Trent begins.

"No." The word bursts out of me, red and ripe with panic.

"Syl." Jackson's voice is soft and firm. "Tell him it's time to get off the phone. We'll be back in LA soon. You are not losing this resort. Don't even think it."

Over the headset, I hear Trent clear his throat. "Syl?"

"I should go," I say robotically.

"Yeah, well, there's one more thing. It's not only the *Round-Up* that's got this. They were just the first."

"I know. You said."

"Yeah, but what I mean is that they're not just repeating that he's a suspect. They're speculating about motive and all that shit."

My stomach twists and I immediately reach for Jackson's hand. "Motive?" I fight the urge to bite my lower lip.

"The movie. The assault. Pretty much what you'd expect," he says, and I can practically hear him cringing. Honestly, I feel like cringing, too. Beside me, Jackson uses his left hand to fumble my tablet out of the seat pocket. He taps it, then curses when a signal doesn't magically appear.

"Listen, you can read it yourself as soon as you hit the ground, and Damien said to tell you that your meeting tonight will cover everything."

"Right. Fine. Sure."

"Are you okay?"

No. Not by a long shot. "I'm fine. I'll be fine. Thanks. Thanks for watching my back."

There is a pause, and then he says softly, his voice full of rough emotion, "What did you think, Sylvia? That I'd throw you to the wolves?"

"I, no—" I begin, but it doesn't matter. He's already hung up.

"Tell me," Jackson says, and I sum up the *Round-Up* article and tell him about Dallas.

"Fuck." The curse is heartfelt, and I silently second it. "And the rest? You said there was talk about motive."

"That's all I know. The movie. The assault. That's all Trent said. That, and the story's spreading." I press my palm gently against his leg. "We'll get through this," I say. "The resort. The trial. All of it."

I want him to repeat the words back to me. To press his hand over mine and gently squeeze my fingers. I want him to put his arm around me and pull me close and tell me that no matter what, we are in this together. I want to feel closer to him, but what I want apparently doesn't matter, because when Jackson lifts his head and faces me, it suddenly seems as if I'm looking through the wrong end of a telescope and things that should be close are suddenly very, very far away.

"Jackson?" His name is a whisper, but also a plea. And for a moment it goes unanswered. He sits there, stiff and distant, his expression hard, his eyes like arctic ice. A riffle of panic rises through me, and I actually clutch the armrests tight in defense against it. He's said nothing—done nothing—and yet I know with absolute certainty that Jackson is moving inexorably away from me. And I neither understand it nor know how to stop it.

I am about to cry out his name again, but then his shoulders sag and his posture relaxes. He glances at me, and I go weak with relief when I see that the ice in his eyes has melted.

He raises his hands, then drags his fingers through his hair as he bends forward so that his elbows are on his knees and his hands are on his head. "Christ, Syl, I've screwed everything up."

I freeze, just a little, as one possible meaning of his words slaps me hard across the face. *Does he mean that he killed Reed?*

And if so, where does that leave us?

I reach to press my hand against his shoulder, needing that physical contact almost as much as I need oxygen.

I don't make it.

Instead, in the next second, I'm screaming and clutching at the armrest as the tin can we are flying in bounces as if we are on a trampoline. My tote, which had been on the floor by my feet, goes airborne, smashes against the ceiling, then falls to the floor, its acrobatics punctuated by my own shrill screams.

The sound of my voice is broken by a harsh crackling. It's the intercom, and Grayson is speaking. "Sorry about that," he says as the plane levels out. "We hit one hell of an air pocket on descent, but everything's fine and we'll be on the ground in about fifteen minutes."

When he's finished, I gasp, then realize that I've been holding my breath. I try to let go of the armrest, but my hand is stuck fast. I'm still so flustered by our near-death experience, that for a moment I'm genuinely confused. Then rational thought returns, along with the realization that Jackson is holding tight to my hand. His thumb is gently stroking the back of my wrist, and he's murmuring softly to me. "It's okay, Syl. It's okay."

I draw in a shuddering breath, so full of relief and hope that my head feels light. "It's okay," he repeats as I turn and meet his eyes. Gently, he lifts my hand to his lips and kisses my fingers. "It's better now."

I sigh and nod, my heart still beating a wild rhythm in my chest.

He's comforting me, yes, and god knows I need it.

But that doesn't mean I believe him.

three

"Have you heard from Mr. Stark?" I'm surfing social media sites while I talk with Rachel Peters, Damien's weekend assistant. At the same time, I'm walking across the tarmac in front of Hangar J, one of Stark International's private hangars in the north field of the Santa Monica airport.

The company actually has ten hangars, as well as the Rec Room, which is what we call the large, nondescript building that houses the flight crews' offices, a kitchen and dining area, a well-stocked bar available to incoming passengers and crew, a huge recreation area with a pool table and giant television, and two private sleeping chambers that the crew has access to on an as-needed basis.

I'm heading that way now, a few minutes behind Jackson, who took off with Darryl on the promise of a drink. "It's almost happy hour," Darryl had said. "And frankly, you look like you could use one."

Since I needed to make this call, I promised to follow, and

then walked more slowly as I did my multitasking thing. I want time to scope out the social media flurry before I talk with Jackson. Because frankly, I think we both need to be prepared for the storm that's about to pummel us.

"I haven't heard a word from him," Rachel says in response to my question.

My work on The Resort at Cortez has taken me off Damien's desk more and more frequently, and as a result Rachel's weekend gig has spilled over into the week more than we'd initially expected. She's doing a good job, though, and Damien has made clear that I'm supposed to be grooming her to take over my responsibilities if and when I move to a full-time management position in the real estate division.

Since that is absolutely my goal, I'm all about the training. And the most important thing Rachel needs to realize is that you can't be Damien's assistant and not have your finger on the pulse of what's going on elsewhere in the company. Not have it and keep the job, anyway.

Which is why I prompt her with, "You haven't heard a word, but . . ."

"*But,*" she says, following my lead, "Dallas called about fifteen minutes ago asking if I could book him the suite at the Century Plaza."

"Did he? And what does that tell you?" I know what it tells me, and I mentally cross my fingers that Rachel understands, too.

"That he's not pulling out. At least not yet. And even if he is thinking about pulling out, he hasn't told Mr. Stark as much. But honestly, I think he's in for the long haul. Because taking advantage of Mr. Stark's hospitality and then cutting off the investment funds would only piss Mr. Stark off. And even a man like Dallas Sykes doesn't want to be on Damien Stark's bad side."

"Not bad," I say. "What else?"

"Well, the rest is a bit more dicey. I may be completely off base."

"That's the job, Rachel. A doormat assistant who can only do exactly what Mr. Stark tells her is no use at all."

"Right. Well, I don't think that Dallas is a very good barometer. About what the rest of the investors will do, I mean." Though her words are statements, her voice rises at the end, as if she's asking a question.

"Okay," I say, biting back a smile as I recall how nervous I was when I took over as Damien's primary assistant. "Why's that?"

"It's just that he's such a wild card. A tabloid fodder bad boy, you know? Which means the other investors might still pull out, especially in light of everything that happened today. Which means we're still fucked."

I laugh out loud at that final assessment, and she sucks in air on the other end of the line.

"I *so* wouldn't have said it that way to Mr. Stark."

"It's okay," I promise. "I get it." And frankly *"fucked"* pretty much sums it up.

I've got my earbuds in so I've been able to look at the web browser on my phone as we talk. And while I haven't scrolled down to read any of the actual articles, I've seen enough to know that Trent is right. This shit is everywhere. It's all doom and gloom, with everyone predicting that the investors are toast and the resort is doomed. And I'm certain that Jackson has seen it by now.

"Do you need me to send you Nigel's statement?"

"Nigel?" I repeat. I only know one Nigel. He's a friend of Damien's who works at the Pentagon and was a helpful contact earlier in the year when Stark Vacation Properties purchased Santa Cortez island, where the resort is being built. "Nigel Galway?"

"About the land mines."

I come to a dead stop on the tarmac. "Rachel, what the fuck are you talking about?"

"Trent didn't tell you?"

"Trent told me about the leaks about Jackson. About the speculation on motive. If you're referring to a metaphorical land mine, I'm right there with you. But otherwise, I need you to tell me what the hell we're talking about." I'm speaking very slowly and very distinctly.

My stomach is tight and my skin is clammy, and I have the very unpleasant feeling that I know where this is going—and it's not going anywhere good.

"The investors all got emails saying that Santa Cortez was seeded with land mines. Part of the military training operations."

"Shit. Fuck. *Damn*." The curses roll off my tongue. I take a deep breath. "Nigel made a statement?"

"Aiden and Damien talked to him about an hour ago—I can't believe Trent didn't tell you. I guess he figured it's been handled. And it has. Really. I mean, there might be blow-back, but—"

"I swear to god, Rachel, just back up and tell me what happened."

She does. Finally. Apparently the investors received a leaked copy of a Pentagon memo proposing to bury land mines on Santa Cortez island back when it was being used as a naval training facility. That proposal was rejected, and no mines were ever buried on the island, a fact which Nigel has put to paper and which Damien has relayed to the investors.

On the whole, it's a minor blip, which was easily resolved.

But it's a blip that's indicative of a bigger problem—someone is still messing with my resort. And they really show no signs of stopping.

Since about the time Jackson came on board, The Resort

at Cortez has been plagued with strange incidents. Security footage leaked to the press. Private emails taken viral. Nuisances, mostly. But troublesome enough that they've eaten into my time and into the investors' confidence.

I'd thought that they were over.

Apparently, I'd been wrong.

I tell Rachel to forward me Nigel's statement so that I'll be up to speed, then I end the call and pick up my pace, both because I now have energy to burn, and because I want to catch up to Jackson.

As soon as I step through the doors of the Rec Room, I stop and scan the interior for him. The room is essentially empty—I happen to know that we were the only flight arriving on the property today, and the staff doesn't normally work Sundays—so I expect to find him easily enough. But while Darryl is cooling his heels at the bar, there is no sign of Jackson.

"Is he in the restroom?"

Darryl looks up as I approach. He's a thin man with a hangdog face that makes him look older than his twenty-eight years and perpetually sleepy. I know it's an illusion; you only need to look at those sharp gray eyes to see that Darryl is as competent as they come, and I fully expect that he'll inherit Grayson's job one day.

"He just left. Asked if I could drive you home. Said he needed to take care of a few things before his meeting tonight." He pauses, his eyes narrowing as he studies my face. "I'm guessing that's a problem?"

Hell yes, that's a problem, but all I say is, "Don't worry about it. I'll use one of the company cars. I've got a few errands to take care of myself."

I really want to run, but I don't want to reveal that I'm worried. So I calmly head behind the bar to the refrigerator and pull out a bottle of Perrier. Then I hitch my tote over my shoulder, grab my rolling bag, which Darryl has left by the side door, and walk slowly out of the room.

Once I'm out, though, I practically sprint around the corner to the row of covered parking spaces that abut the back of this building. These are cars that Stark International keeps for the use of clients, investors, consultants, and the like who arrive at this airport. I'm totally mangling company policy by snagging one for my personal use, but at the moment, I don't much care.

Jackson's been playing emotional hide-and-seek with me ever since the cops showed up in Santa Fe, and now he's taken that to the next level.

Well, too bad for him that's not a game I'm in the mood to play.

A lockbox is mounted to the side of the building, and I punch in the code, then grab the keys for a bright yellow Mustang. I hurry over to it and fire up the engine, gratified by the way the motor purrs as I back it out. It's a responsive car, a hell of a lot spunkier than my five-year-old Nissan, and I hope that it's got enough power to catch up to Jackson.

He can't really lay on the gas until he's off airport property, but I'm more than willing to break the rules and do exactly that. I hope he hasn't passed the gates, because I'd never find him on the city streets. But surely he hasn't been gone that long. Has he?

There's a single road that winds its way through this Stark-operated section of the airport, and I'm certain that is Jackson's path. But I know how to cut across on the service feeder that runs behind the Stark hangars and, hopefully, catch up with him by Hangar C, which is where the main road and the feeder converge.

I'm not entirely sure what I'm going to do then, but I'm not above tailing him all the way to wherever the hell he's escaping to. Because I know damn well that he's not going home. He needs a fight—he needs to lash out. He needs to pummel the world into submission, until the universe rights itself again.

What he doesn't seem to need is me, and the thought that he's not just running from me but actually escaping out the goddamn back door makes me want to curl up in a ball and cry. Fortunately, my anger has overshadowed that emotion. I'm fired up, riled by my fury. I'll melt down later; right now, all I want is to find him, to shake him, and to tell him to get the fuck over it. Because he's got enough problems right now, and dammit, I'm not one of them.

My temper has been rising with my thoughts and I realize that I've pushed the car up to almost ninety, which is completely forbidden on airport property.

I press harder, edging the speedometer up even more. I'm not worried about safety—this part of the airport is primarily used for storage of planes and parts, and even during the week there are rarely people around. But even if it were bustling, I'd still floor it. Because right now, the rules are the last thing on my mind. My descent into anarchy is rewarded when I pass a cluster of planes anchored on the tarmac just past Hangar D. They are on my right, and just beyond them I see the black streak that is Jackson's Porsche.

I'm even with him, maybe just a little bit ahead, and I floor it, barely even slowing when I reach Hangar C and make the sharp right turn to take me up the building's north edge, which will put me perpendicular to him right about the time he's about to pass the hangar.

I pound on the steering wheel, as if that will force the car to go faster, and Jackson's black Porsche comes into view on my right the moment I'm clear of the hangar. I slam on the brakes, bringing me to a dead stop in his path, with just enough room for him to hit the brakes.

I cringe as his tires squeal, and too late I realize that the consequences will be very bad if he hits me. Not just injury to me, but damage to his Porsche.

And that really won't sit well with Jackson.

But it's not the Porsche I have to worry about. He's brought it to a stop mere inches from the Mustang, and he's out of it and at my door so quickly it makes me gasp. His palm slams down hard on the roof and I jump, then have to fight the urge to lock the door and stay safe inside.

But this isn't about being safe.

This is about getting into that goddamn thick head of his.

"What the hell are you doing?" he demands as I burst out of the Mustang.

But I don't answer him. Instead, I surprise us both by lashing out and slapping him hard across the cheek.

four

"What the fuck?"

"You need a fight?" I demand, my voice harsh. My skin feels hot and prickly. I'm walking on dangerous ground, and I know it, but I can't go back now. "You need to hit something? To lash out? I told you once, Jackson, and I meant it. Whatever you need."

"I need to be alone."

"Bullshit," I say, even as I raise my hand to hit him again.

He catches my wrist, then twists, so I have no choice but to move where he wants me to go. Now it's his back that is against the car, and I'm standing with nothing to support me except Jackson's hand holding me up.

He releases me, backs away. Then slowly walks toward me, stalking me. His eyes are feral. Wild. And his face is all hard lines and angles, dangerous and edgy. The hint of copper in his coal black hair flashes like fire, a sharp contrast to the cold, hard blue of his eyes.

I lick my lips, then swallow as I take a corresponding step back. Then another and another as he just keeps coming.

"What kind of game are you playing, Syl?" His voice is a tight coil.

"Yours." I draw in a breath. "Dammit, Jackson. Did you think I wouldn't notice? Did you really believe I'd let you push me away? Tell me," I demand. "Talk to me. Or if you won't do that, then fuck me. Because we had a deal, and I'll be damned if you're going to go off on your own and beat the crap out of someone."

"Don't." He lunges toward me, startling me, and I try to take another step back. But there's nowhere to go. I'd parked the Mustang close to the hangar, and now we've reached the metal exterior.

He slams me back against it. The impact reverberates through my body and I'm thrumming with energy. With need. But this isn't about sex—not yet. It's about communication. About getting through to him. Because I am afraid—so terribly afraid—that I am losing the man who fought so hard to get me back.

We've walked through fire, he and I, and I can't stand the thought that in the end it will be Robert Cabot Reed who destroys us.

I'm breathing hard, and so is he. His arms are around me, caging me in place. And just then I'm thinking that this moment could go anywhere and that maybe I've made a mistake, because Jackson has a temper and sometimes he really does need to beat the shit out of something, and right now I'm a little scared that something might end up being me.

I watch his face as he forces himself to breathe. As he grabs on to control like a lifeline. "Don't push me, Syl. Not today. Not now."

"Screw that, Jackson. We had a deal. You want to run off

and fight? Want to kick the shit out of something? You don't run to the ring, remember? You run to me."

"Not today." His jaw is tight, his voice equally so. He's trying to hold it together, but I am determined to break it. To force the explosion. To make him break through and lash out and to finally—*finally*—work through all the shit that has been building up inside him.

"Why not, Jackson? Why not today?"

"Because, goddammit, I'm not running toward a fight. I'm running away from you."

His words are like a knife, and they slice through me, cold and unexpected. My eyes sting, and I look away, blinking furiously, not wanting him to see that he has hurt me. Because Jackson Steele is the one person in all the world who would never, ever hurt me. He's my warrior. My knight. My goddamn protector.

And that's when the truth hits me, as hard as the slap I'd laid upon his cheek. I get it. That's what this is about.

I turn my head so that I am looking at him, though he will not meet my eyes. I lift my hand and cup his cheek. A muscle twitches beneath my palm, and I feel the tightness of his jaw. He's doing everything he can to hold it together even as I'm doing the only thing I can think of to make him let go.

"You're a fucking idiot," I say gently. "I made you leave me once before because I was trying to protect myself. I'm not letting you leave now because you think you're doing the same thing."

"I'm the idiot?" His voice is low, with a dangerous edge. "You're wrapped up with a man who has a child. A man who might be going to jail. A man who is the reason the project you care most about in the world is going to fall apart, because you're going to lose your architect to a goddamn prison."

"You're wrong. You're what I care about most in the world."

He winces, just a little, and I continue on.

"You're scared," I say. "Do you think I don't get that? Hell, Jackson, I'm fucking terrified. I can't bear the thought of losing you. And I hate the universe for even threatening to take you from me. And I sure as hell couldn't survive you leaving."

He looks at me now, his blue eyes boring straight into mine, and I can see everything, right to the heart of him. Frustration. Rage. Need. And, dammit, I can't just stand there and wait for him to make his choice.

I lunge.

The kiss is wild and hard. A sensual battle that I am determined to win. Teasing him with my tongue. Tormenting him with my teeth. At first his lips are hard, resistant. But then everything shifts and he's claiming, demanding. And the knowledge of this small victory spreads through me, lighting my body with a wild desire that I am determined to see satisfied.

I slide my hand to the back of his head, pulling him closer because I want the kiss deeper. Harder. I want him wild. I want to break him. To push him past this thing that has been keeping us apart. This cold barrier that I couldn't get through.

But I'm getting through now, and that knowledge is the most potent of aphrodisiacs.

He pulls away, and I almost scream in protest. But then I see his face. The heat and power and ferocious need. There's danger, too, and I welcome it.

"Jackson," I whisper. And this time, that is all it takes.

He thrusts me back roughly, slamming me against the corrugated metal. "Is this what you want?" he growls. "You want to be fucked? Used? Because you're here and I need it?"

The words are harsh, designed to make me back away.

But I hear what he is really saying—*Because I need you.* And dear god, I need him, too.

I look him hard in the eyes. "Yes," I say. "Oh, please, yes."

I watch, relieved and aroused, as a rising heat melts the coldness in his eyes. I'm wet with desire, every bit of skin on my body a direct link to my cunt. Not only because I will always respond to Jackson's touch, but because it excites me to know that he needs me like this. That he is claiming me. Using me to make himself whole.

He crushes his mouth over mine, hard and wild, his tongue demanding, taking, *fucking,* before he pulls back, his teeth tugging at my lower lip.

I hear his breath, wild and fast like my own. And when he yanks up my T-shirt then flips open the front clasp of my bra, I gasp, both in surprise and delight, but also from the way my body clenches, wanting more. Wanting Jackson.

The air is cool, and my nipples tighten even more. He brushes a fingertip over one, the touch so light it is almost negligible.

But oh, dear god, what it does to me. It is as if he's touched me with an electric wire, and the sensation shoots all the way to my core. I explode—the orgasm ripping through me, wild and incredible and completely unexpected.

I don't even realize I've closed my eyes, but when I open them, I see Jackson watching my face, his expression hungry. *Yes,* I think. *More.*

Those are the only two words in my head. The only thoughts I can form, and even when he tells me to turn around, my mind doesn't process it until he physically moves me.

"Bend over," he says as his fingers make easy work of the button on my jeans. "Hands on the wall." He's right behind me, and I can feel his cock straining against the denim of his jeans and pressing against my ass.

He slides my zipper down, and then uses both hands to tug my jeans down. For a brief moment, the sensual fog that has surrounded me lifts and I realize where we are. But the truth is, I don't care. We're mostly blocked by our two cars and this section of the property is unused, this hangar devoted to storage.

Most of all, he needs this. I need this. And I'm not going to risk stopping—risk sending him off to some damned boxing ring or who knows where else when I'm so close to having him back.

My jeans and panties are pushed down to just above my knees. I'm bent forward, my shirt shoved up and my bra open so that my breasts are exposed. I'm wet—so damn wet—and when he slides his hand between my legs and over my clit, I shiver with need.

I hear him take down his zipper, then feel the head of his cock stroke the curve of my ass. I whimper and try to spread my legs wider, but I'm bound by my jeans. I feel wild. Shameless. And if he wasn't running this show I would happily strip naked and fuck him on the asphalt.

"You need this as much as I do," he whispers. It's not a question, nor is it a statement. It's an expression of wonder. Of connection.

"Yes," I say. "Oh, god yes."

"You slapped me." Now there's a commanding edge to his voice, and I shiver in anticipation, my body clenching simply from the heat and power in his voice.

I may have started this, but I cannot deny that I want Jackson to finish it. I want to lose myself in his demands. To go soft and wet with the pleasure of submitting. And more than that, I know that if we are going to get past this, he has to grab control.

And oh, thank god, he is.

"Naughty girl," he says playfully, and then lightly smacks

my ass. "Very naughty," and this time he spanks me harder again and again and again.

I gasp, both from the sting and from the sweet pleasure of it, and then I moan in wanton need when he uses his palm to soothe my heated rear before slipping his hand between my legs again and thrusting his fingers roughly inside me.

My muscles tighten around him, wanting more—and thankfully, so does Jackson. He's right there, the tip of his cock pushing against my core. His hands are on my hips and he holds me steady as he thrusts inside. Gently at first, and then harder, until he's pounding into me, wild and powerful.

I bite my lower lip to keep from crying out, but that goes all to hell when he bends over me further, one hand crushing hard against my breast as another teases my clit. I keep my arms stiff, my hands flat against the side of the building so that there is little give as he thrusts into me, over and over, harder and faster. Using me even as he pleasures me.

I am lost in the sensation of being touched and filled by him. Of being needed by him. My fears have been tossed away, destroyed by the brutal power of this claiming. *He needs me.* And oh, how I need him.

I can feel his body tightening, readying for an explosion. His fingers close painfully over my breast, and I moan with pleasure as hot threads of sensation shoot from my breast to my cunt. I'm needy and hot and ready. And when he demands that I come with him, I submit even in that, my body breaking apart under this wonderful, sensual destruction.

I do not remember taking my hands off the wall. I don't remember sliding to the ground. I know only that I am curled up against him, my jeans pulled up but not fastened. My body glowing. My skin wonderfully sensitive.

"Thank god for you." His voice is low, rough. "Thank god you're a better fighter than I am."

I can't help my smile. But when I speak, I'm completely

serious. "I won't ever stop fighting for you. You need to get that through your thick skull."

"I think you've managed to drill it in."

This time, my smile turns into a laugh. "I think you did that," I say, making him laugh, too.

His arms tighten around me, and I know we should get up. We're sitting on the hard concrete with the scent of gasoline and oil lingering in the air and the roar of planes in the distance. But I don't want to move and neither does he. Not yet. And so we simply stay still, lost in each other's arms.

I've closed my eyes and am drifting when his voice pulls me back. "I went there," he says, and I stiffen in his arms. "I was in his house the night that he was killed." The words are flat and firm. As if Jackson is simply taking care of business, announcing this bit of news like someone else might state the weather.

I open my eyes and swallow, not sure what I should say. Not sure that I want to hear more.

"I already told Charles. There will be evidence," he says. "A fingerprint. A security camera. Who knows? But they'll find it." He presses a kiss to the top of my head. "And whatever the police know, you will know first."

"All right." There is no point in arguing. Of that, I'm certain. I shift on the ground, needing to sit up so that I can see him. "Why did you go?"

"Why do you think? To threaten him. To tell him to give me the photos or pay the consequences."

"You'll tell the police that?"

His smile is so tender it melts my heart. "No. If I tell them anything at all, I'll tell them it was about the movie. But the pictures—what he was threatening to do to you—that much stays hidden. I promise."

He is already hugging me close, but I hug myself now, too, needing the comfort to support me for what I'm about to say.

Then I draw a breath for courage. "Are you going to take the Fifth? Because if you don't, you have to tell them everything, Jackson. Hold something back, and if it comes out it'll bite you in the ass."

"Sweetheart, they're going to swallow me whole, and we both know it."

"*No.*" I grab hold of his arm and cling to him. "You're going to be cleared."

He makes a noise, somewhere between a laugh and a derisive snort. "We can try to believe that, baby. But we both know it's not true."

"It has to be." I say the words defiantly. And before I can stop myself, I hear myself asking the one question that I know I shouldn't. "Did you kill him?"

"What does it matter?" he asks. "The system is capricious. You know it as well as I do."

A faint dread washes over me, not because I'm afraid that Jackson killed him, but because he is right. If he did kill Reed, the system will make him pay, even for the death of a monster. And if he didn't kill Reed, it won't matter. He will be an innocent man falsely convicted, punished for the potency of his hate rather than the reality of his actions.

"Would it change anything?" he asks me. "If I killed him, would it change anything between us?"

"No." I say the word fiercely, because he needs to know how much I mean it. That there is even some small part of me that hopes—maybe even believes—that it is true. And, yes, that is humbled and excited by the knowledge that Jackson would kill to protect me.

He closes his eyes—just for a moment—but I see some of the tension escape him. When he looks at me again, I see a vulnerability that he rarely shows.

"I'm scared." His voice is low, and even this close, I have to strain to hear him. "And that's not an emotion I'm comfortable with. But lately I'm becoming more and more familiar with it. I'm afraid of losing you. Ronnie. My freedom."

I can hear the pain and the confusion in his voice, and I understand it. His daughter is in limbo as much as Jackson's freedom is. And for a man who needs to hold tight to control, limbo is a horrible place to be.

"I can survive anything. I'm certain of that. But that doesn't mean I'm not scared of where this is going. And I don't like you having to see me carry all this shit."

"You can't push me away because of this investigation. Not unless you want me to slap you again."

I'm rewarded with a wry smile. "I get that," he says. "But I'm not just talking about the murder. It's Ronnie, too. I don't like you seeing me flounder."

"Flounder?" I think about how good he is with her—so naturally comfortable in a way I can't even fathom—and am genuinely baffled.

"What the hell do I know about being a father? God knows mine was no role model."

"You're amazing with her," I say, and though I'm being a hundred percent honest, I do understand what he means. Children have never been on my radar for exactly that reason—my parents screwed me up so much that I'm not sure I have a decent parenting bone in me.

"She's the one who's amazing," he says. "But that's not even what I mean. It's like every decision is a test, and the wrong answer could mess up her life. Do I step in as her dad? Do I continue as an uncle? Do I leave her with Betty? There's an infinite number of choices at every juncture and then a whole new set of choices after that. And there's no way of knowing if I'm following the right path."

"You think the fact that you're struggling means you'll be a bad father? It's just the opposite, Jackson. Don't you see? It matters so much to you—hell, it's consuming you—and every step you're taking is with her best interest in mind. That's the definition of a good father, Jackson. You and I know that better than anyone." I offer him a small smile and a gentle kiss on his cheek. "It's pretty sexy, actually."

He doesn't laugh, but the tension in his face relaxes a bit.

"You're doing the right thing for Ronnie," I insist. "The best thing. You're focusing on Ronnie because you want her life to be better. Because you love her. Leaving her with Betty isn't a mistake. It's a choice, and it's the right one."

"Maybe. But that doesn't mean I haven't made other mistakes. And I'm afraid that I'm going to have to pay for them sooner rather than later. I'm afraid Ronnie's going to pay, too. And Syl," he says, sliding his fingers through my hair to cup the back of my head as he looks deep into my eyes, "I'm afraid that you're going to pay as well. I'm afraid you already are."

"No." I say the word fiercely, as if I can erase the shadows from his eyes simply by the force of my will. "Don't go there, Jackson. Don't you dare slide off into melancholy with me. Ronnie is better off having you in her life, and I am, too. I love you, and there is no price I wouldn't pay to be with you."

He looks at me then, as if he is absorbing my words. As if he's weighing the truth of them. He looks at me for so long, in fact, that I'm almost compelled to speak, but then he does that first.

"Being with you in Santa Fe . . ." He trails off.

"What?"

I see something like pain flicker across his face. "I know I was an ass. It was because of Ronnie. Well, because of all of it. But I think it was mostly her."

"Oh." An icy chill snakes up my back, and I tense, certain I know where this is going. I'm not her mom. I haven't the faintest idea how to be a mom. And right now Jackson needs to focus on two things: getting cleared and being a father. Which means he needs to not focus on me.

"It's just that I caught myself thinking that it would be good—a comfort, I mean—if I knew that Ronnie would be safe on the outside with you if the worst happened."

I frown, no longer sure where he's heading. "And that turned you into an ass?"

The corner of his mouth actually curves up. "Have you not been paying attention? You found out about five minutes ago that I have a child. A child you've spent barely any time with. And yet in my mind I already had you filling the gap in her life when I end up behind bars. Auntie Syl, right there. Helping to take care of her. Protecting her. I mean, hell, sweetheart, I practically had you in the role of Mommy."

My chest tightens, emotion flooding me. He wasn't pulling away from me because he didn't want me. Just the opposite.

"It's selfish of me, and unrealistic, and—"

I can't help myself. I burst into tears.

"Oh, Christ, Syl. Oh, shit." Jackson wanted to kick himself. What the hell had he been thinking?

That was easy. He was thinking that he wanted her. Forever. For always. *He* wanted her. And he had to go and run off at the mouth without thinking about what she wanted.

"I'm sorry," he rushed to say. "I shouldn't have told you. Shit, I shouldn't have said anything. That's why she's with Betty now, because of course I don't really expect you to—"

"You're such a fool."

Her voice was thick with tears, and for a moment, Jackson was certain he must have misunderstood.

"Do you have any idea what that means to me? That you

have that much faith in me? That you'd trust me with the most precious thing in your life?"

He stared at her, a little bit shell-shocked. Had he heard her right? Did she understand what she was saying?

"I haven't got a clue how to play Mommy," she continued. "But I love you, Jackson—those aren't just words, and they sure as hell aren't temporary." She brushed her hand over his cheek. "Whatever you need, remember? And those aren't just words, either. For better or worse, we're getting through this. And we're doing it together."

He didn't answer. Not yet. All he wanted to do was look at her. To breathe her in and let her words fill his head. Because they were damn good words.

For better or worse . . .

Someday, he thought. Someday she'd say those words to him again and he'd put a ring on her finger.

But first, they had to survive everything that was yet to come.

five

Our destination—the office of Bender, Twain & McGuire—takes up three floors in 2049 Century Park East, one of the two iconic triangular shaped towers that comprise the Century Plaza Towers in Century City. They rise up ahead of us, shining against the night sky, as Jackson maneuvers his beloved black Porsche down Santa Monica Boulevard, cutting a straight path from my condo to our destination.

I've always loved these towers—the sleek, clean lines and the soft gleam of the aluminum facade. The towers truly shine when they are set against the backdrop of the blue California sky. But even after dark, they stand like monuments, reflecting the power and prestige of the area and the people who live and work here.

"He's on my regret list," Jackson says, pointing to the towers.

"He? You mean Yamasaki?"

Jackson grins. "I should have known you'd be familiar

with him. Along with Frank Lloyd Wright, Minoru Yama-saki is one of the people I always invite to dinner when I play that game."

"Who you'd have at your table, either living or dead?"

"Exactly. Wright passed away before I was born, and I think I would have been about four when Yamasaki died. I was building things with my Legos back then, but even if I had clued in to my desire to be an architect, I don't think he would have taken my call."

I can't help my smile. "Probably not. He's on my list, too," I admit. "There's such an elegant majesty to his buildings, you know?" Minoru Yamasaki may have been the original architect for the towers in Century City, but he's most well-known for the original World Trade Center.

We stop at a light, and Jackson turns to me. "I haven't taken you on an architectural tour of Los Angeles yet. We should do that soon. Maybe next weekend."

"Don't," I snap, my voice harsher than I'd intended. "Don't try to keep my mind off what's going on around us. Don't try to pretend that everything is fine. Like it or not, this is reality now."

"Syl . . ." The light changes, but he doesn't move forward.

"No, I mean it," I say, as a car behind us honks. I turn around and glare at the idiot in the convertible—some overly made-up blonde who looks like she doesn't have a care in the world, then I turn back to Jackson, even more irritated than I was before. "*Go,*" I say, but he's already moving.

We drive in silence for another block. Jackson's got both hands on the wheel, and an uncomfortable tension has filled the car, completely obliterating the sense of normalcy that had been between us just a few moments ago.

Good.

Because this isn't normal. Nothing is normal. And we have to remember that. We have to fight it.

Except, dammit, how do you fight the evidence? The police? A horrible reality that's edging closer and closer?

"Do you think I don't understand the stakes?" Jackson's voice is level, but firm.

"I think you're trying to make it better for me," I say. "And you can't. Not like that." I kick off my ballet flats and pull my legs up onto the seat, then rest my chin on my knees as I hug myself. "You need to do what they say, Jackson. Evelyn. The attorneys. I mean it. Exactly what they say."

"Christ, Syl." I hear the temper in his voice. "I'm not paying them to then ignore them."

"No, but you fly off the handle sometimes." I know that I should just shut up now, but I can't seem to close my mouth. "You can't do that anymore. You're already on trial in the media, and you need to be careful. You need to be smart."

He slows to make a right turn, and as he does the streetlights illuminate his face in the same moment that I am looking right at him. I see the hard lines. The harsh angles. "I know," he says simply. No argument, no reproach. And just that simple acknowledgment makes me sag with relief.

"It's just that—" I draw in a breath, then spit it out. "I don't know if you killed him or not, Jackson. I don't know because you haven't told me, and that's fine because I get that Charles doesn't want you to say. But whether you did or not, I know you could have. Hell, I know you probably wanted to. And if I can see that—"

My voice breaks and I draw in a breath before trying again. "If I can see that, then what is a jury going to see?"

There is fear underscoring my voice, and I know that he hears it. But he doesn't reach for my hand. He doesn't try to console me. I'm grateful; right now, I need harsh, cold reality. Not platitudes.

"You see me," he says simply. "You know that I'd do whatever is necessary to protect you. To protect Ronnie." He draws a slow breath. "But a jury won't see that. That's my heart, baby. And my heart is only for you." He reaches over and strokes my cheek. "It will be okay."

"Do you really believe that?"

"I have to."

The underground parking garage is huge, but he manages to snag a guest slot near the elevator bank. As we walk that way, I check my phone one more time. Not that I'm loving being inundated with the social media bullshit, but I can't ignore it. If we're going to talk about the entire picture of Jackson's defense, handling the media is going to come up. And not only do I need to know for Jackson's sake, but also for the sake of the resort. Dallas Sykes may be completely on board, but I'm still not confident about the rest of the investors, and too much bad press just might tip them over the edge.

For the most part, what I find as I surf is more of the same—speculation about the assault and the movie and just general tabloid style gossip.

But as we step onto the elevator, I'm knocked sideways—literally—by the tweet that flashes across my screen, and I grab on to Jackson's arm to steady myself.

"Are you okay—oh, shit," he says when he sees my face. "What is it now?"

I don't want to show him, I really don't, but it's not like I can avoid it. I pass him my phone, trying very hard not to cringe in anticipation of his reaction.

"*Motherfucker.*"

I wince despite myself, then glance over to see the screen even though what it says there is already burned into my mind: *Damien Stark Half-Brother Jackson Steele Wanted for Questioning in Murder of Robert Cabot Reed #Scandal #Stark #Sordid #Steele*

"Yeah," I say grimly. "That just about sums it up."

There's a link, too, and Jackson tries to follow it, but of course we've lost the signal. Doesn't matter. If there's one tweet, there are a thousand, and we both know that the press is now all over the fact that Jackson Steele and Damien Stark are brothers. And that both of these men have been on the wrong end of murder investigations.

"How the hell did they find out?" He turns his attention from the phone to me. "It's not like there's any connection to Damien on my website. If that son of a bitch leaked it—"

"No," I say firmly. "He wouldn't do that. Not without telling you. Not at all." But even as I say these words, I wonder. I truly don't think that Damien would reveal this secret maliciously, but what if Evelyn said he needed to get ahead of it? What if she insisted he leak the story even while Jackson was still on the plane?

I don't know, so I don't suggest it, especially since Jackson is so clearly on edge. As we rise, I stand beside him, feeling a strange mix of relief and sympathy. Sympathy that yet another piece of his personal life has been hijacked by the media. And relief that this time I am not the cause of the tension in his posture or the tight set of his jaw.

When the elevator doors slide open on the twenty-fifth floor, we're greeted by a willowy blonde who introduces herself as a legal assistant and offers to lead the way. Although it's almost eight on a Sunday evening, over half the offices that we pass are populated by young associate attorneys, their faces glowing in the reflected light of their computers. A few assistants and secretaries man desks in the interior cubicles, and the clickety-clack of fingers on keyboards gives the office a busy, vibrant feel.

Bender Twain is one of the country's top law firms, and the activity in these halls—especially so late on a Sunday—goes a long way to explaining why.

Charles's office isn't as large as Damien's, but it's still massive and easily holds Charles's desk, a large oval conference table, a couch with two twenty-something men on it, and several comfortable chairs. Not to mention the bookshelves filled top to bottom with legal treatises, historical fiction, and stacks of files.

We're the last to arrive, and before I can even get my bearings or scope out the room's occupants, Jackson strides past me, my phone still in his hand. "What the fuck is this?" He's aimed like an arrow toward Damien, and I doubt that he sees anything or anyone else in this room.

Damien is standing beside the conference table and barely even glances at the outstretched phone as Jackson approaches. But he does look up, his eyes cool and calm on Jackson's face. "I didn't say a thing," he says evenly. "Believe me. I'm coming to terms with the idea of having a brother, but I wasn't ready to go public yet."

Damien glances at Evelyn, who is seated at the table with an open folio in front of her. "We've been talking about how to handle that announcement, and I wasn't too happy that someone beat me to it." He almost smiles. "I thought it might be you, but based on your reaction, I'm thinking not."

"It wasn't," Jackson confirms, and when I see the way his body relaxes slightly, I know that he believes Damien.

"So how are you holding up?" Damien asks.

"Fine." Jackson's voice is clipped.

"Bullshit. You're scared," Damien says. "And if you're not, then you're not as smart as I thought you were, because you should be."

I stand frozen next to Jackson, and despite my rant in the car about facing reality, Damien's words are making my stomach twist so violently, I fear I might actually throw up.

"If you did it," Damien continues, "you're afraid that someone's going to figure that out. If you didn't do it, you're even more afraid that you'll end up in prison with a tight grip on the soap and your back to the wall, all because you told the wrong guy to fuck off, and that guy ended up dead.

"It's a screwed up situation." Damien's voice, which had started out harsh, now takes on a more conciliatory tone. "And that's why we're all here. To make sure you don't end up fucked."

Jackson glances at me just long enough for me to see relief in his eyes. Then he turns toward Charles, who is approaching from where he's been standing with a familiar-looking woman by the window near the bookshelf.

"Let me make sure you know everybody," Charles says. "Damien and Evelyn are givens, obviously, and you've already met my paralegal, Natalie. Those two are UCLA law students," he says, pointing to the sofa and giving us the interns' names. "And this is Harriet Frederick," he adds, and I have to stifle a little gasp as he gestures to the woman with whom he'd been talking.

Harriet Frederick is one of the most prominent criminal defense attorneys in California. Probably in the country. She's poised and sharply dressed, but still has a semi-casual "working on Sunday" look about her. Her long hair is clipped back at the nape of her neck, and she wears minimal makeup. From what I can see, she doesn't need much. She comes off as competent and sharp, and even if she'd just been one of the interns, I would be glad she's on our team.

But I'm even more glad because Harriet Frederick has been all over the news, and I know she consulted a few times with Charles from stateside when Damien's trial went forward in Germany with local defense counsel. I knew that Charles was bringing someone else on board for Jackson's case—while he was more than capable of bailing Jackson out after the assault, his specialty is corporate law, not criminal. But I hadn't anticipated we'd get Harriet, and seeing her here is more than a relief—it's like getting a shot of undiluted hope.

She moves confidently across the room to shake Jackson's hand. "Mr. Stark's right. Being nervous is par for the course, but if you listen to me—if you're honest with me—we'll have a better chance of keeping you a free man."

I lick my lips, hating what she's not saying, but what I already know. That there are no guarantees. And even though she's one of the most famous and well-regarded criminal defense attorneys out there, even Harriet Frederick cannot guarantee that I won't lose the man I love to prison.

"We'll apply for a change of venue, but we won't get it. And that means the jury is coming from this community, and this is a community that loves movies and celebrities—and that includes Reed. So that means I want you on your best behavior, Mr. Steele."

"I understand."

She looks him up and down as if taking his measure, then she nods in what I hope is approval. "Well, I guess we'll see." She gestures to the table. "Why don't we all sit down and get started?" We all sit, but she remains standing. "It's unfortunate that we weren't able to get ahead of the reveal about your relationship with your brother, but it's relevant only to the extent that your overall persona is relevant. Unfortunately, in a high profile murder trial, your persona will be very relevant."

Jackson is frowning, and I try to catch his eye. I want to know what he's thinking, but he's focused on Harriet, and I'm left to wonder.

"Damien and Evelyn were putting together a plan to get ahead of this revelation. Now we'll rework that to get on top of it."

Evelyn nods. "I'll have something ready by tonight. I

imagine the vultures will be circling Stark Tower tomorrow, not to mention the Beverly Hills PD."

"We'll take Jackson in and out through the back," Harriet says. "No face time with the press tomorrow. And while much of this case will be tried in the media, our primary focus still has to be the evidence and what it's going to look like to a jury."

She crosses her arms as she studies Jackson, looking much like a stylist in a high-end clothing store. "You're not testifying. You're not answering their questions tomorrow. You go, I answer for you. You're relying on the Fifth Amendment, Jackson."

"Won't that make him look guilty?" I ask.

She turns to me with a small shake of her head. "Better than him admitting he was in Reed's house. Or, worse, not mentioning that he was there, and getting sideswiped when the forensics team finds evidence. Stay quiet, the police may never know. They'll have a hard time proving Jackson killed Reed if they can't prove he was at the crime scene."

I nod. I understand all that—and I even get that pleading the Fifth doesn't automatically mean a defendant's guilty—but I can't deny that the thought of it scares me, because I know that's what the media will think. And the speculation will be everywhere.

"Sylvia." Harriet's voice is gentle, and I realize that I've been staring at the tabletop. I look up at her. "As far as the press is concerned, he already looks guilty. Taking the Fifth won't change that. But how he interacts with the public can, which is why he'll be personable and likable. And," she added with a quick glance toward Jackson, "he won't lose his temper."

"Damn right, he won't," Evelyn says. Evelyn Dodge is a Hollywood establishment and knows her way around PR better than anyone. I'm thrilled she's on Jackson's side. I'm even more thrilled that she's a friend.

She indicates Charles and Harriet. "We've been strategizing for the last few hours, and it comes down to you being gracious and charming." She lifts an eyebrow. "Assuming you can handle that."

Jackson almost smiles. "I'll do my best."

"Don't approach the press, wave them off if they get in your personal space—that's fair. But when you comment, you're charming. You're accessible. You're likable."

"Am I?" Jackson says, and across the table, Damien chuckles.

Evelyn raises a brow, and she reminds me of a mom trying to keep her kids in order. The thought makes me smile.

"You hit him—that's fine to admit, it's not like we can hide it—but the rest of it? Well, you toss it back to Harriet and Charles. Damn attorneys making you stay quiet, otherwise you'd spill all. Just like talking to your best friends. Got it?"

"Got it," Jackson says.

"You have a temper, young man," she says once again, as she firmly meets his eyes. "Keep it under control. You don't, and you're fucking the case and yourself. Do you understand?"

His jaw tightens, and I know he's fighting back a retort. Because of course he understands. But all he says is, "Yes, ma'am."

And it's that "ma'am" that breaks the tension. Evelyn tilts back her head and guffaws. "Good lord, Jackson, that wasn't meant to piss you off." She lifts a shoulder in an apologetic shrug. "This, though . . . well, this may rile you up a bit."

As she speaks, she's pulling a photograph out of her folio and sliding it across the table.

I gasp at the same time Jackson says, very firmly and very evenly, "No fucking way."

The picture is of Ronnie.

"We need to get ahead of it," Harriet says gently. "She's in your life. And, honestly, there's not much the press likes more than a single dad fighting for his kid. You want the press to love you? Let them see you caring about that little girl."

Jackson says nothing, but he puts his palm over the photo, as if doing that can keep his daughter safe from all this.

For a moment, no one says anything. Then Damien stands, circles the table, and leans back against it beside Jackson. "It's going to come out." His voice is firm, but gentle. "And when it does, everyone will see the connection between your daughter and the movie—and it will be crystal clear why you didn't want the movie to go forward. Get on top of it, and we can soften the impact. Wait, and it's going to be brutal."

"I'm not throwing my daughter to the wolves." He is tense, as if one wrong word from anyone in this room will cause him to bolt. "Not until it's absolutely necessary."

"Jackson—"

But Evelyn cuts off Damien's protest. "No, we can make this work." She glances at Harriet, who nods almost imperceptibly, then turns her focus back to Jackson. "But you keep your eyes on the prize, okay? And that's staying out of jail. That's being around to watch that little girl grow up."

Jackson says nothing, but he's watching Evelyn with interest.

"We'll play it your way for now, but that might change. I need to take the media's temperature. See if they warm to you, or if that ice in your eyes spills over. Too icy, Mr. Steele, and we may need to attach a sweet little girl to your image. Do you understand that?"

His jaw clenches, and one hand grips tight to the edge of the table. But all he says is, "Yes."

Evelyn nods, satisfied.

"What *is* going to happen tomorrow?" I blurt out the question, as much because I want to know as because I want to change the subject. "Are they going to arrest him? Can Jackson post bail?" I can hear the panic in my voice, and I'm touched when Jackson takes his hand off his daughter's photo so that he can grasp mine.

"They might arrest," Harriet says, as if she's commenting on the possibility of rain. "Normally in a high profile case like this I'd assume not, but in this case Jackson did assault both the screenwriter and Reed, though we don't know if the police are aware of the first incident. And he did visit Reed the day of the murder. The prosecution may not know that. But maybe they do. Maybe they're going to disclose it tomorrow. And maybe they're going to parlay that into an arrest."

Jackson nods, looking a little bit shell-shocked.

My mouth is completely dry, and though I'm holding tight to Jackson's hand, I can't feel his fingers. It takes me a couple of tries, but finally I can form words. "You said normally you'd think not? Why not?"

"As a rule, the police don't want to act prematurely because once they arrest, the clock starts ticking. And especially in a high profile case, they like to have time to get their ducks in order."

"But don't they want to order those ducks here, too?"

Harriet looks straight at me, and though I hate the way she doesn't pull punches, I can't deny that I respect it. "My fear is that the ducks are already all lined up."

"Wouldn't we already know? I thought the police have to disclose evidence." I can't seem to be quiet. I have to wrap my head around it. "Or is that just the way it plays out on television?"

This time, Harriet does smile, at least a little. "They do, yes. But not yet. Certainly not before there's an arrest."

"Oh." I finally get it. She fears that tomorrow Jackson will be subjected to a full song and dance presentation of the evidence, and the grand finale of the show will be putting him in cuffs and carting him off to a cell.

Oh god.

"If the worst happens, we'll move for bail, of course," Charles says. "Until then, we're going to hope it doesn't happen."

The meeting continues for almost two more hours, covering so many details and plans that it feels like all the information is going to spill out of my ears. Even I've been given marching orders. Like Jackson, I need to be polite and charming to the press. But I have the added benefit of being able to say that he was with me at a party the night of the murder. Of course, that Halloween party was just over the hill in Studio City, and any reporter worth his salt will know that Jackson could have easily gone from Reed's to the party.

That part, I won't be saying.

As for my calls to the investors, I can reassure them that Jackson was with me, then segue neatly into Jackson's talent—not to mention the fact that a little bit of drama attached to the resort probably won't hurt the opening week receipts.

Jackson is told to stop doing his community service. Charles is going to square that with the court. "But we don't want to draw attention to the fact that you got such a light sentence after the assault. No appearance of perks. No suggestion of special privileges. It will come out, of course," he adds cynically, "but why shine a spotlight?"

Harriet had taken a seat, but now she stands. "I think

that covers everything but motive. As it stands, the prosecution can come at this from either the movie angle or the assault angle—and the movie angle gets stronger once the media finds out about Ronnie. But," she adds quickly, "I'm willing to wait to address that, so long as you're aware of the potential downside."

"I've already said that I am," Jackson says.

I'm frowning at something else she's said. "They'll really think Jackson killed Reed to keep him from filing a civil assault suit? Is anyone else seeing the irony?"

"Trust me," Harriet says. "People kill for the stupidest of reasons. The police know that, and they'll push. And who knows what they'll uncover if they investigate multiple angles." She looks hard at Jackson. "So if there's any other possible motive out there, I need to know about it now. Something pops out later and surprises me, it can destroy your entire case. I want you to be very clear about that."

I sit perfectly still, but I'm terrified that the room can hear my heart, because it's about to pound out of my chest. I don't look at Jackson, but I'm certain he's thinking the same thing. *The photos of me.* Reed threatened to expose them if I didn't get Jackson to agree to the movie.

And, yeah, that's definitely motive.

But all Jackson says is, "That's it. Nothing else."

I release a breath I didn't know I'd been holding. *He's still protecting me.* Even though this secret could land him behind bars, he's still protecting me.

Am I really such a coward that I will let him do that?

"All right," Harriet says. "Let's move on to—"

"There's more." My whisper is so soft that the words are barely audible. I keep my eyes on the table, not on Jackson.

"I'm sorry, Sylvia?" I look up to see Charles peering at me. "I couldn't hear you."

I draw in a deep breath and squeeze my hands into fists.

"Sylvia." Jackson's voice is hard. Demanding.

I look at him, hoping he can see the apology in my eyes. Then I turn my attention back to Harriet and Charles.

"He was blackmailing me." I'm no longer whispering. I'm saying it flat out. "Reed. He had photos. I used to model for him and—well—some of them were explicit. I—I wouldn't want them coming out. I—" I swallow. "I'm not sure I could handle that at all."

Very slowly, Harriet puts her notes on the table. "I see."

I turn just enough to see Jackson. To see the tiny shake of his head and the pain in his eyes. But I continue. "He said he'd release them if I didn't convince Jackson to quit trying to block the movie."

Charles and Harriet exchange glances.

"Well," Harriet says. "You're right. That definitely goes to motive."

I swallow. I know that she is right.

"Do you have these photos?" Charles asks.

"She doesn't." Jackson's voice rings firm. "We burned the ones he sent to her." That's a lie, but since I don't think it matters—and since I really don't want them to see the photos—I don't challenge him.

"So presumably there are still copies?" Harriet asks. "Unless whoever killed Reed took them?"

I shudder, but nod.

"Anyone else know about this?" she asks.

"*No.*" I blurt the word out before Jackson can mention my dad or Cass. I want the attorneys to know about the blackmail because that matters to Jackson, but I can't bear the thought of wrapping my dad up with us like that. "And please—please don't let it leave this room."

This time, I look to Damien, who nods once, and I know that he understands what I am asking, and why it is so important to me that he keep this secret, even from Nikki.

When she speaks, Harriet's voice is gentle. "This isn't information we have to turn over. And with any luck, Reed buried his copies of the photos in his backyard under a rosebush and no one will ever find them. But thank you for telling us. It really does help Jackson's defense."

I nod. I know. Lord knows I didn't have any other reason for sharing.

The rest of the meeting dissolves into task assignments and scheduling, and as soon as Jackson has worked out when he will meet Harriet tomorrow so they can drive together to the police department, he and I take our leave.

I can tell he's tense as we walk toward the reception area, and when he doesn't take my hand, I know that the tension is more about me than the meeting in general.

I sigh, and when I'm certain that we're far enough down the corridor to avoid being overheard, I say softly, "I had to."

"The hell you did." There's a tightness in his voice. Maybe anger. Maybe sadness. I'm really not sure. "I told you I would protect your secret."

"Jackson—"

He whirls on me. "No. Goddammit, Syl. You should have waited. It might not even come out. And we could have dealt with it if the police found the originals."

"I can't be the reason this goes south for you, Jackson. Don't you get that? I love that you want to protect me, but right now it's my turn to protect you."

"*Fuck.*" He turns violently, and it's only when he smacks his fist against his own palm that I realize he's looking for something to hit.

"Jacks—" I begin, but my word is cut short by the way he grabs me and drags me to him. His mouth closes hard over mine, and he holds me by my wrist pressed against my spine, my arm twisting uncomfortably. He pulls me up against him, our bodies pressed hard together.

I can feel him, hot and hard against me. It's not a kiss of passion, but of claiming. Of demand. And when he backs away from me, gasping, his eyes are hard. And when he speaks, there is danger in his voice. "Do you think I don't understand what it does to you? Even thinking about what he did to you? About how much you gave up to even tell them that it happened?"

I press my lips together and nod. Because it had been hard. But it would have been a hell of a lot harder before Jackson was in my life, and I tell him that. "You've made me stronger, Jackson. Don't you get that? I could tell them because of you. Because I know that if it gets bad—if the nightmares creep up—that you're there to help me fight them back."

My throat is thick with unshed tears. "As for what I gave up—well, I'll be giving up a hell of a lot more if I lose you. And I'll do whatever it takes to not let that happen."

"You shouldn't have to protect me." He is still holding me fast, but his voice has lost its edge. "I'm the one who sucked you into this."

I only shake my head. I am breathing hard, aroused by the tension crackling between us. By his passionate need to protect me. And, yes, by the hard length of his body pressed so enticingly against mine.

Finally, I force myself to speak. "We're in this together, Jackson. And I want to keep you out of jail as much as you do. Because I love you, dammit, and I can't bear the thought of losing you. But also because I need you to finish my damn resort."

I stare at him, perfectly serious. And the bastard bursts out laughing.

"Oh, baby." He releases my arm, and this time when he kisses my lips there is such tender sweetness that I go a little limp.

"I can't lose it," I say. "And I can't lose you. So, yeah. If I can help you, I will. And if that pisses you off, then that's just too damn bad."

We're in the reception area. A wall of windows exposes the twinkling lights of the city and the ocean beyond.

He looks at me, his expression soft. Calm. He nods once. Just a simple incline of his head, but I see the apology in it.

I sigh, then walk to the window and press my palm to the glass. It's easy to see the line where the city meets the impenetrable depths of the ocean. But beyond that ribbon of black, I see the faint, twinkling lights of Catalina Island. And beyond that, unseen, is Santa Cortez.

Jackson comes up behind me and very gently reaches around to lay his hand atop mine. "We're not losing it."

I want to believe him, but I can't deny that I'm still scared. Scared of losing my island. Of losing him. Of having everything I've worked so hard for—that means so much to me— ripped away.

But just knowing that he understands me so well—that he can see my face and read the direction of my thoughts— comforts me.

We ride the elevator down in silence, holding hands. I'm exhausted, both mentally and physically. It's been a very, very long day, and a hard one. And ending it on this meeting hasn't made it easier. There is no certainty for me. Nothing I can look at and say, yes, this is how it will end because no other result is possible.

I turn to him, knowing that he might not tell me. Knowing that I shouldn't even ask. But I'm grappling here, searching for something to hang on to. Something good to hold close. Something bad to fight against. *Something*. Because this uncertainty is killing me.

"I need to know," I finally say. "I need to know if you killed him."

Jackson looks at me, and for the first time I cannot read

the expression in his eyes. For a moment, I'm afraid that he will argue. That he'll cite the rules and his attorneys' instructions. But then he simply sighs and shakes his head.

"I wanted to. Christ, I wanted to so much I could taste it." He draws a deep breath, then drags his fingers through his hair. "But no," he finally says, though he doesn't quite meet my eyes. "I didn't."

I nod, but I don't feel better. On the contrary, I feel strangely disappointed, as if by not killing Reed, Jackson has failed me in some perverted way. More than that, I'm not certain that I even believe what he has said.

In the end, though, it doesn't matter, and I shiver as I dig deep and acknowledge the real core of my lingering fear—it's that even Jackson, a man to whom control is everything, is helpless. Because guilt or innocence doesn't really matter. It's not about reality. It's about evidence and motive and judges and juries. Twelve people who have their own beliefs and biases. And no matter how much I want to believe in the system, I can't quite seem to manage.

six

I'm screwing around on my phone when Jackson turns from Century Park East onto Santa Monica Boulevard. So it's not until he makes another turn in relatively short order that I look up, because unless traffic is a mess and he's searching for a shortcut, it should be one straight shot to the 405 and then down to the marina.

But there is no eighteen-car pileup. It's just Jackson, who for some reason is not only heading away from the beach but is now steering us into Beverly Hills.

"Are we taking the scenic route?"

"Something like that." He keeps his eyes on the road as he speaks, and while there's nothing inherently odd about that, I can't ignore the chill that flickers up my spine, making the hairs at the nape of my neck prickle.

I'm about to say something—to ask just what exactly is he doing—when he makes a left turn. I see the house that dominates the end of the block, and the answer to that question becomes blazingly, horribly, obviously clear.

"What the hell are you doing?" I demand. "Shit, Jackson, anyone could be watching."

"I just want to see it." He grips the steering wheel so hard that his knuckles are white. I'm looking at his profile, and his jaw is firm, but a muscle in his cheek twitches. He's trying to hold it in—anger, fear, all of it. And dammit, this is not the place he needs to be.

"Jackson, I mean it. We should get out of here."

"It's a crime to drive by the house of a dead man? A dead man who fucked with my life? Who threatened my girlfriend? Who's screwing with me even now that he's in the grave?"

"A crime?" I repeat, my voice rising. "I don't know. Is stupidity a crime?"

For the first time, he turns to me, his motion sharp and quick, and I see the fire of temper light his eyes.

I sit up straighter, because I know that I am right, and I am not backing down. "It's not a crime, but driving past the house of the man you're accused of killing just screams bone-headed to me. Especially when we already know you were here the day of the murder—and that they just might be taking you into custody tomorrow." My voice breaks a little, telegraphing my fear.

"They're either going to arrest me or they won't." His voice is flat. "Where I drive today isn't going to change anything."

He's right. I know he's right. But that doesn't change the fact that I want to lash out at him. To pound some sense into him. Or maybe I just want to kick and scream and throw a tantrum, because nothing is going the way I want it to right now, and I hate this sensation of staring down a track at the headlight of an oncoming train. I force myself to breathe. To just breathe as I try to keep my shit together, if for no other reason than I need to be strong for Jackson.

Finally, Jackson puts the car in gear and starts to drive. He's silent at first, but after a few blocks, he pulls over and sighs deeply, his attention entirely on the house that faces us from the lot at the end of this cul-de-sac.

"They're on it, you know," I say gently. "Harriet's team is going to find out who really did this."

Jackson's hands tighten on the steering wheel. "I know. If her team can bring in other viable suspects, it increases reasonable doubt. It's just that . . ." But he doesn't finish the sentence. Instead he trails off with a shake of his head, then leans back and closes his eyes in what looks like an expression of complete exhaustion.

A knot of fear tightens in my stomach. "Jackson—" But like him, I don't finish my thought. What am I supposed to say? *Are you scared they won't find anyone else because you're the one who did it?* Or maybe, *I hope you killed him because the bastard deserved it, but at the same time I'm terrified I'm going to lose you?*

"Jackson," I begin again, but once more I lose the words.

This time, he takes my hand. "Oh, baby, it's okay. *I'm* okay." He hesitates, his eyes on me, as if he is feeling out my mood. "I just hate not being the one calling the shots. Hell," he adds, his mouth quirking up into the slightest hint of a smile, "maybe I should be the one investigating. At least then it will feel like I'm doing something. And who knows how many suspects I could track down?"

The knot in my stomach loosens. "I get that," I say. "Hell, I get you, and I know it's driving you nuts not to be in control. But you have to be careful, Jackson. You may look like a movie star, but this isn't a movie, and you can't traipse around like you're Sherlock Holmes or something."

The corner of his mouth twitches. "I don't traipse," he says, and relief flutters over me, as soft as a butterfly, because the cloud over him seems to be lifting.

"Fair enough. You don't prance, either. I'm going to say that's a good thing."

"I'd do both if I thought it would help me aim the cops' spotlight on somebody else."

I start to tell him that he can't control the whole world, and he needs to let his attorneys do their job. But the words just sit in my head, stale and stupid. Because this is Jackson, and if he can't control the world, who can? And frankly, if it were my freedom on the line, I wouldn't be able to sit still, either.

"Well, we can't risk having you prance or traipse," I say airily. "Do you want me to talk to Ryan?" I figure if anyone would know how to help with an investigation, it's Stark International's security chief.

But Jackson shakes his head. "No. I'll handle it."

I study his face. "Are you going to hire your own consulting detective?"

"Actually, I think I'm going to ask for a little brotherly advice."

"Really?" I can't help the way my voice rises in surprise.

"The guy knows how to get his hands on information." He glances sideways at me. "And I think it's fair to say he knows how to defend against a murder charge, too. If nothing else, he knows who to pay when he needs results."

"So maybe he's worth knowing, after all?"

"Well, you respect him," he says dryly. "So how bad can he be?" But he's grinning, and I know he means it. For the most part, anyway.

I settle back as Jackson maneuvers onto the freeway. Jackson and Damien may never be as close as I am with my brother, Ethan, but at least they've left epic acrimony and distrust behind. Then again, considering who their father is, maybe they'll bond over their mutually wretched childhoods. That would put them leaps and bounds ahead of me and Ethan, because as much as I love my brother, I haven't shared with him the hell I went through during our youth. Not only because I don't want his pity, but because I don't want his guilt.

Ethan knows that I modeled, and that the money I earned went toward the medical treatments that saved his life. But he doesn't know how much those treatments cost or what exactly our father was selling to Reed. Not just my image, but me. To photograph, to touch. To use.

And though I hated every goddamn minute of it—though I begged my father to make it stop—I never did the one thing that was always in my power to do. I never ran. Because I knew that we needed the money. That despite the horror of it all, somehow I was helping to save my brother.

I shift uncomfortably in my seat, because now my father is in my head, and I really, really don't want him there. I'd pushed him out after he called me in Santa Fe, and I'm not at all pleased that I've let him back in.

"Dammit," Jackson says under his breath, and for a moment I actually think he's commenting on my thoughts.

When I come to my senses, I'm absurdly grateful for the distraction. "What?"

"I completely forgot to call Ronnie at bedtime, and now it's almost eleven there." He slams his hand against the steering wheel. "Shit. So much for father of the year."

"Text Betty," I suggest. "Tell her not to answer her phone. Then call and leave a message for Ronnie that she can play to her in the morning."

Jackson pauses at the road that turns into the marina where his boat is docked. Then he shifts in his seat and stares at me.

I squirm a little under his inspection. "Um, what?"

"Maybe you should get father of the year. That's brilliant."

A delighted laugh bubbles out of me. "I aim to please."

He reaches over and slides his hand very slowly over my jean-clad leg. "And you do it very, very well."

I'm still tingling from the sensual tone of his voice and the heat from his touch as we approach the entrance to the marina. It's marked by a guard station with a gate that lifts and lowers to allow residents and their guests to enter. Never once, however, have I seen it down, and usually the guard who sits in the small station simply waves us through.

Today, though, the gate is lowered—and it's easy enough to see why. Dozens of reporters line the drive—some are even perched on camp-style chairs or sprawled on the ground, as if they've been waiting for hours. But they rise to their feet as Jackson's Porsche approaches, and rush toward us *en masse,* almost like a swarm of bees zeroing in on a target.

"Fuck," Jackson says, and I silently second the curse, even though we both know that we should have expected this.

"Jackson! How long have you known Damien Stark is your half-brother?"

"Did you follow your brother's trial in Germany?"

"Sylvia, did you know your boss and your boyfriend were related?"

"What's the status of the Fletcher house movie, Jackson? Is it tabled now that Reed is dead?"

Jackson is inching the car forward, though I have a feeling he wants to gun it and maybe run over a few toes in the process. He reaches the guard station and rolls the window down to talk to the man inside.

"How long has this been going on, Charlie?"

"Couple of hours, Mr. Steele. The property managers are hiring extra security. We'll keep them out of your hair."

"I'll pay for the extra men." Jackson's voice is tight.

"Well, sir, I guess that's up to you. We've got the cameras on and there'll be extra men walking the property tonight. But you be sure and lock the gate to your dock and the doors on the *Veronica*."

"I will. Thanks, Charlie. And sorry."

"Not your fault, Mr. Steele," the guard says loyally, though I can tell from Jackson's face he disagrees.

He remains tense all the way to his parking slot in front of his boat, and once he kills the engine, he turns to me. I shake my head and press a finger over his lips. I don't know if he's about to curse them or apologize for them, but I don't want to hear either. Instead, I want to make him forget. And so I lean toward him as I lower my hand and press it over his thigh, just close enough to his cock to let him know that the paparazzi are the very last thing I'm interested in at the moment.

He says nothing, but I can feel the shift in his body. A different kind of tension forming. And when I drag my teeth over my lower lip, I see the heat build in his eyes.

"What exactly do you think you're doing, Ms. Brooks?"

"Me? Just thinking."

"About what?"

"About a man I know."

His brows raise. "Oh?"

"Mmm. He's utterly gorgeous. Wildly sexy. The touch of his hands is like magic on my skin."

The corner of his mouth twitches and a victorious trill runs through me. "I think I'm jealous."

I slide my hand up, my pinky brushing lightly against his hardening cock. "It's been one hell of a day. What do you say we go inside, get naked, and help each other forget?"

His eyes are like blue flames. "I think that sounds like an exceptionally good idea."

The heat in his voice makes me gooey in all the right places.

I reluctantly pull back, then open my door. "In that case, mister, follow me." We get out of the car, and I take his hand and lead him through the gate then down the dock to his boat. There's a small gangplank permanently set up; it opens to a door onto the deck. I've been here enough to know the routine, and I take charge, leading the way.

I step carefully onto the sometimes slick deck, glance around the familiar area, see the man—and scream.

Jackson moves in front of me even before the echo of my scream dies away.

I'm breathing hard, my pulse pounding, my body ready for flight. But that's just a lingering reaction. My fear has faded.

The man isn't one of the paparazzi. For that matter, he's not even an intruder. Or, at least, not the kind I'd imagined.

Then again, this kind might be even more dangerous.

This intruder is Jeremiah Stark.

seven

Jackson stared at his father, trying to convince himself that the man was only an apparition. Some sort of horrible revenant. Not actually Jeremiah Stark.

Not here.

Not today.

"About time, boy. I was just about to give up on you."

Jackson didn't move. He didn't say a word. Instead he just stood there with Sylvia behind him, her scream still lingering in the air.

It took every ounce of Jackson's willpower to keep his feet planted and his hands at his sides. Because right then he was certain that very little in this world would feel better than wringing Jeremiah's neck.

When he was certain that he could move without launching himself at his father, he stepped sideways and then back so that he could slide an arm around Syl's waist and pull her to him. It would look, he knew, as if he was comforting her.

But that was only an illusion. He needed her in his arms right now. Needed to hold tight and let the feel of her steady him. Because he'd been pulled tight as a wire all day, and he was dangerously close to snapping.

He focused on his father's face, his gaze unflinching. "You want to tell me how the hell you got on my boat?"

"Not hard," Jeremiah said. He held up his phone. "Lot of pictures of me and my sons on the internet today. I just flashed one at your guard, told him it was urgent that I saw my boy, and he let me right through. I'm surprised you didn't notice my car out there."

"I'd say I'll pay more attention next time, but there isn't going to be a next time. Get the hell off my boat, *Dad*."

"We need to talk," Jeremiah said.

"You need to leave."

"What I need is to convince my son not to be a goddamned idiot."

"Your son? Is that what I am today? I've never really been able to keep that straight." His entire life had been structured by the whim of a father whose focus was on another family— Damien's family. Jackson had been forced to keep the truth of his paternity secret, because god forbid the public should learn that tennis superstar Damien Stark had a secret bastard half-brother squirreled away.

For years, Jackson had resented Damien, channeling the anger and frustration that rightfully belonged to his manipulative, narcissistic father toward the brother he didn't even know. A brother who seemed to have everything in the world at Jackson's expense. A brother who, Jackson was only beginning to learn, had also suffered at the hands of their father, and pretty damn brutally, too.

All of which meant that Jackson wasn't inclined to play the good son simply because Jeremiah was wearing his daddy hat. As Jackson was learning the hard way, being a dad was about one hell of a lot more than biology.

"I did what I had to do so that you could have a good life, and now you're about to toss it all into the crapper. Ms. Brooks," Jeremiah said, turning his attention to Sylvia without warning, "you should go inside. Jackson and I have a few things to discuss."

"I'm not going anywhere." She spoke with such bold finality that Jackson had to bite back a grin. He'd forgotten that she knew his father, of course. Jeremiah Stark might not be close to Damien, but Jeremiah was the kind of man who'd infiltrate himself anyway. And undoubtedly that meant that Sylvia'd had the dubious pleasure of dealing with him on more than one occasion.

"Suit yourself," Jeremiah said. "I'll say what I came here for and then I'll leave. But, boy, you need to get in front of this thing. You need to publicly endorse that movie."

The words, so out of left field, struck Jackson like a blow.

"What the hell are you talking about?" It was Sylvia who asked the question. Jackson was still reeling from the absurdity. "Why on earth would he do that?"

"Motive," Jeremiah said. "Do you think I want to see a son of mine behind bars? You need to play this game smart, son. You need to make sure any argument they might have as to motive is soundly shut down."

"That movie is not getting made." When it had been a question of movie or blackmail, Jackson had made the choice to protect Sylvia. To stop fighting the movie and protect his little girl with love and care. To hold her close, keep her safe, and try to protect her from the glare of an unwelcome spotlight.

But Reed's death had neatly solved the problem of the blackmail photos, and Jackson was no longer pulled in two directions. Now he was going to fight as long and as hard as he could to keep Ronnie out of such a scandalous spotlight. Hell, he'd fight it from a jail cell if he had to, but there was no way he was sitting back and allowing a film about all the tragedy in his little girl's life to hit the screen.

"Then you're a bigger fool than I thought," Jeremiah said. "Because that movie's going to happen whether you try to stop it or not. You think you have that kind of power? Think again. And now that they know Damien is tied to you there's going to be even more push to get it made. And what if you cause enough of a stink that they rewrite it as fiction? So what? Everyone will still know. The gossip will still be out there."

Beside him, Syl was squeezing his hand, sharing her strength. And dammit, right then all he wanted was his father gone and his woman in his arms. Forget the photographers, forget the press, forget the man standing right in front of him. In that moment, Jackson needed nothing more than Sylvia. To take her hard, to bend her body to his. He craved the feel of her against him, and the desire to push her to the edge—to manipulate her pleasure—cut through him like a wild thing, fierce and demanding.

His pulse kicked up as he anticipated watching passion build in her eyes, knowing that he was responsible for taking her far. That if nothing else, he had control over this woman—her body, her release, her satisfaction.

So much around him was fucked up—spinning out of control. His father. Reed's murder. Even the bullshit sabotage of the resort. His life was a goddamn tempest, and Syl was the eye of the storm. Right now, he needed her.

Hell, he fucking craved her. And it pissed him off that he couldn't take her right then, right there, because the man who was his father was still standing in front of them, blathering on. "Say you support the movie, and you'll have erased motive. No point in killing him if you don't care about the damn film, eh?"

"You need to leave," Jackson said coldly. "We're going inside. You're not invited."

"I'm trying to look out for you."

"Is that what you're doing?"

"Dammit, son—"

"Son? Are you sure about that? Because from where I was standing I was never your son. I was some obligation tucked off in a corner somewhere. The little boy no one was supposed to know about. God forbid Mom or I caused a scandal and messed up the flow of gold-flavored milk from your cash cow."

He heard the fury in his voice—the decades' old hurt—and he wished he'd said nothing. The last thing he wanted was to reveal himself to this man.

"I was only looking out for you and your mother." His father was an attractive man with the air of a well-aged movie star. Now, though, he just looked red in the face and flustered.

But those words were empty excuses, and the look of disdain that Jackson shot at his father said as much.

"I was bringing money in," Jeremiah continued. "Keeping food on the table."

"Yeah. You're a real saint." Beside him, Syl shifted. The movement was almost imperceptible, but he knew what she was thinking. She wasn't seeing Jeremiah, but her own father, and Jackson was struck by the similarity between those two men who played their children like pawns on a chessboard.

"Jackson—"

"What were you doing at my screening?" The question, seemingly out of left field, cut off the protest and had his father taking a single step backward.

"You know damn well I'm on the board of the National

Historic and Architectural Conservation Project with Michael," he said, referring to Michael Prado, who directed *Stone and Steele,* the documentary about Jackson and his design of an Amsterdam museum. It had screened not long ago at the Chinese theater. That night was burned into Jackson's mind not because of the film or because his father had shown his face, but because that night was the first step to getting Sylvia back. And for that, Jackson would happily declare the date a national holiday.

"But even if I weren't, I still would have attended," Jeremiah added in the face of Jackson's continued silence. "I wanted to celebrate my son's achievements."

After a moment, his father shifted his weight from one foot to another as if trying to decide what to say next. When he didn't come up with anything, Jackson casually asked, "Did you know Reed?"

Jeremiah's mouth pulled into a frown. "What the hell kind of question is that?"

"One I'd like an answer to."

"No. Not really. I've met him a time or two."

"About what?"

"What the hell, boy? Is this the third degree?"

"Maybe it is. You're awfully interested in that movie."

"I'm interested in saving your ass," Jeremiah spat back.

"I can take care of my own ass, thanks." He pulled Sylvia closer. "And now it really is time for you to go. Trust me when I say you've worn out your welcome."

"Jackson, please. I'm your father."

"I suggest you don't say that again."

For a moment, it seemed as if Jeremiah was going to argue, and Jackson felt the tension build in him. Hell, he almost hoped the bastard tried to stay, put up a fight. *Any excuse. Any excuse at all.*

So Jackson was disappointed—but reluctantly had to

admit it was probably for the best—when Jeremiah turned and headed off the boat. He paused after a few steps though, then looked back to where Jackson stood with Sylvia at his side. "You shouldn't have told Damien you're his brother, but I guess it's good you did before it came out. Less pain for both of you."

"Do you really think I believe that you give a fuck about what's best for either of us? Your focus has always been on Jeremiah Stark, and no one else."

"That's not true."

"I don't know what your angle is, old man, but I know you came here with one. And whatever game you expect me to play, I'm not biting."

"No games. I'm your father. I'm concerned." He drew a breath, then shoved his hands in his coat pockets, and for a moment he just looked tired, and a lot older than his sixty-plus years. "We've had a rocky relationship. But I care about you. I'm your father, after all."

"That's just a word," Jackson said. "And right now it feels pretty damn hollow."

eight

I watch Jackson as he watches his father disappear into the night.

My whole body aches, and I realize that I haven't relaxed since we arrived and found the paparazzi camped out.

For that matter, I haven't really relaxed since we left Charles's office. Since we left Santa Fe. Since the detectives arrived with the news of Reed's murder.

Now we're just hours away from Jackson walking through the doors of the Beverly Hills Police Department. And I'm so damned afraid that he's not going to walk back out again.

Hell, maybe I should thank Jeremiah and the damn story vultures. Because for a few minutes at least, I wasn't afraid. Instead, I was just angry. At the paparazzi. At Jeremiah. At my own father.

I take a deep breath. I don't want either of those men in my head right now. I just want Jackson, but his back is still to me, his eyes on the now-empty dock.

"Jackson?" I say his name tentatively.

He turns and although the anger on his face fades when he looks at me, I can see that it still lingers behind his eyes. "I knew we'd have to deal with the press at some point, but he had no right coming here. He had no business interrupting us, coming unannounced, bothering us at all."

"No, he didn't. But he's gone now." My voice is soft. Right now, I want only to soothe.

He runs his fingers through his hair and sighs. He looks so tired, and I just want to pull him close and hold him. I reach for him and gently take his hand.

"You're exhausted, and you have to be at the police station in the morning." I give his hand a tug as I start to turn away. "Come on, you need to sleep."

I lead him below deck to the area that serves as his office, then start toward the door that leads down to the stateroom.

Jackson pulls me back. "No." The word is rough, and I turn back to see his face and the wild hunger that I should have expected. Because it is not sleep that Jackson needs now. Not when the world is crashing down around us.

He pulls me to him, giving me no choice but to stumble toward him. I crash against him, breathing hard, my body trembling with answering desire.

"How could I sleep when tonight might be our last night? When the goddamn guillotine is poised to cut off my head?"

"Don't," I beg. I know the truth too damn well, and I don't want to hear it out loud.

"Don't what? Don't touch you? Don't need you?" His lips brush my ear as he speaks, deliberately misunderstanding me. "Don't take everything I need from you so that I can hold it close to me tomorrow, and the next day, and the next?"

"Please, Jackson. I don't want—"

"The truth?" He pulls his head back so that he is looking straight into my eyes, and I look away, ashamed because that is exactly what I want to avoid. "I'm not hiding from reality, baby, and neither are you." He trails his fingertip over the curve of my ear, then slowly down my neck. "I need you, Sylvia. I always need you. But tonight—if you pushed me away tonight—"

"What?" Already, I am limp with desire. Already, I am his to do with what he will.

His mouth curves into a slow smile, and I see a dangerous kind of heat flare in his eyes. "I'd just take what I want, however I want." With a violent tug he slams my pelvis against his. He's rock hard, his hand on my ass giving me no place to go, nowhere to shift, while his other hand cups my breast roughly even as his mouth crashes hard over mine.

It's a full-on assault, startling in its swiftness, its heat, its power. "Yes." The word is a groan, my body molding to his as electricity rips through me, filling me with spark and sizzle and making my body hum.

"Tell me you want it," he whispers when he breaks the kiss. "To bend to my will. To hand me the key to your pleasure. To be the instrument of mine."

With each word I am getting wetter, and my breasts are painfully tight inside my bra. I want to shift my hips and move in slow rhythmic motions until I find some satisfaction. I don't. I force myself to remain still.

"Tell me, Sylvia," he repeats. "Tell me I can take you. Whenever and however I want."

I tilt my head up. I look him in the eyes. "No," I whisper, as a wild, forbidden heat washes through me, soaking my panties and making my nipples so sensitive that even the slight motion from breathing is like a sensual assault.

He holds my gaze for a moment, and this time his eyes are flat. The twitch of a muscle in his cheek is the only evidence of any emotion that I see.

Then he roughly cups his hands over my breasts. He

squeezes, his thumbs and forefingers finding my nipples and teasing them through the thin material of my blouse and the lace of my bra. "I'm going to fuck you so hard," he says, as his fingers send wild currents of heat ripping through me.

Swiftly, he claims my mouth in a kiss that leaves me gasping once he's moved on, brushing his lips over my neck, then over my blouse to tease my already sensitive breasts.

I try desperately to stay upright despite the fact that I'm feeling just a little dizzy. He drops to his knees and tilts his head back to look up at me. And though it is Jackson who is on his knees, there is no doubt that he is the one in charge. "Take off your clothes."

I shake my head.

His brow quirks just slightly. "Take off your clothes." This time, each word is stressed.

I lick my lips. "No."

The corner of his mouth twitches, and he stands up slowly. "No?"

I meet his eyes defiantly. "I thought you were taking what you wanted."

"I am," he says. "What I want is your submission."

"Oh."

I see a flash of victory in his eyes before he starts to walk away. "Decide how you want to play the game, sweetheart. But know that I'm only willing to play by my rules."

He is almost to the steps that lead back to the deck when I call out to him. He turns, his brow raised in silent query.

I slip off my ballet flats. And then, as he slowly walks back toward me, I peel myself out of my jeans, taking my underwear with them. He reaches down, then uses the tip of his finger to lift them off the deck of the boat. "Lace. Very nice."

"I'm glad you approve." My voice sounds breathy. I'm standing there in only a T-shirt and bra. The window facing the ocean is open, and the cool night air teases my already soaked cunt until I am right there on the edge, waiting to go over, and wanting that push so badly that I'm not sure I can survive the anticipation.

"No more," he says, and it takes me a moment to realize he means the panties.

"I—what?"

"Don't wear them." He meets my eyes. "When I think of you, I want to think of you bare. But do wear the necklace. From now on. Until I say otherwise."

"Oh." Little tremors of pleasure course through me. The necklace is a chain with a small pendant that is actually a vibrator. It's lovely and classy and deliciously effective. And I haven't worn it since before we left for Santa Fe.

I nod. "Yes," I say. And when he lifts a brow, I amend to, "Yes, sir."

"Good girl. But you're still not naked."

"Oh." I'd gotten distracted. "Right." I pull my shirt off and toss it on the deck, then drop my bra on top of it.

"You're so beautiful." He brushes a single fingertip up the curve of my hip. "It's a rare thing to get to touch something of such beauty." As he speaks, he draws his finger higher, the contact light but oh-so powerful. He traces a line beneath my breast. The touch is as gentle as a butterfly's kiss, and yet so intense it sends shuddering waves of electricity rolling through me.

When he pulls his finger away, breaking the contact between us, I whimper.

"In museums, the rules are clear. Anyplace, in fact, where there is something of beauty, no touching is allowed."

He bends to whisper in my ear. He is not touching me, but his breath as he speaks is as potent as a caress. "But those rules don't apply to an owner. So tell me, Sylvia. Are you mine?"

"Yes. Oh, god yes."

"Touching," he repeats as if I hadn't spoken. "Exploring and teasing." As if in illustration of his words, he draws a single fingertip lightly over my body. My arms. My shoulders. The back of my neck.

There is nothing particularly sensual about any of the places he explores, and yet he fires my senses everywhere he touches, and threads of electricity stream from his fingertips all the way to my core, making me weak and wet and terribly impatient.

He drops to his knees, his hands now holding me steady at my hips. He tilts his head back and I look down and meet his eyes, and the desire and heat I see there humbles me.

He eases forward, pressing his mouth to my abdomen, then trails kisses down, lower and lower, following the landing strip of pubic hair to the soft skin at the juncture of my thighs. I am lost now, floating in some wild place where I have been reduced to little more than sensation and need, desire and demand. And when he uses his tongue to gently lave my clit, I arch back as crackling threads of pleasure shoot through me to converge at my sex.

I'm right there, floating on the edge, and all I need is one tiny push to send me over. Another flick of his tongue. Another stroke of his finger. I have been reduced to pure need, to desperate want.

Jackson, however, denies me.

He takes his hands from my hips. He pulls his mouth from my body. And then he rises slowly, his smug grin making clear that he knows exactly what he is doing to me.

"Go down below," he says in a voice that promises all sorts of wicked pleasures. "Get on the bed. Spread your legs, and close your eyes."

I hurry down to the staterooms below. I look back once to see if he's coming, but he's not there. I hesitate, but only for a moment. This is a game, I know. This is what we need. This is a way to get lost in each other. To forget what is coming. And, yes, to have something to hold on to later.

I settle myself on the bed and lay there spread open for him, my eyes closed, my imagination humming. He likes this. Me waiting for him. Me wet for him, wanting him. Laying here, wide open, for him to use however he wishes.

And the truth is, I like it, too. The anticipation that comes with being spread out naked and wet. The soft kiss of the air over my skin. The tease of the boat's creaks and jolts, which keep my body thrumming because I am not sure if it is the sound of the boat or the sound of footsteps that I hear.

But what I like most is the pleasure of giving in to his demands. Of letting myself go completely and knowing that not only will he take me far, but that he will bring me back safely.

I don't know how much time has passed when I feel a shift in the air. I turn my head to the side and my ear brushes his lips.

"Beautiful."

That is all he says, but the heat in that word sends ripples through me, like a swarm of electric butterflies that settle between my legs, the lightness of their touch drawing me to the edge, but not quite over.

I catch the scent of mint on his breath and think that's odd, because Jackson doesn't suck on mints or chew gum as a rule. I don't ask, though, as I know he doesn't want me to speak. And, frankly, my curiosity is satisfied soon enough, because without any preamble at all, he runs his hands up my thighs spreading me wider, then closes his mouth over my clit.

Oh. My. God.

His tongue is teasing me in the most exceptional way, but that is not what has truly sent me reeling. It's the mint. Icy and hot all at the same time, arousing and enticing with just a hint of pain.

I squirm, trying to escape this onslaught of sensation that threatens to overwhelm me, but Jackson holds me fast. I can go nowhere. I can only submit to pleasure. To pain. To the brilliant, fiery heat that thrusts me up and over until I am arched up in the bed, my hands tight on my breasts as Jackson's tongue reduces me to nothing but ashes.

Only when all the tremors have passed do I actually breathe again. But even then I have no respite because Jackson grabs me by my hips and slides me down the bed so that my ass is right on the edge. He lifts me, then thrusts hard into me.

I melt with the pleasure of it. Of being taken. Of being fucked hard.

And when I slip my hand down to tease my so-sensitive clit, I hear Jackson's soft growl of approval as his body slams into mine again and again and again.

I feel the tension build in him, and my muscles grab tight, wanting to heighten the explosion, to make it hard. To make it wild.

And when he finally explodes inside me, my body milks him until the last tremor of pleasure has swept through us both.

Once we are recovered enough to move, he tells me I can open my eyes. I find him smiling at me, his expression warm and satisfied. He slides up the bed, then holds out a hand for me to do the same.

I take a different route, though. I kiss my way up his body. His calf. His knee. His taut, toned thigh.

I see the newly inked tattoo that Cass gave him right beside his pubic bone—my initials, SB—and I gently kiss it. Then I gently lick up the length of his semi-hard cock, making him growl softly.

I glance up, grinning, and notice the tin of mints on the bedside table.

I start to reach for them, but he laughs and grabs my hands, sliding me up his body until I am balanced atop him and his arms are around my waist.

"No fair. I want to try them."

"And I want to hold you."

He rolls us over so that we are spooned side by side, his fingers idly stroking my shoulder and down my arm as I start to drift.

I am right on the verge of sleep when the words come. I don't know what makes me say them—perhaps I want Jackson to know that we have exorcised not only the ghost of Jeremiah, but my father, too.

"My dad called me."

I whisper the words, but I know that he has heard me when his arm tightens almost imperceptibly around me. "When?"

"In Santa Fe. You were outside with Ronnie. I'd just taken a shower."

"Why didn't you tell me before? Wait," he immediately amends. "I know why. I was being an ass."

I roll over, because I need to see his face. "No," I say, then kiss him gently. "You were trying to protect me. In a bone-headed way, sure," I add, drawing a small smile from him. "But the thought was there. And I didn't tell you because you had enough on your plate with Ronnie and the news about Reed."

He flashes an ironic grin. "So you were trying to protect me, too. Aren't we a pair?"

My smile is wide and easy. "I like to think so."

He continues to stroke my shoulder, and I sigh, simply enjoying the sensation. But after a moment, I prop myself up on my elbow, frowning. "Why did Jeremiah not want the connection between you and Damien revealed? I mean, it made a little bit of sense back when Damien was the golden boy with his face on cereal boxes. But now?"

Jackson shakes his head. "I don't know. To be honest, I wonder if he might be the one who leaked it."

"The father doth protest too much?"

"Something like that."

"But why?"

"No idea," Jackson admits. "And right now, I'm not interested in thinking about it." He draws me close and I tuck my head against his chest. "Sylvia, tomorrow at the—"

"I don't want to talk about tomorrow. Please. Can we just not?"

There is silence for a moment, and then he says, "All right. But it's coming whether we want it to or not."

I know that. I do. But for a few more hours I want to hold tight to the illusion.

And maybe, if I wish hard enough and hold Jackson tight enough, I can make the fantasy real.

nine

As police stations go, it probably doesn't get much better than the Beverly Hills Police Department. I'm no expert, but I've watched enough cop shows to know that most police stations sport walls with dull gray paint that probably used to be white, Plexiglas barriers that are so clouded they're no longer transparent, and lots and lots of faded, crumpled notices tacked to walls.

Not so this station. I'm sitting on a polished wooden bench in a long hallway. It's not travertine tile, but the flooring is clean and polished. For that matter, everything is clean and shiny, from the building to the people who work here. And right now, I'm focusing way, way too much on all of it. Because if I spend my time noticing the way the light from the window makes a geometric pattern when it hits the opposite wall, then maybe I won't completely freak out about the fact that Jackson has been in an interview room with Harriet and two detectives for almost an hour.

They'd arrived before I did at eight this morning. Jackson had told me not to come. "You can't go into the interview, so you'll be sitting by yourself worrying. Go to work. Do something. Don't think about it. And I'll be with you before you realize any time has passed at all."

It was a great plan in theory, and when Jackson dropped me by my condo on his way to Beverly Hills, I was totally on board. But then my car decided it had other plans, and I ended up on Rexford Drive at the art deco–inspired building.

Now I'm doing exactly what Jackson said I would be doing—worrying instead of working.

And, yes, I know that he won't be saying anything except, "On the advice of my attorney, I refuse to answer," yada yada yada. But what if they arrest him? What if the last moments he had free were last night?

What if today is the day that I lose him?

I pull out my phone to call Cass, but on Mondays she doesn't open the studio until two, and so she tends to sleep in. I know she won't mind if I wake her, especially under the circumstances, but she and Siobhan haven't been back together that long, and I hate to interrupt. Especially since I'm so happy that Siobhan is back in Cass's life—and Zee is so very out of it.

I stroke my thumb idly over the surface of my phone, debating. But in the end I slide it back into my purse. I'm a big girl, after all. I can go it alone.

Oh, god.

Those words slice through me, because I do not want to go it alone. Not now in this hallway and certainly not for the rest of my life.

Breathe. Just breathe.

I do, and that's my mantra for about ten minutes—*just breathe.* But as each minute ticks by, my fear is ratcheting up, too. And when I can't stand it anymore, I yank my phone out of my purse and am just about to dial when I hear my name from the wrong end of the hallway.

I glance automatically toward the doors through which I expect Jackson to emerge. He's not there, of course, and when I turn in the other direction, I see Orlando McKee striding toward me.

"Ollie?"

Ollie works as an associate at Bender Twain, but I can't imagine why he's here. I leap to my feet, suddenly panicked. "What is it? What's wrong?"

"Nothing. I haven't heard a thing. Nikki asked me to come."

"Really?"

I must sound as astounded as I feel, because he laughs. "I guess Damien told her you weren't at the office, and she figured you were here. Worried. So she called me."

"That's incredibly sweet." I'm genuinely touched. I like Nikki a lot, and we've become friends, but in the grand scheme of things we still don't know each other that well— the only truly close friend I've ever had is Cass. But I think it's a friendship worth working on, and the simple fact that she sent Ollie to hold my hand tells me that she feels the same way.

"How's Cass?" he asks. "Has she decided what she's going to do?"

"She wants to go forward," I say, referring to Cass's plan to franchise Totally Tattoo. "I'm sure she'll call you soon about the next step, but right now she's in that blissful new relationship stage. Renewed, actually, but why split hairs?"

"Good for her. I hope it sticks."

Since I happen to know that his attempts to renew a relationship were less than successful, I change the subject. "I'm having drinks with her and my brother tomorrow night. I'll tell her you said hi. Maybe that'll nudge her."

"Definitely tell her hello for me, but no need to nudge. She needs to take her time and be sure."

"You sound very lawyerly."

"I practice in the mirror every morning," he deadpans, making me laugh.

"You're looking very lawyerly, too." His long hair has been cut short, and his glasses have been replaced by contacts. Basically, Orlando McKee has gone from hippie to hot.

"I decided—well, I decided it was time to grow up a bit."

I smile in response, but the truth is that I've surpassed my small-talk quota. I turn away from Ollie to stare at the closed door at the end of the hall. The door that leads to the bull pen and the detectives' offices and an interview room with Jackson in it.

"I'm starting to really get scared." My words are so soft that I'm not even sure that Ollie has heard them.

"I know." He hooks an arm around my shoulders and I lean against him. "But even if they arrest him, that's not—"

He doesn't finish the sentence because the door opens at the end of the hall. For the flash of an instant, my imagination runs wild, and I picture Jackson in an orange jumpsuit, his wrists bound in cuffs.

The image is so vibrant, so horrible, that it propels me to my feet. And when I really do see him—unfettered and striding toward me with his usual confident air—I can't help myself. I race to him and launch myself into his outstretched arms.

"You're here," he says as Harriet moves away toward Ollie to give us privacy.

"Of course I am."

My legs are wrapped around his hips and he's holding me up by the waist. Now, he releases me, and I slide down his body, relishing the sensation of being with him. Of being able to touch him. Of the world having righted itself.

When my feet are on the floor, I hook my arms around his neck and he bends forward, his forehead pressed to mine.

"How was it?"

"I'm not in a cell. I'm counting it as a win."

I frown. "Don't joke about that."

"Sweetheart," he says, "I'm not joking."

I look at his face—at the tension there, at the exhaustion. And worry swirls in my gut. "Oh, god. What do they know?"

He runs his hand over his hair. "Not much. Not yet." But then he meets my eyes. "My number on his cell phone. I called him on Halloween before I went to his house."

"Oh, god." I reach for the wall and then drop down onto the nearby bench. Jackson immediately sits beside me.

"No," he says. "*No*. All they know is I called. And as Harriet says, why would I do that if I was going to kill him? Leave an electronic trail? That wouldn't be smart." He tilts my chin up with the tip of his finger. "And we both know I'm smart."

I hug myself to ward off a chill, but I nod. He is. Smart enough to double back, create false leads. To plan a murder if he wanted to. Or angry enough to fly off the handle and let all that intelligence fly right out the window. Either way the cops play it, that's a piece of a much larger puzzle. A piece that I wish didn't exist at all.

Jackson's hands twine with my own. "Hey," he says softly. "I'm a free man right now. Let's celebrate that, okay, and not the what-ifs?"

I nod, feeling raw and hollow and like I could use a good long cry. I'm overwhelmed, I know. Battered by emotions. But what I want to be is numb.

"I'm glad you're here," he tells me again. "I don't think I could get through this without you."

I manage a tremulous smile, because I know that he needs to see it. "You won't ever have to," I say, and even as I speak, the horrible, awful reality that has been poking at my sub-conscious breaks through, and it is all that I can do not to bury my face in his shirt, hold him close, and cry.

Because I have spoken the truth: I will always be there for him.

But if he's arrested—if he's convicted—the same won't be true for me.

I'll be alone.

And I honestly don't know if I'm strong enough to survive without Jackson at my side.

"This one is completely impossible," Rachel says as she hands me an envelope addressed to Damien.

I've spent the last hour helping her sort through various pending items that have built up as she's manned Damien's desk. I'm glad for the work. Jackson and I had a quick cele-bratory breakfast on the way to the office, but just because the ax hasn't fallen doesn't mean it's not still poised to do just that. And I can't spend the day wondering what's going to happen next.

With Rachel—with the job—I'm forced to focus. And that's a good thing.

I pull a card from the envelope and see that it's an invita-tion to Senator Robertson's daughter's wedding, and Senator Robertson is the kind of man with whom conglomerates like Stark International want to stay friendly. Considering the stress in Rachel's voice, I realize that she knows that. I also know why it's impossible—Damien will be in China, along with the heads of other multibillion-dollar corporations, to discuss all manner of business with Chinese government of-ficials.

"Should I just decline and send a gift?"

"Yes, but Damien needs to send a personal note, too, ex-plaining that he'll be out of the country. And," I add as I remember something, "there's one more thing." I'm standing behind her desk so that we both have a view of my—well, today it's her—computer monitor. I bend so that I can reach the mouse, then open up the file we keep on Senator Robertson. Then I lean back, smiling with victory as I point at the screen. "There."

Rachel skims the article that I've copied into the file— a small piece from the *Washington Post* about the senator's wife and her involvement in a retired greyhound adoption program. "Check with Damien, of course, but that's a cause he'll support."

"Send a note to the senator along with a donation for his wife's cause?"

"See how good you're getting at this job?"

She makes a face. "I spent the entire morning rearranging meetings and dealing with Dallas."

"Sykes? Or the city?" Cold fingers of worry flicker up my spine.

"The man—no, no, it's not the resort." She hurries to re-assure me, and I realize my face must be revealing more than I want it to. "He's throwing some party in San Diego to celebrate a new store opening and he wants Nikki and Damien to go, but both their schedules are insane, and—"

"Yeah," I say, putting my hand on her shoulder. "Believe me, I get it."

"Advice?"

"Learn the subtle art of saying no."

She scowls.

"Hey, if you want this desk . . ."

"If we weren't at work, I'd have to call you a nasty name." She smiles brightly. "But I'm at work and on my best behavior, so I'll just leave that to your imagination."

I laugh, genuinely amused. The more time I spend with her, the more I like Rachel, and I'm glad that she'll be taking

over for me when I move full-time to the real estate department. *If* I move full-time, I amend. That's not happening until
the resort happens—on time, on budget, and with all the
other trappings of success. But with land mines, scandalous
photos, hacked emails, and murder trials, I'm having to fight
harder and harder to get my resort off the ground—all at a
time when I'm horribly distracted.

"So how are you doing?" Rachel asks, and I jump, realizing that I'd slid off into my own little world of anxiety. "I
mean, the two of you, and all this stuff with Jackson's arrest.
Are you okay?"

I nod. I'm not okay, of course. I'm a nervous wreck. I'm
terrified that Jackson will be taken away from me. I'm terrified of what it will mean if he is. Of what it will mean for me.
For Ronnie.

Jackson and I haven't talked about that since the one
vague conversation on the airport tarmac. And that is scaring
me, too. That uncertainty. If he goes to jail, do I become Aunt
Sylvia? Do I become Mommy?

And if so, what do I do then? How the hell am I supposed
to cope without him?

I give myself a solid mental shake, because those are the
kinds of things that I'm not letting stay in my head. That way
lies madness. Or at the very least, bone-deep terror.

So instead, I force a smile that I am certain looks lame.
"It's been hard. But we're good." I lift a shoulder. Just one
more martyr making it through the day.

"Oh, Syl." Rachel's voice is full of genuine pity, and I really do appreciate that she cares.

I glance down at the floor, as if I can see through the car-
pet and concrete to where Jackson sits many floors below in
his office, working at his drafting table. "The work helps,
you know? It keeps him sane."

"You, too," she says, and I have to nod. There are only

two things that pull me out of the path of the nightmare that is barreling down on us—getting lost in Jackson and getting lost in my work.

"How about you and Trent?" I ask, because I want to change the subject. Her cheeks turn a little pink, and I grin. "Did you guys have a hot weekend in Santa Barbara?"

The pink fades and her mouth turns down and I want to kick myself.

"Santa Barbara?"

I shake my head. "Sorry, I just assumed. I had dinner with my old boss, and he mentioned that he'd bumped into Trent in Santa Barbara. And I know you guys are going out, so I thought . . ." I trail off with a shrug and a weak smile, a string of *shit, shit, shit* running through my head.

"Nope," she says, her voice just a little thin and possibly a little hurt. "But maybe he was scoping out a place for a wild weekend."

"Probably. Or more likely it had nothing to do with anything. Maybe he has family there."

Her head tilts to the side. "Actually, I think he does." She nods firmly, as if she's just solved a sticky problem and is ready to put it away. But there's still a haunted look in her eyes, and I have a feeling that I may have just opened a nasty can of worms for Trent.

Honestly, considering how discreet I can be about Damien's personal business, you'd think I would know how not to open my mouth and insert my foot.

Damien's door opens and he steps out, and I swear I want to kiss him just for breaking up the moment. "Rachel, I'm going to meet Aiden at the Stark Plaza site before my meeting with Dallas."

I frown. "Should I come? Are you talking about his investment?"

"Not at this meeting, no. Dallas is still on board." He

meets my eyes. "I'm sorry, Syl, but Tarrant Properties pulled out. I don't have confirmation, but I think they've been courted by Lost Tides," he adds, referring to the competing Santa Barbara resort that is my nemesis.

His voice is tight, reflecting my own coiling anger.

"Do you know who made the overture?" The developers of Lost Tides have been playing PR games, keeping the participants under wraps, with their early marketing documents claiming that it's the resort that matters, not the names behind it.

To me, all that means is that they don't have a name as big as Jackson's.

Damien shakes his head. "Once they start actively signing investors, they'll have to be more transparent."

"Good," I say. Whoever started that damn resort copied the idea from me. Even if I can't stop them, I want to know who it is I hate.

Damien's expression is knowing. "Don't worry about the competition," he says. "Just worry about making Cortez the best it can be. The rest will fall into place."

"Assuming we don't lose all our investors."

"No one else has bolted."

"But there's no arrest yet." I don't mean to say that. I don't mean to shift the focus from the resort itself to Jackson. But the words slipped out—the worry that Jackson is going to end up behind bars is just too close to the surface with me.

"And if it comes to that, we'll deal with it, too," Damien says gently. "We'll meet for an update after my lunch."

I nod, and he's heading toward the elevator when the doors open and Jackson bursts out. "Have you seen the latest bullshit?" he asks as he thrusts his phone into Damien's hand.

"Well, hell," Damien says. "Though I can't say that I'm surprised."

I hurry to them—and even Rachel abandons the desk to

join us. I stand between the men, my hand on Jackson's shoulder so I can rise up on my toes to see better.

All I can read is the headline—*Another Alcatraz off the California Coast?*

I look at Jackson, confused. "What—?"

"It's a bullshit editorial. About Reed's murder. The assault. And my alleged involvement in both of those and the Cortez project. And then, to milk the absurdity properly, the writer pulls in Damien, too."

"A murderous dynamic duo," Damien reads, his mouth curving down with a frown before he looks up at Jackson. "You can be Robin. And I'm not wearing a cape."

I take the phone from Damien and start to skim.

"It's not funny," Jackson says.

"No. It's not," Damien says. "But it's also not unexpected."

I'm barely listening to the two of them. Instead, my stomach is twisting more and more as I read. "This is another dig on the project," I say. I look at both men in turn. "Like the land mine bullshit. This isn't gossip about Jackson or your relationship or Reed or any of it. This is about shutting down Cortez. *A tainted island*," I read. "*Bathed in blood and tragedy.* How much do you want to bet that every one of the investors will get this in their inbox?"

I see Jackson and Damien exchange glances. "She's right," Damien says.

A burst of fury cuts through me. "I swear I will strangle whoever is behind this."

Jackson reaches over and takes my hand, and I find the change in our positions both comforting and amusing. Usually I'm the one cooling his temper.

I glance at him, and see that he is watching Damien. "Listen," he says, as he glances at his watch. "How's the rest of your afternoon? Can I buy you a drink at happy hour?"

For a moment, I'm confused. Then I remember Jackson's

comment about doing his own investigation into Reed's killer, and asking Damien for help. Unfortunately, I happen to know that Damien's heading out to see Aiden, and after that his schedule is jam-packed late into the night, so that ball isn't going to start rolling today.

"I'm busy," he says evenly. "But it's nothing that can't be rescheduled. Rachel," he adds, turning toward her desk, "Take care of it for me."

"Of course, sir," she says, as Jackson shoots me a smug grin. My eyes, I know, are wide with surprise.

I'm still gaping as the two of them step onto the elevator, and when the doors shut, Rachel lets out a long sigh.

I laugh. "It's not that bad. Just call everyone and tell them something came up. With a man in Damien's position, it's hardly unexpected."

"Oh, that's not it," she says. "It's this." She taps her monitor and I hurry around her desk to stand behind her, dread building as I do.

The moment I see the screen, I exhale, my breath forming a single word—"Shit."

I'm looking at a scene from last night on the boat. It's an image of the three of us, with me standing just behind Jackson, who is looking at his father with an expression of calm, contained fury. His stance conveys power and control, and though this must have been taken by one of the paparazzi with a long lens, the shot is so clear that the scar that bisects Jackson's left eyebrow is in sharp focus.

The caption—*Daddy Trouble for the Man of Steele?*—is little more than a snarky irritation. But the photo itself scares me, and not just because of how closely the paparazzi have crept in, managing to take shots of conversations that should have been private.

No, what scares me is what I see in the image. What the entire world can see now.

Because the camera has captured a man who goes after what he wants, even if that means walking into battle. A man who will protect what is his. A man who will kill if necessary.

A man who, I think, has done just that.

And now I fear that the whole world knows it, too.

ten

Phil, the bartender at the Gallery Bar, slid two glasses of scotch in front of Jackson and Damien. "Anything else, Mr. Steele?"

"Thanks, no. We're good."

The bartender hesitated, then nodded. "Well, if you change your mind," he offered, before moving on to take care of a couple sitting close together at the far end of the long, polished granite bar. Jackson hid a smile. He'd been served by Phil a few times now, and he understood that the young man's simple comment was more than just an offer of another drink. It was a sign of support as Jackson navigated the rough seas of the tabloid world.

"Friend of yours?"

"No, but he's good at his job, discreet, and seems to be a good judge of character. He likes me, after all."

Damien laughed, then took a sip of his drink. They'd left the Tower together, then ignored the calls and questions from the flock of paparazzi that had taken to lingering on the grounds in front of the building.

Questions and camera clicks had followed them as they walked down the hill together. Jackson had felt his nerves twitching—all he wanted was to get out of that spotlight— but he had to admire the way his brother had blinders on, ignoring the shouted questions and demands for photos even as he continued to chat with Jackson as they walked. Damien had put up with this shit for a long time, and now that Jackson understood what it was like to dodge the press, his respect for the brother he was only just getting to know grew even more.

Their destination was the Millennium Biltmore hotel and this historic bar, which was one of its showpieces, not to mention Jackson's favorite bar in the city. Damien had headed automatically toward a table in the corner, but Jackson had demurred, then led them to the bar. He liked sitting there in the view of the carved wooden angels with the room behind him. He felt at home at the bar, whereas at a table, he felt like a guest subject to the whim of his host.

The thought of whims made him frown. "Do you think she's right?"

"About the saboteur and the Alcatraz article? Probably."

"Fuck." Jackson punctuated that articulate sentiment by tossing back a long swallow of eighteen-year-old Macallan. "We need to know who's screwing with us. And," he added, keeping his eyes off his brother as he set his glass back on the bar, "I need to know who really killed Reed."

He turned to find Damien's eyes on him. "Honestly, I thought you did."

Jackson hesitated, then covered the silence with another sip of his scotch. "There's a lot of that going around. I need to know who else wanted that fucker dead, and why. It plays to my defense. And, frankly, I'd like to shake that man's hand."

Damien studied him, and Jackson was certain his brother was weighing the truth in Jackson's words. Was this for real? Or was Jackson manufacturing new pieces of the puzzle, so that if the police asked, Damien could honestly say that Jackson asked for help finding the real killer, so surely that killer wasn't him.

He was silent for so long, that Jackson began to fear his brother was going to tell him to fuck off. "Arnold Pratt," Damien finally said. "He's a private investigator I keep on retainer. He works primarily for the company—Ryan sends him all our background checks to handle—but he's done some work personally for me. A few matters that required both digging and finesse. If he has the time, he'll take the job. And if he doesn't have the time, my guess is that for the right fee, he'll make time. Syl has his number. Why didn't she just suggest him?"

"She probably would have. I told her I wanted to talk to you."

"A little brotherly advice?" Damien asked, with a hint of irony.

"Brotherly? I don't know. But you trade in information. And when I need help, I search out the best."

Damien lifted his glass as if in a toast. "Touché."

"Speaking of brotherly, have you asked Pratt to look into who leaked our relationship?"

"I haven't."

"Any reason why not?" As far as Jackson was concerned, that question and the identity of the saboteur were second only to the question of who killed Reed.

Damien tossed back the last of his scotch, then lifted his glass to signal Phil. "Because I don't need Pratt to find the answer. I already know it. And so, I think, do you."

"I've considered that it might be Jeremiah," Jackson admitted. "But it doesn't make a lot of sense."

"On the contrary. It's the only answer that does make sense. I know I didn't leak it. You say that you didn't, and I'm inclined to believe you."

"Thanks so much."

Damien's mouth twitched, but he continued. "We both know that neither Sylvia nor Nikki said anything."

"There are others," Jackson added. "Cassidy knows, and so do Jamie and Ryan. But I can't imagine any of them telling."

"The only other person who knows is your mother," Damien said. "And Penny's not in a position to talk to anyone at the moment."

"You know about my mom?" Penelope Steele had developed early onset Alzheimer's ten years ago. She lived now in a facility in Queens, a relatively easy jaunt from Jackson's office in New York. He visited frequently. Most of the time, she had no idea who he was.

"As you said, I like information. You grew up knowing all about my family. I thought it was only fair I learn something about yours."

"You could have just asked." The idea that Damien had been poking around in Jackson's life pissed him off. Not that this was a new sensation. He'd experienced the same sense of violation when Damien had found his petition to establish parental rights, along with the evidentiary DNA test results confirming that Ronnie was his daughter.

"Now I would. Back when I looked, I didn't trust you. And, frankly, you didn't trust me. I could have asked, but you wouldn't have told."

Jackson didn't answer; Damien was right. Instead, he finished his own drink, lifted his finger to signal to Phil that he should pour a fresh glass for him as well. As soon as the drink was in front of him, he took a long swallow, savoring it before speaking again. "He chewed me up one side and down the other for coming to work for you. And then he got in my face about telling you the truth. Doesn't that cut against our assumption?"

"Do you think it does?"

Jackson sighed. "No. I think that Jeremiah Stark has and always will have his own agenda, and trying to second-guess that man is like trying to predict the lottery."

"Glad you get it," Damien said, then he shifted on his stool so that he was facing Jackson more directly. "I want to show you something." He pulled out his phone, swiped the screen a few times, then handed the device to Jackson.

"*Goddammit.*" The word burst out the moment he saw the image from last night—Jackson, Syl, and Jeremiah on the deck, right about the time that Jackson was telling his father to get the fuck out off his boat. He didn't even bother to read the caption, just passed the phone back to Damien. "Those *fucking* pricks."

Honestly, it was just as well he hadn't seen this picture before he and Damien walked down the hill, because he sincerely doubted he could have kept his temper in check.

He fought a shudder as he remembered what had happened after Jeremiah had left. He'd almost taken Sylvia on deck. Demanded she strip for him. That she stand naked under the stars as he stroked her, touched her, fucked her.

His stomach roiled at the thought that she'd come so close to having her privacy violated to the extreme, and he clenched his fists against his harsh and immediate reaction to move out. To stay at a hotel. To tuck tail and run because these lowlifes were messing with him.

Fuck that.

"You're pissed," Damien said mildly.

Jackson glared at him. "Some asshole I don't know has a camera aimed at my home and is snapping pictures of me and my girlfriend."

He glared at Damien, as if the fact that his brother handed him the picture made him responsible for all this shit. "Damn right I'm pissed."

Damien nodded as if the response pleased him. "It's a safe bet that Jeremiah's not pissed at all. On the contrary, he's soaking up the attention." He paused just long enough for the words to soak in past Jackson's still-bubbling anger. "Don't trust him, Jackson. Just a little bit of brotherly advice from me to you."

Jackson pushed down the lingering anger as he considered the other man. "You know, I used to wonder what happened between the two of you. I thought that you were such a shit to him. I mean, I had reason to hate him. He was always gone. Kept me and my mom hidden away. But you had him—and yet I looked at you and thought you were a complete prick. Demanding. A prima donna. Too goddamn full of yourself."

"So glad your impression has changed," Damien said wryly.

Jackson chuckled. "About some things. Not others. But seriously, after I learned about Germany—after it all hit the press—"

He cut himself off with a small shudder, thinking of the things his brother had endured, all with their father's knowledge and without his protection. He thought of Sylvia, who had suffered so similarly, and he had to fight a sudden rush of anger against Jeremiah, Reed, and Sylvia's father. Not to mention a universe in which even one child had to endure such horrors.

He took a sip of scotch, blinking back a wave of emotion, because now Ronnie was at the forefront of his mind, and he really couldn't understand the way those men had sacrificed their children, because there was nothing—*nothing*—he wouldn't do to protect that little girl.

"Anyway," he finally said. "I understand why you set up your foundation. It's a good cause. I'll be back volunteering as soon as they let me."

Damien nodded, but didn't say anything more. Jackson hadn't expected him to.

"My point is that after all that shit hit the tabloids, I understood your issues. But I still thought you were a shit. I knew all about you after Brighton, remember? Or at least I thought I did." He'd recently learned, to his chagrin, that Damien's last-minute land buy in an Atlanta-based development deal five years ago had saved Jackson's ass, not screwed him. If Damien hadn't swooped in and destroyed the deal, most of the key players in the Brighton Consortium would have been sucked into a RICO case, their fortunes and their reputations destroyed.

Most of the players, however, didn't realize that Damien had saved their ass.

"As far as I was concerned," Jackson continued, "you were heartless. Ruthless. You had to be. How else could you climb so far so fast?"

"I can be all those things," Damien said easily.

"Can be, yeah. But it's not who you are." He downed the last of his scotch. "I've seen what you've done for Syl's career. I've seen how fiercely you watch after your wife, and I've heard about what you've done for her friends. And I know now that you weren't trying to fuck me or anyone over on Brighton."

He flashed his most charming smile at his brother. "Make no mistake, I'll call you out the second I think you're doing something to fuck up Cortez, but as for Damien Stark the man? Maybe you're not the devil I thought you were."

"Don't spread it around," Damien said. "I have a reputation to protect, after all."

"My lips are sealed." Jackson glanced down to check his watch. "Should we head back?"

"In a minute. Detective Garrison asked me to see him tomorrow," Damien said flatly, referring to one of the two detectives who'd spent the morning grilling Jackson.

A cold, hard knot formed in Jackson's gut. "Why?"

"Presumably because they think my half-brother committed murder. More specifically, because you also work for me, and as I think I mentioned once, I've met Reed a time or two. But all that is just speculation."

"Well, shit. I'm sorry."

Damien's brows rose slightly. "Sorry?"

"That this mess is screwing with you, too."

"Murder isn't the kind of thing that stays contained."

"So what are you going to say to him?"

"That I don't think you did it."

Jackson studied him. "That's not what you said a few minutes ago."

Damien didn't smile, but Jackson saw the hint of amusement in his eyes. "I'm not talking to the police right now, am I? I'll tell them that I don't know you that well, but I do know you're not stupid. And killing him just a few days after beating the shit out of him would be very, very stupid." He waited a beat, then leaned closer, his elbows on the bar. "Jackson, stupid doesn't run in our family. Jeremiah's a shit, but he's not stupid, either. If he did leak our relationship—he had an endgame."

"Like what?"

Damien leaned back. "I have no idea. But you wanted to know who else might want Reed dead. I say add him to the list of possibles. Jeremiah knew Reed. You said so yourself."

Jackson considered, then nodded slowly. "I'll talk to Harriet. Have her keep an eye on him. Maybe he'll end up being my reasonable doubt."

"You don't have to do that," Damien said.

"No, you convinced me."

"I mean, it's already done."

Jackson narrowed his eyes at his brother. "Is it?"

Damien lifted a shoulder. "Like I said, Jeremiah Stark always has an endgame. I'd like to know what it is. Besides," he added with a significant look to Jackson, "maybe he did kill Reed."

"Anything's possible," Jackson said dryly. "But what would he gain?"

"I don't know," Damien admitted. "If he were another man, I'd say maybe he was trying to protect you. Keep the movie from being made. Keep Reed from suing you for the assault. Maybe even protect his granddaughter."

"He doesn't know about her," Jackson said tightly.

"Are you sure?" When Jackson stayed silent, because, dammit, he wasn't sure, Damien continued. "It doesn't matter. My point is that Jeremiah Stark looks after one person and one person only."

He met Jackson's eyes. "So watch your back, Steele. Because you may not see him coming."

eleven

Since it is already the end of the workday and I am still too riled about that damn photo to focus, I decide to grab a few files and head home to work there.

Home, of course, is the operative word. Because Jackson and I have been spending more and more time on his boat since his drafting table and other work tools are there. And as for me, I like to stretch out on his comfy lounge chairs with a glass of wine and relax to the sound and rhythm of the ocean. I'd like to do that tonight, in fact. But I can't, and that pisses me off.

Because tonight, the boat isn't my destination; my condo is. Not that I don't love my condo—I do. But I'd rather be in my place because I'm craving my own stuff. *Not* because the damn paparazzi are messing with our lives.

And, yes, I trust that the property managers at the marina are doing their job. None of those cockroaches are getting access to the boat or even the parking lot. But that didn't stop them from taking those pictures last night, and that was invasive enough for me.

Tonight, I sleep in my own bed.

It occurs to me as I reach Santa Monica that the press might be staking out my place as well, but when I pull my Nissan up to the entrance to the underground parking garage no one is there, and my shoulders dip in relief. It's possible there are a few stragglers by the main entrance to the building, but that's outside on the Third Street Promenade, and since I'm coming in through the garage, I don't even have to see them.

As I head to the elevator, I shoot Jackson a text—*Safe and sound in the condo. See you soon.*

I still don't have a reply by the time I get upstairs, but I'm not surprised. He's with Damien, after all, and on top of everything that's happened recently, they have a lifetime of catching up to do.

So do I, I realize, as I step into my condo. Or maybe not a lifetime of catching up, but at least several days' worth.

I wrinkle my nose, because the place has that closed-up smell that is one part dirty laundry and two parts something left in the trash I forgot to take out.

I remedy that first, emptying the trash from all of the rooms, then shoving a lemon down the disposal and turning it on while I run the trash to the chute. I hit the button for the back door as I step into the hall, and by the time I return thirty seconds later, my garage-style door has almost completely ascended, letting in a nice, cleansing ocean breeze.

On a normal day, I'd be irritated with myself for doing something as stupid as forgetting to take the trash out. Today, however, is not normal. I want a distraction, and cleaning seems like just the ticket.

Within half an hour, I've gone through the pantry and refrigerator and tossed every bit of old food. An hour after that, I've vacuumed, added some essential oils to the pot-pourri I keep on a table in front of the couch, completed one load of laundry and started a second, and am telling myself that I wasn't worried by Jackson's lack of response two hours ago, and I have no reason to be worried now. We'd all left work early, so it's only seven. For all I know, drinks turned into dinner. And if that's the case, I should be happy. After all, I love Jackson and I respect Damien; I want them to get along.

But despite telling myself that, the sense of dread in my stomach doesn't ease, and though I really don't want to, I pull out my phone. This time, I'm not going to text Jackson.

This time, I'm searching social media.

And, dammit, there he is. Not just one picture, but several.

Jackson and Damien walking down the hill to the Biltmore, presumably taken by one of the photographers who've taken to camping outside Stark Tower just on the off chance another prime shot like the one of Megan kissing Jackson comes along.

Then there's a shot of them entering the Biltmore, then several of the exterior of the hotel with the hashtag #Stark-SteeleWatch.

Great.

Of course, there's nothing inherently bad about any of these pictures. It's just the fact of them that bothers me. That they exist at all, and that they exist because a layer of Jackson's privacy has been stripped away.

Damien has always been news-fodder, of course, but for the most part, nobody camps out at the Tower anymore, primarily because there's no Stark scandal at the moment. Or, at least, there wasn't.

Now there's murder and sabotage and sibling speculation, and the frenzy has started up all over again.

I sigh, knowing that it won't die down until after Jackson is either cleared or tried. And so long as I'm tied to Jackson, I'm in the thick of it, too. Right now, the press is only interested in me as Jackson's girlfriend and the resort's project manager. Yes, they know that I was a model for Reed years ago, but those photos are so tame that they've died down on social media. But the more I'm caught in the spotlight that shines on Jackson, the more likely the press will dig.

And if they learn about the blackmail—if that goes public—

I shiver, because that is a thought that I really can't let into my head.

With an effort, I force my mind away from all this. I plug my phone into the small speakers in my kitchen, and my favorite playlist starts blaring out *Basket Case* from Green Day. That'll work, I think, as I crank the volume and then go to change the sheets. That, and then vacuuming, will keep me busy for another half-hour.

And if I haven't heard from Jackson by then, I'll call Nikki. If I can't find my boyfriend, maybe she at least knows how to find her husband.

I strip the sheets, then ball them up and start to carry them from the bedroom to the small laundry closet that is just off the kitchen. But the moment I turn around, I drop them, and a small, startled "oh!" escapes me.

"Let's go," Jackson says. He's by my breakfast bar tapping the key I gave him against the granite counter. He stands tall and straight, his eyes hard, his expression defiant. But what it is that he is defying, I really don't know.

"Go?" I repeat. "Go where."

A flicker of irritation crosses his face. "Back to the boat."

"Are you kidding me?"

"I'm not. No."

I gape at him, my head shaking a little bit as I try to wrap my mind around what he's saying. "Jackson," I say gently, "there are paparazzi everywhere. I saw the pictures of you and Damien walking to the Biltmore, so I know you've seen them. And last night at the marina? And if you didn't already know it, then let me be the first to tell you that those fucking bastards have splashed pictures of you and me and your dad all over social media."

"I saw."

"Well, then, hello? The boat is really not the place we want to be now."

A muscle in his cheek twitches, and I tense, because more and more it's become clear that he's not just in *a* mood—he's in a *dangerous* mood.

"Okay," I say. "What happened?"

"The walk down was fine, but when we were ready to leave we saw that they'd practically swarmed the Biltmore. Phil got us out the service entrance," he says, referring to the bartender he chats with sometimes. "And I felt so damn smug all the way back to the Tower and into my car, because Damien and I went into the Tower the same way, through the loading dock in the back."

"So you beat them."

"We snuck around like rats," he said. "Or like criminals." He meets my eyes as he says the last, his voice harsh and hard and angry.

"Jackson—"

"*No.* I'm not living my life that way. We're going to the boat. We're going about our business. We're going to pretend like the fuckers don't even exist." He draws a breath. "Pack your things, Sylvia. You're coming with me."

I press my lips together, because I get it now, fully and completely. I understand where he's coming from. What he's trying to do.

I once told Jackson that his work was all about power and

control, and he agreed with me. But he'd taken it further. *"It's not just what I do. It's who I am."*

Those words from so many years ago come back to haunt me now, because that is the root of his anger—his inability to control the scandal, to tame the media storm. He wants to press a reset button and return everything to normal, and he can't.

So yeah. I get why he's frustrated. Why he's hurting. And, yes, I understand why he wants to go back to the boat.

I understand it. But I'm not going along with it.

Slowly, I shake my head. "We're staying here tonight."

"The hell we are."

"Goddammit, Jackson," I say, my temper rising to match his. "I'm sorry the world isn't operating to your liking right now, but you can't kill a man and then act like nothing has changed."

He'd taken a single step toward me, but now he takes one back, his head cocked slightly to the side as he studies me. I stand there, breathing hard, aware that something has shifted for him, but not entirely sure if I've made my point or simply pissed him off further. Finally, he speaks, his words coming slowly and without inflection. "I think if I kill a man, that's exactly how I should act. Not guilty."

"I'm talking about being smart. I'm talking about just staying the hell away from the press. Don't go walking in right under their noses. Don't give them any fodder."

His expression softens. "You truly think I killed him."

"I—" I close my mouth, suddenly unsure.

"And yet you're still right here."

"Where else would I be?" My voice is gentle. "Whatever you did, you did for me. For Ronnie. We've talked about this, Jackson. I know you'll always protect me. All I'm trying to do now is protect you, too."

He closes the distance between us, this time coming so

close I am breathing in his scent. Musk and wood and just the hint of scotch. "Baby," he says, his voice filled with heat, "that's not what I need from you right now."

I gasp as he pushes me against the wall, then lifts my arms and holds them in place above my head, his right hand encircling my wrists. I open my mouth to speak, but his mouth closes hard over mine even as his left hand slips down into my yoga pants. His fingers roughly stroke me, then thrust inside. I moan, my body responding immediately as it always does to Jackson's touch.

But while there is no question about the desire that has flared between us—that heated connection, that primal need—I don't know its source. Is this about control? Is he taking from me what he can't get from the world?

Or is this about anger? At the paparazzi. At me.

Or is it simply the ignition of the sparks that are ever-present between us?

I truly don't know, and I think this is the first time that I have been unable to read him.

I want to ask, and yet I say nothing. Part of me is afraid of the answer, but another part of me is simply melting under the long, firm strokes of his fingers and the pressure of his mouth against mine, his tongue taking and teasing.

And it is only when my phone rings sharply—a series of chimes that indicate that the caller is my brother—that my senses return, and Jackson backs away, breathing hard.

"You should answer it," he says.

"Right. Yeah. I should." I scramble away and grab my phone from where I'd left it on the kitchen counter. "Hey, what's up?"

"Any chance we can have drinks tonight instead of tomorrow? I talked with Cass, and she's good if you are."

"Oh." I glance over at Jackson. "I'm not sure tonight's the best idea. Why the change?"

"I had to get away from the house," he says. Considering he's living temporarily with our parents, that's a sentiment I completely understand. "I got in the car and ended up here. And I'd just really like to see you."

"And you don't want to drive up again tomorrow?" I tease.

"That, too."

I sigh. "Listen, I don't think I should. It's just not—"

"Go." Jackson's voice is firm and clear.

I blink. "What?"

"It's Ethan, right? And he wants you to go tonight instead of tomorrow."

I nod, acknowledging that he got it right.

"You should go."

I want to protest—to tell him I don't want to go, because now going feels like I'm being pushed away. But at the same time I don't want to argue or play games. And I really do want to see my brother.

With my eyes on Jackson, I speak into the phone. "Okay," I say. "When and where?"

As soon as the details are worked out, I end the call and look back at Jackson. "Do you want to meet us later?"

His mouth curves up. "I thought this was the no-significant-others gathering. Cass without Siobhan. You without me."

"Maybe I don't like you without me."

The corners of his eyes crinkle with his smile. "Maybe that's good to know."

"Jackson," I blurt. "Are we okay?"

He steps forward so that he can press his hands to my shoulders, then kisses me tenderly. I close my eyes, relishing the connection, the heat that inevitably comes merely from his proximity. I have come to depend on this sizzle. This spark of awareness. But today, when it all feels slightly off, I cannot help but fear what will happen if that flame is ever extinguished.

"Of course we are," he says, and I wait for relief to flood me.

It doesn't, though. Because the truth is, I'm not quite sure that I believe him.

twelve

I hesitate on the sidewalk outside Gemini Rising, one of the trendy bars that are forever opening and then usually folding in and around Santa Monica. This one is owned by twins, one of whom Cass dated almost a decade ago, and she assures me that the atmosphere is great—as in you can actually have a conversation—and that both the food and the drinks border on orgasmic.

Which, of course, is why she chose this place.

The thing is, even though I've been looking forward to drinks with my best friend and my brother, now I'm not so sure I'm in the mood for conversation. I'm too busy pretending like my entire world isn't teetering on the brink of complete and total disaster.

In other words, I'm a mess. And while an evening out is probably a great idea, I really don't want to dump all my problems on Ethan and Cass. But I have a feeling that once

I've gotten some wine into me, that's exactly what's going to happen.

With a sigh, I grab hold of the door handle and give it a tug, the motion fueled by a mental shrug. After all, that's what friends are for, right?

The lighting inside is dim, and it takes a moment for my eyes to adjust. I finally find them at a table all the way in the back, and as I head over there, I have to agree with Cass's assessment—the place is funky and fun, but not so loud you can't come to catch up with friends.

A circular bar is the centerpiece of the room, and as I walk past it, I hear the familiar sounds of flirting, pickups, and the hum of new relationships. The sound is bittersweet, because a week ago, I would have walked smugly past the bar, secure in the knowledge that I was with the only man I ever truly wanted—and certain that he wanted me right back.

Tonight, though, I'm weighed down by the fear that I am going to lose him.

I force the thought away, then school my features into a happy smile of greeting when I see them at a back booth.

Cass is dressed simply in jeans and a fitted white T-shirt with some graphic on it that I can't see from this angle. Even casual, she looks awesome. The shirt covers her shoulder, but there's no ignoring the vibrant colors of the tattooed tail feathers that trail down her arm. Her hair is raven black with streaks of blue, and she wears no jewelry that I can see—with the exception of the occasional glitter from the diamond stud in her nose.

My brother looks equally amazing. And if he wasn't my brother, I'd go so far as to say he looks hot. He's also in jeans and he's wearing a light cotton button-down that he's left untucked. He has a casual I-don't-give-a-fuck air that goes with his slightly mussed hair. He almost looks like a beach bum, but his bearing suggests otherwise. Yeah, sister or no,

I'll say that he looks hot. And if the women in the bar shooting him interested glances are any indication, I'm not the only one who thinks so.

He and Cass sit opposite each other at a booth, and they're deep in conversation as I arrive.

"Hey," I call as I get closer. "Sorry I'm a little late."

Cass looks at me, then frowns. "Are you okay? Other than the obvious, I mean. I've seen all the social media bullshit." She must decide it's too intense a question to start out with, though, because before I have time to even think how to answer that, she looks at my brother. "The bloom must be fading. I don't think she got laid this morning."

Ethan actually chokes on his drink, and I laugh. A genuine laugh, which reminds me why I love Cass.

"Actually," I say, as I scoot into the booth beside Cass. "You're right." I grin wickedly. "But last night was exceptional."

"No, no, no, no, no," my brother says, his interruption so on cue that Cass and I look at each other and grin. "Do not even go there, or I will have to start running down the list of women I've met in Orange County. Laguna Beach is a happy hunting ground, I kid you not."

I debate silence for a moment, but I just can't deny the truth. "Sorry," I say to Ethan. Then I turn to Cass and say, "Honestly, Jackson is just so—"

Across the table, Ethan groans as if in pain.

"Fine," I say, then turn my attention back to Cass. "How's your love life?"

"Oh, hell," Ethan chimes in. "Why not skip the romance and jump straight to your sex life?"

We both turn to him, and he grins and raises his hands. "Hey, girl on girl and no sister in the picture? I'm perfectly fine with that."

I smirk at Cass. "You'll have to forgive my brother. He's an ass."

"But such a cute one, don't you think?"

"He is pretty adorable," I say, and though we're bantering to get a rise out of him, the fact is it's true.

I adore my brother, and I always have. He's the only good thing, in fact, that came out of the horror of my childhood, because when it was all said and done, he walked away healthy.

He's been living in London and only recently returned to the States. And between work and the soap opera that is now my life, I haven't gotten to see him nearly enough. He's got a few weeks off before he starts back up at his job, so he's been using our parents' house as a home base. That's not a situation that's conducive to visits as far as I'm concerned, because the only thing I want less than to shove bamboo under my fingernails is to visit my parents. So I was beyond thrilled when he called and suggested drinks with me and Cass. "No significant others," he'd said. "Jackson's awesome, but I want the dirt."

Apparently he meant it, because now he's all about the gossip. He kicks back, looks me square in the eye, and says, "I've read all the tabloid shit. What's the real story?"

The waitress arrives with the fried avocado, tuna tartare, and specialty martinis they'd ordered before I arrived, so I wait until she's gone to run down all the drama. At least, all the drama I'm willing to share.

"No way," my brother says. He grabs a slice of fried avocado and points it at me. "He didn't do it."

"Kill Reed?" Cass asks, as though we could be talking about anything else.

"I spent time with him. Jackson's not a killer."

"Thanks for the assessment." It's one I agree with, actually. Jackson isn't a killer. But he is a man who would kill when necessary. And if he ends up convicted, how the hell will I live with the knowledge that he killed for me?

"Anytime." Ethan smiles, but it seems a little sad.

"What?" I demand. "What happened with Mom and Dad to send you racing up to Los Angeles?"

He waves the question away. "Nothing. Really. I just needed my space. And I wasn't even thinking about that. It just sucks that you have to deal with this murder stuff and all the crap that the tabloids are printing and posting all over the web." He lifts a shoulder. "It's just all a mess."

Since I can't argue with that, I don't.

"I think the hardest thing on Jackson is that he didn't get to bring his daughter home," I say.

"Well, yeah," Cass says. "You guys went all the way to Santa Fe and then got slammed with the news he's a prime suspect. It sucks," she adds, in what might be the understatement of the century.

Ethan's reaction is entirely different. He's staring at me as if I've lost my mind. "Jackson has a kid?"

I nod, realizing that although Cass has known this for almost as long as I have, I never told my brother this little family secret. "The media doesn't know. He wants to keep it quiet to protect her from, well, from all of this mess. So don't, you know . . ."

I trail off, and he swats my words away as if they are a nuisance. "Of course I won't say anything, but Jesus, Syl. You're dating a guy with a kid?"

"He's just a guy," Cass says. "Fatherhood isn't his defining characteristic."

Ethan cuts her a quick glance. "No. No, it's not. But if it's serious between you and Jackson, and if you're thinking that he's your guy and maybe there's marriage down the line—"

He doesn't finish the thought. He doesn't have to. At least not to me. Because he and I have had more than our fair share of conversations about parenting. And in every single one of them we both acknowledged the fact that with parents like ours, we needed to stay far, far away from that particular vocation.

Ethan doesn't know the hell I went through with my dad, but he does know how distant I am from both our parents. And even though they treated him like a prince when he was ill, the truth is that even his relationship with them is strained, because they never really saw him as a kid. More like a fragile commodity. And while he is willing to spend time with them and truly loves them, he's told me at least a dozen times that he's not sure he could be a dad, because what the hell does he know about genuine closeness?

I don't know if he's right about his parenting skills, but I see that distance in the way he handles his relationships with women. Hell, I saw it in my own, too. Or, rather, I saw it until Jackson.

"What's the matter with you?" Cass snaps the question at Ethan even as she takes my hand and squeezes. "You've told me she's a little angel, right?"

"She is," I say, glancing at my brother as if to underscore the point. But the moment I see his face, I regret looking that way.

I see all the years of my childhood. All of my pain—most of which he doesn't even know about. I see the way my mother ignored me. I see my anger at my father and his distance toward me.

I see the fragility of children, and the knowledge that it is so easy to fuck up a life.

I see it, because that fragile child stares back at me every morning from the mirror, and the woman she is now has no idea how to be a mom. Hell, that girl isn't even certain how she survived childhood.

"I don't want to talk about it anymore," I say.

"Oh, shit. Syl—"

"Forget it, Ethan. It's okay. It's just been a long, weird

couple of days. And the fact is, Ronnie's not really at the top of the problem pile, you know? Keeping Jackson out of jail is what's keeping me up at night. Not whether or not I'll be watching *Sesame Street* every morning."

I turn pointedly to Cass. "So. All well with Siobhan?"

Thankfully, Cass understands my need to change the subject. "Everything is perfect," she says. "I'm in that lovey-dovey floaty place." She releases an exaggerated sigh and then pats her hand rapidly over her heart. "I'm all pitty-pat and gooey and sweet. It's disgusting, really. On anyone else, I'd want to smack them for being a walking case of sugar shock. But I'm just giddily floating along."

I lean over to shoulder-butt her, then raise my brows as I look at my brother. "Of course, she'd drop Siobhan in a heartbeat if Kirstie Ellen Todd was available and willing."

Cass tosses her hand up to her forehead like a Victorian-era woman with the vapors. "Alas, she's off the market again. She and Graham Elliott made up. Pregnant," she adds in a stage whisper.

Ethan looks at me, a little hesitant at first, but then his grin widens with Cass's antics.

"She has a little crush," I say.

"Hell, who can blame her? Todd is hot."

"Exactly," Cass says. "Of course, Siobhan is hotter. Be still my heart."

Ethan tosses an olive from his drink at her, and I ask Ethan about his love life.

"Happily non-monogamous," he says. "Or did you miss the part where I pointed out that Laguna Beach is like a buffet of hot women?"

"Neanderthal."

"And proud of it."

We move from insults to his house hunt. "All I really need is two bedrooms in a complex with an exercise room. I'm not picky, you know? Mostly I just want to get out of Mom and Dad's house."

"I don't blame you," I say dryly, and beside me Cass grabs my hand under the table. She's known part of my story for years, but it's only been recently that I told her about my dad's role in what happened to me as a teen. Ethan doesn't know any of that, and I will go to my grave protecting that secret.

"Dad said he's been calling you," Ethan says. "I really think—" He cuts himself off. "You know what? Never mind."

I should just drop it, but I don't. "You really think what?"

"I just think—you know. You should see what he has to say." He doesn't look at me when he answers, and the tuna sits uncomfortably in my stomach. Because I have no interest in hearing what my dad has to say. And Ethan knows that.

Beside me, Cass winces, and I realize that I've been squeezing her hand so hard it's a wonder the bones are still solid. I shoot her a silent apology and release her hand. As for Ethan, I just shake my head. "We don't have anything to talk about."

"He pissed you off at dinner," he says, referring to the dinner he, Jackson, and I shared with my parents the night Ethan got home from London. The night that Jackson— damn him—told my dad what Reed did to me.

"I get that," Ethan continues. "But don't you think—"

"No." I really was pissed as hell at Jackson, and we worked past it. But that doesn't mean I want to get all warm and fuzzy with my father. That, in fact, is the last thing I want.

"Silly . . ." He trails off, leaving my nickname hanging in the air.

I pull out my phone and check the time. "Listen, I have to go," I lie. "I told Jackson I'd meet him after drinks."

"Shit, now you're mad."

"I'm not," I say. "Really. Just don't push me on this, okay?"

He hesitates, then nods. "Don't," he adds, when I start to put cash on the table. "I've got it."

"Thanks. I'll see you later, all right?" I lean over and give Cass a hug. She squeezes tight, whispering, "Are you okay?" I nod in reply, then give her another squeeze.

Ethan stands as I leave, and I hug him close. "I love you. But I can't deal with—"

"Yeah," he says, then shoves his hands in his pockets and looks at the floor. "I know."

I'm still not sure what's up with my brother. I mean, I get that he wishes we could be one big, happy family. I wish that, too. Or I used to, a long time ago. But I've made peace with the fact that my parents are not and never will be part of my inner circle. Or, frankly, my outer circle. And I wish that Ethan could make peace with that, too. Because if he's going to keep pushing on the parental reunion thing every time we get together, that's going to get ugly.

I want my brother, but I really, really don't want the baggage.

I'm in the car and firing up the engine when I see Ethan sprinting toward me. I'd parked next to my parents' silver Camry, but I don't think Ethan is racing for his car. No, he's making a beeline to me.

I roll down my window. "I don't want to talk about it."

"I know. I get that. I'm sorry," he says. "Listen, can I get in for just a sec?"

"I—okay." I adore my brother too much to deny him—or to stay mad at him. "Get in."

He does, and then he just sits there. His hands are in his lap, and he's picking at his cuticles. It's a habit that he broke when he was a freshman in college, and seeing him doing it now only reinforces what I've already figured out—whatever he has to tell me, it's bad. And while I'd started out thinking that this was about me or our father, now I'm wondering if there's something else on his mind.

"Are you in trouble?" I ask.

"No—no, I'm fine. Well," he adds with an odd little shrug, "I'm not fine. But that's not the point. Oh, hell. Listen, I want to say I'm sorry about that. About Jackson's little girl, I mean. It's just that you surprised me. And I was on edge after the stuff with Dad yesterday, and—*shit*. Dammit, I wasn't going to say anything about that. *Fuck*."

"Is he sick? Come on, Ethan, you're scaring me." I may not have the greatest relationship with my dad—hell, I may not have any relationship with my dad—but I don't wish him ill. If for no other reason than I know that losing our father would hurt Ethan.

Beside me, my brother takes a deep breath. And then, very fast, he says, "He told me."

For a moment, I truly don't have any idea what Ethan is talking about. But then the horror sets in. My stomach twists into a knot, and my hand slowly rises to my mouth. I want to cry out, to protest, but I can't seem to form words.

"Oh, god, Syl. I'm so sorry. I'm so, so sorry." He leans forward, his elbows on his knees, his forehead in his hands. He's breathing hard. He may be crying.

"Why?" My whispered word is muffled behind my hand, and I'm surprised I can even force it out. I'm no longer real. I'm ice. I'm frozen. Trapped someplace harsh and unfair. Someplace where secrets are revealed and nightmares are re-lived and it never, ever stops no matter how much you think you've gotten past it all.

That one word keeps running through my head—*why why why why*—and there's nothing else. Just darkness and betrayal and the haunting pull of my nightmares.

It's not until I feel Ethan's hands on my shoulders and hear him saying, "Syl? Dammit, Syl—oh, hell, oh, *shit*," that I realize I've gone away. And although I don't want to, I know I have to come back. Because this is Ethan and I love him, and I never wanted him to know how much I suffered. But now he knows, because his words have kicked me under.

Breathe, dammit. Just breathe.

"*Syl.*" He puts his hand on my shoulder, then leans over so his whole arm can go around me. "It's okay. It's okay. And I'm so sorry you went through that, and I'm so sorry it was because of me, and—"

"*No.*" The word bursts out of me from the dark place, so forcefully that my throat hurts from the effort of it, and I sit up straight. "No, don't you dare feel guilty. Dammit, Ethan, I didn't want you to ever know. Why did he tell you? Why would he put that on you?"

"He—he said he didn't really understand what was happening—"

"Bullshit."

"He said that now you were being blackmailed. That Jackson told him. Is that true?"

I nod.

"He said I needed to know—"

"No! I never wanted you to know!"

"He said I needed to know in case it came out," he continues, his voice soothing. "He said it might because it was Reed who took the pictures, and with the murder the police or the press might find out. And if it goes public you'd need me."

"That's bullshit," I say. "He doesn't care about what I need. He never did. He's protecting himself. Making sure you learn the truth about the money from him and not from the tabloids."

"Syl, no. He's really sorry. He wants—"

"*No.*" I scream the word then slap my hands over my ears. "I don't care what he wants."

Beside me, Ethan sags. "I'm sorry," he repeats, then pulls me awkwardly to him again. He rocks me gently. "I'm so, so sorry."

I let him hold me for a few minutes, because I love him and I know that he's hurting, too. But I need to be alone.

I pull out of his embrace, then blink at him through my tears. "Ethan, I—"

"I don't want to leave you alone," he says, and I am grateful that at least I do not have to explain that I need him gone.

"I'll be okay. I just need—I just need to sit here for a bit. Please, Ethan? I'll be okay." I'm not actually sure that I will. I'm holding on by a thread, but the last thing that I want is for him to see me snap and fall. "Please," I repeat.

He looks at me, as if trying to assess how serious I am. Then he nods. "Yeah. Okay." His voice is soft, and a little too careful. "I'll call you tomorrow?"

"Yes. Thanks." And then, because I know that he is hurting, too, I grab for his hand, catching him just as he has pushed open the door. "It wasn't your fault, Ethan. You know that, right? *It wasn't your fault.*"

He looks at me, his eyes full of sadness. "I know. But that doesn't make it hurt less." He leans over and kisses me on the cheek. "We'll be okay, you and me."

"Promise?" I can't bear the thought of losing my brother, and the fact that my father has so blithely risked everything the two of us have built over the years only fuels my anger.

"Cross my heart."

He slips out quietly, then shuts the door. I watch as he climbs into the car parked next to me, then I tilt my head back and force myself to breathe. My instinct is to call Jackson, but I tell myself not to reach for my phone. I'm still too unsettled from our parting. I want him—god knows I want him—but I need to get my shit together first.

I hug myself and breathe deep, then jump at the sound of an engine firing. I've been so lost in my own world that I didn't realize that Ethan has been sitting in the Toyota beside me all this time.

He turns my way, and his parting smile is both sweet and sad. I smile back, then blink away tears when he blows me a kiss before pulling out of the space. As soon as he disappears from sight I lean back again and focus on breathing. On trying to calm down. To quell this rising fear.

And even as I'm fighting, I think how much has changed. Before, I would be jamming the key into the ignition and driving blindly to someplace like Avalon, with cheap drinks, dim lights, and a pounding beat. I'd be finding a guy. Taking him. Fucking him. But with *me* in control. Me, proving to myself that I can keep it together. Me, saying fuck you to the world.

And then, goddammit, I'd go to Cass and have her ink that fungible man's name on my thigh, just one more toss-away man I cared nothing for, who only served to prove that I could keep my shit together. That I wouldn't lose control. That I could keep the nightmares at bay.

Now, I don't want to keep control. Now, I want to let go.

Now, I want Jackson.

I want to surrender to him. To let him hold me, to let him help me.

Want, yes. But more than that, I need it.

Need it so badly in fact that it scares me, because how would I get through this without Jackson? How will I manage if I lose him? If he's behind bars.

I squeeze my eyes shut tight, because I can't think about that. Not now. Not when I'm so damn raw.

And despite my lecture to myself about waiting until I got my shit together, I grab my phone from my purse. Fuck waiting; right now, I need the man I love.

I am about to dial when the phone vibrates in my hand— *Jackson*.

"I'm on my way," he says, the moment the call connects, and it is only when my body sags with relief that I realize just how tense I have been.

Ethan, I think as I clutch the phone tight like a lifeline. *Thank god for Ethan*.

"Don't hang up," I beg. "Stay with me."

"I'm right by your side, baby," he says. "I'm always by your side."

thirteen

"That son of a bitch," Jackson says as he pulls me from my car and holds me tight. There is a wild tension to his body, as if he is being held together by some invisible force field that is now cracking under the strain of his effort, and the power that he is giving off warms me. But it does not calm me, and my nightmares are still reaching for me out of the shadows that surround our cars.

Nightmares of my father. Of Reed. And of my fear that things have shifted between Jackson and me.

I shift, moving out of his arms.

"Jackson." His name is tight. A plea. A protest. "Are we okay?"

"Oh, baby." Something like regret washes across his face, and he presses his palm to my cheek. "I'm not sure if I'm the most selfish man on the planet or the luckiest. But yes, of course we're fine. How could we be anything else?"

I blink, and as I do, warm tears trickle down my cheeks. "I thought—I wasn't sure. It felt like we were miles apart."

"No," he says as he pulls me close to him again. "Not miles. Not even inches. I'm right here."

I nod, because he is—thank god he is. But I don't need to be held. Not tonight. Not now.

I know what I do need—Jackson is the one who taught me. I used to think that to fight my nightmares I had to take control. Had to fuck my way out of danger, taking what I wanted from men and keeping my own emotions at bay. Cool. Controlled. Like a shark trolling waters full of men.

But what I actually need is to surrender. And I need it desperately right now. Because the dark has cold fingers and they are starting to grab me.

"Come on," he says, gripping my arm and firmly steering me toward the Porsche. "I'm taking you home."

"No." I swallow. I can't say more. Can't put into words what I need. Because part of what I need is for him to understand.

For a moment, he just looks at me, his expression hard, wary.

Then he pulls me to him, and bends to whisper in my ear. "You don't get to say no, sweetheart. You say 'yes, sir,' or you say nothing at all."

Immediately the tension leaves my body. *He gets it. Thank god, he gets it.* And more, I think, he needs it, too.

"Yes, sir," I say, as my body tingles and I feel an intense pressure in my core. The need to be taken. Penetrated.

He steps toward me, closing the distance between us. It's dark in this corner of the lot, and his face is hardened by shadows. But his eyes blaze. "You want to be fucked?"

I swear I almost whimper. "Yes."

"You want it rough?"

"Yes."

He strokes my cheek, sliding his hand back until he has taken a handful of hair. "Yes what?"

"Yes, sir." I'm breathing hard, both excited and apprehensive. This is different than what we've done before. *He's* different. And though I trust him—though I will always trust him—I do not know what to expect.

And oh, dear god, that excites me.

"You want me to spread you wide and fuck you hard?"

"Yes, please, sir."

"Then you need to be a good girl."

As he speaks, he's pushing me to my knees, his fist in my hair guiding me. I descend willingly. Enthusiastically. I can think of nothing but this moment; everything before is gone. Ethan. My dad. My fears.

This is just me and Jackson and pleasure and submission. Letting him take me there. And letting him take control. Jackson, who needs this as much as I do.

"Go ahead," he says, and I reach out and press my hand flat over his erection, now struggling behind the pressed cotton of his slacks.

I am eager, but I force myself to slowly draw down his zipper. I slip my hand in and free his cock, so hard that I imagine he must be close to exploding.

His fingers are still twined in my hair, and when I tease the tip of his cock with my tongue he tightens his grip. "No."

I can't tilt my head up, so I can see him only by lifting my eyes skyward, making me feel like even more of a supplicant. "I want that pretty mouth of yours," he says, and then, instead of me sucking him off, he holds my head in place and actually fucks my mouth.

It isn't easy—he's thrusting hard and hitting the back of my throat, and I'm trying to find a rhythm and fight a gag reflex. But at the same time, I like it. For the first time, he's using me—truly using me—just as I've wanted him to do every time he was gunning for a fight. And I know that's part of it. Because he needs this as much as I do. Needs to take control hard and fast and completely.

This is about his pleasure, not mine, and that simple fact excites me, twisting it around and making it about me, too, because there is pleasure in knowing that we satisfy each other. That like a lock and a key, we fit and make each other whole.

Though we are in the dark, hidden by the shadows and the cars, I think for a moment that anyone could see us, me on my knees on the asphalt and Jackson fucking my mouth hard.

The thought makes me moan, and I'm so damn wet now, the evidence of my excitement creaming my thighs. As Jackson had ordered, I'm not wearing underwear, and I'm tempted, so tempted, to slip my hand under my skirt. But that, I think, is against the rules.

"Christ, Syl, that mouth of yours." The tightness in his voice tells me how close he is, but just when I think that he is going to explode, he pulls out and hauls me to my feet. He yanks up my blouse, then unfastens the front clasp of my bra before bending me over the hood of my car.

The metal is cool against my skin, and my nipples tighten almost painfully.

"Tell me you liked that," he says as one hand strokes my back and the other one slides up my thigh. "Tell me you liked my cock in your mouth."

"Yes," I say. "Oh, god, yes."

He slides his hand between my legs and groans softly. "Oh, yes, baby. That's how I like you. Wet and ready for me." He hikes my skirt up around my waist so that I am completely bare from the waist down, with the exception of my shoes.

"Spread your legs, baby. I'm going to fuck you hard." I do,

and true to his word, he spreads me wide and shoves his cock hard inside me, his powerful thrusts making me slide across the top of the car, giving me small friction burns on my breasts and belly.

I feel the buildup to his orgasm, and my body responds, claiming him, clenching hard against him, until finally, he explodes inside me, his low groan of pleasure echoing in the dark.

He doesn't pull out, though. Instead, he holds my hip with one hand and uses the other to reach around our joined bodies and find my clit. I'm so turned on already that it takes very little, and soon the wild tremors of my release cut through me and my cunt clenches tight around him as he continues to tease and play me, not relenting until my knees are weak and it is only his hand and the car that are keeping me from collapsing.

When he has cleaned me up and fixed my clothes, he takes my hand and eases us both to the ground on the darker side of the car. I am limp with satisfaction as I curl up against him by the tires. His arm is around me, and I snuggle close, wanting there to be no distance between us at all. "Thank you," I whisper. "Sir."

He chuckles, but then says seriously, "I needed it, too," revealing what I already knew. He presses a kiss to my forehead, and I feel a low buzz of pleasure from that simple touch. "I was so goddamn angry at your father." He meets my eyes. "And at myself."

I look away. I was furious when he told my father flat out what Reed had done to me. When he revealed that Reed was still tormenting me, this time by blackmailing me. And he made it damn clear that Jackson and I both know that my father knew all along that Reed wasn't just taking innocent advertising shots of me.

I've gotten over the fury, but that doesn't mean I want to

relive the moment. But it does mean that I understand what Jackson is talking about when he says he needed it, too. He was angry. At my father. At himself.

He was angry and he needed a release.

I was angry and needed to be claimed.

I smile a little thinking about it, but my smile fades soon enough. "It scares me a little," I admit.

"What does?"

"This. With you." I tilt my head so that I can look at his eyes, and I see the confusion and the worry in them. "The way I let go completely. The way I want to be used. I get the root of it—I do. It's about the pleasure that comes from giving up control. It's fighting back against Reed, who stole that control from me over and over. And, honestly, the wilder it is the more I like it. The intensity—it keeps me grounded. It makes me feel alive.

"So I understand," I continue. "I do. But I want to be stronger, Jackson. And this need to surrender to you is so powerful, that sometimes I'm afraid that I won't be able to cope without you beside me."

"You think giving yourself to me makes you weak?" He brushes his hand over my cheek. "The hell it does. Weak is closing yourself off. Weak is being too afraid to ask for what you want. Do you think being strong means not needing anybody else? It doesn't. It means knowing yourself. Knowing your desires. And not being scared to demand what you truly want."

"I want you," I whisper.

"I know. But that doesn't mean you can't stand on your own. If you need to—when you need to—you will do just fine."

"How do you know?"

"Because I know you." He kisses me gently. "And sweetheart, I need to tell you something."

I nod, fighting back a fresh wave of fear.

"I didn't kill him."

"What?" I'm not sure if my response is surprise at his statement, or bafflement that he's brought the subject up now.

"I didn't kill Reed. You've stuck by me, believing you knew what happened. It's only fair I tell you the real truth."

"Oh." Relief overwhelms me, and yet there remains an undercurrent of some odd disappointment. Because the truth is that I liked the thought of Jackson being the one who erased the man who tormented me.

"So you don't need to worry. The truth will win out, and I won't go to prison. I'll always be beside you."

I nod, because I know that he is saying it to soothe me. But at the same time, it's cold comfort. Because innocent or not, that is one promise that it's no longer in Jackson's power to keep.

fourteen

I wake up naked and alone in my bed, and I immediately sit up, afraid that Jackson changed his mind and decided to go back to the boat after all.

He'd taken me home because I had told him I needed my own bed, and in that moment, I'd been wrecked enough that he hadn't argued. But the disagreement or fight or whatever-the-hell-it-was that we'd had about the paparazzi and the boat had still lingered between us.

I know that we will have to deal with that, especially since we will need the boat to get to the island today. Granted, we could take one of the Stark International boats. Or even, god forbid, a helicopter. But Jackson's office is on his boat, and if he wants to make the most of the trip, then he needs to have his computers, software, and other various gadgets and gizmos with him. But surely he didn't already leave me to go there. Did he?

My body is stiff as I toss the sheet aside and then sit up in bed. I hug my knees to my chest, my attention drawn to the tattooed star on my ankle. Idly, I trace its design, as if by doing so I'm claiming it all over again. I want to claim it, because this star represents strength. It marks an escape—my flight from the home I'd grown to hate to boarding school in my sophomore year of high school.

I draw a breath, then get slowly out of bed, this time brushing my fingers over the ribbon inked at the juncture of my thigh, a ribbon covered with initials of men I cared nothing for, but needed in order to prove to myself that I was in control. Not Reed, who'd so greedily stolen control from me. Not those men whose initials now mark my legs.

Just me.

Me taking. Me holding. Me keeping so tight a grip on my world that there was no way it could spin out of control.

Slowly, I ease my hand around to my back and the intricately inked "J" entwined with an "S." Cass had inked that tattoo five years ago, after I'd so brutally broken up with Jackson in Atlanta, shredding both our hearts in the process. At the time, I'd thought I could never have him back, and yet I couldn't bear the thought of surviving without him. And so I'd kept a piece of him on me, a quiet reminder that he would always have my back—would always give me strength—even if he didn't know it.

I close my eyes and sigh as I continue to move my hands over my body, this time coming to rest on the newest tattoo— a flame on my breast. Cass inked this one less than a month ago, when I'd pulled Jackson back into my life despite my better judgment. Out of the frying pan, she'd said, because I was leaping headfirst into the fire.

Hadn't I learned the hard way that my nightmares were too close to the surface with Jackson? That the passion that pulsed between us wiped away all my control, leaving me soft and vulnerable—and too damn close to the nightmares and memories of Reed?

But I was desperate to save my resort and so I'd taken a deep breath, clothed myself in battle armor, and walked through the door into my own personal hell.

Jackson, of course, stripped all my defenses away. More than that, he'd turned everything around. And the man who had once conjured my demons now slays them. He keeps me sane. He keeps me safe.

He makes me feel loved and cherished and beautiful.

With Jackson, I can surrender control without opening the door to fear. To self-loathing.

With Jackson, I can lose myself to submission. To passion. To love.

We've come so far, he and I, but now I fear that we are about to hit a wall. That we've taunted the gods, and the gods are pissed.

I'm scared to death that he's going to be arrested for murder. That he's going to be yanked from me forever, and I hate that it is not just him that I am scared for, but myself, too. Because while I used to rely on my tats to give me strength, now I rely on Jackson.

I do not want to be a woman without the strength to stand on her own. But at the same time, I know that I am stronger with him than without him.

And oh, dear god, what will I do if I lose him?

I shiver, suddenly cold, and put on the T-shirt he'd left hanging over the back of a chair the last time we stayed here. It's for Dominion Gate, a heavy metal band that he likes, and the hem hangs down almost to my knees and the whole shirt seems to swallow me.

My phone is on a table beside the chair and when I glance

down and see that it is past four in the morning, my self-analysis turns into worry.

The door to my bedroom is shut, but now that my eyes have adjusted, I see that there is the faintest glow of light creeping in from the gap below the door. I open it, then step into the tiny area between my bedroom and my living room, moving quietly so that I don't wake him if he's fallen asleep out here.

As soon as I pass the utility closet and can see into the living room, I see him. Not inside, but out on my patio. He is perched on the side of the chaise, bent forward so that he is using the fold-up chair that Cass usually sits in as a make-shift desk. He's got his tablet propped up and he's sketching furiously on a pad of paper in his lap. His dark hair is tousled, as if he has been running his fingers through it, and I can hear the gentle scrape of lead against paper.

I want to go to him. I want to step behind him, put my arms around him, and hold him close.

But that's only my own selfish desire.

What Jackson wants—no, what Jackson *needs*—is to get lost in his work. I can practically feel the concentration and pleasure rolling off him, and I don't want to be the one to take him from that. Not now. Not tonight.

I'm about to turn around when a woman's voice stops me. "I'm back. Sorry. This early, coffee is a necessity."

"Thanks for this, Amy," Jackson says. "I didn't actually expect you to answer my email until later."

For a moment, I'm confused, then I see that he's on a video call. I shift to the left so I can see the tablet screen, and realize that he's talking to Amy Brantley, his estate and family law attorney in Santa Fe.

"It's almost six here, and I've started getting up before dawn to go to the gym. I figured I'd rather talk to you.

Are you hanging in there? Ms. Frederick doing all right by you?"

"She's doing as good a job as she can, but we both know there are no guarantees."

"No," Amy says. "There aren't."

"I spoke with Stella yesterday. Betty won't say a word, but her health is deteriorating fast."

"I know," Amy says. "I was actually going to give you a call later today. Right now, if anything happens to Betty while she's caring for Ronnie, custody shifts to you pending establishment of your paternal rights. But if you're incarcerated, then the next in line is still Megan, at least on paper. Are you okay with that?"

He hesitates, and though I know that it pains him to admit it, he says very simply, "No."

It's the right choice, of course. Megan may be Ronnie's biological aunt, but she's checked herself into a clinic as she battles mental health issues, and though I know it breaks Jackson's heart, she's in no position to take care of his daughter.

"I didn't think so," Amy says. "And frankly, with Megan having admitted herself to a clinic, the court might refuse to put Ronnie with her. She'd end up in foster care unless Arvin takes her," she adds, referring to Megan's father. He's the man who hired Jackson to build the Santa Fe house that is now the focus of the movie that Reed was determined to make. And although Arvin Fletcher is Ronnie's grandfather, he has distanced himself far, far away from the child.

"That would be worse," Jackson says dryly. "And we both know Arvin would never accept custody. But the truth is, I've been thinking about all of that; it's one of the reasons I'm calling. That, and to make some financial arrangements." He drags his fingers through his hair. "I've been up all night thinking about it. I know Ronnie inherited money from Amelia," he says, "but that's in trust and it shouldn't be used for her day-to-day care."

Amelia is Ronnie's birth mother. More than that, she's the reason the movie is even on Hollywood's radar. Though no script has been officially released, it's no secret that the movie centers around tragedy at the Fletcher Residence, an amazing Santa Fe house designed and built by Jackson. The project, actually, that put Jackson Steele on the map and turned him from a simple architect into a starchitect—a celebrity architect with all the baggage that goes with the title.

Back when Jackson was building the Fletcher Residence for Arvin—one of the country's wealthiest men—Jackson began dating Amelia's identical twin sister, Carolyn. Amelia wanted Jackson for her own, and was crazy enough to impersonate her sister in bed, a single night that left her pregnant with Jackson's child—Ronnie. After the house was built and Jackson had moved on, the little girl was born—and that's when Amelia went completely off the rails. She killed her sister and then she killed herself, leaving Ronnie to be raised by the twins' older sister, Megan—and attracting the attention of Hollywood's scandal hounds.

Since Amelia had quite the lineup of men going through her bedroom, the Hollywood people don't know that Ronnie is Jackson's daughter, and they probably won't make that connection until the court confirms paternity or Jackson's petition finds its way to the press. They see only a murder-suicide that centers around the amazing house that made Jackson's career and the love triangle that destroyed two young women, both of whom wanted the same man.

When Jackson learned that Ronnie was truly his daughter, he considered petitioning for custody right away, but he also knew that the scandal surrounding the house and the buzz about a possible movie would thrust the little girl into a media feeding frenzy. She was safe and loved with her aunt

Megan and her uncle Tony, with her great-grandmother Betty helping from the sidelines. Jackson took on the role of uncle, visiting her and supporting her financially.

Now, though, things have changed. Tony passed away, and Megan's mounting bipolar issues mean that she is no longer a good choice for guardian. Neither is Betty, in light of her failing health.

More than that, though, Jackson simply wants his daughter back. And until this damn murder trial reached out and slapped us in the face, that was what he was in the process of handling.

"So you want to designate a contingent guardian, and then set up a trust to use for Ronnie's daily care?"

"Exactly."

They talk for a few more minutes, with Jackson explaining that the trust will be funded with his share of the Winn Building, a retail and residential high rise in Manhattan, and also the first project he both designed and developed—and kept a piece of the income stream. "I've got a forty percent interest and Isaac Winn has sixty. He's been looking to acquire a bigger percentage since day one. If we need the cash for Ronnie, he'll buy me out."

"I'll seed the trust with ten percent," Amy says. "You can add more if you need to."

"Fair enough."

"And the guardian?" she asks, after reminding Jackson that until his parental rights are established by a court order, he is not the one who can force this issue. "But I'm sure that Betty and the court will take your opinion into account."

"I want Sylvia," he says, as I press my hand over my mouth to hide my gasp. "And I want you to go ahead and set the paternity hearing."

"The hearing? Jackson, are you sure? What if—"

"I want her to have a father. I'm tired of waiting. I want

my daughter, Amy. And if the worst happens, then I want to know that the woman I love is taking care of her."

"And Sylvia will accept the role?" she asks as my heart thuds painfully in my chest and I hug myself, not sure what I'm feeling, only certain that I am numb. "The court will only offer guardianship. They won't force her to take it. If she says no, Ronnie could be looking at foster care."

"We've talked a little. And we'll talk more. But I think she will. I need this done, Amy. I'm living in limbo right now, and I don't know how much longer I can stand it. I need this to be handled. I need my daughter. And I need you to make it happen sooner rather than later."

"All right, Jackson," she says, her voice gentle. "I should be able to get a court date in a couple of days."

"Thank you," he says, and there is such relief in his voice that my eyes sting with unshed tears.

I don't actually notice when he ends the call. I'm lost in a world of maybes. A world where Jackson is gone, and where I am raising his daughter.

Oh, god.

A tremor of fear runs through me, because I am suddenly struck with just how real that possibility is. And I can't escape the overbearing reality that no matter how much I love Jackson—how much I adore his little girl—I have no idea how to raise a child. My mother has treated me as a zero ever since my brother became ill. And my father—oh, god, I can't even think about my father.

I shudder, then stumble back to bedroom, my stomach in knots. I lurch into the bathroom and kneel in front of the toilet, certain that I'm going to throw up. I don't. But I clutch the porcelain until I feel steady enough to stand.

I meant what I said at the airport—I do want to be there for Jackson, and I am humbled that he would trust me with his daughter.

But this?

Oh, god, this?

I stand, then force myself to breathe deep and tell myself that it isn't going to happen. Jackson didn't kill Reed. He's not going to be arrested. He's not going to prison.

Ronnie will be in our life, yes, and that's great. I can do this with Jackson at my side. I can handle being a mom so long as he's holding my hand.

I tell myself that again and again, then realize that even as I have been lecturing myself, I have been inching my T-shirt up so that I can once again see my tattoos in the mirror. Only this time, I'm not thinking about the battles that each one represents. Instead, I'm thinking about a new battle. I'm thinking that, if I'm going to manage this, I need the ink that marks the child.

I close my eyes, hating that I am so weak when Jackson needs me to be strong.

When I open them again, I see Jackson's reflection in the mirror; he is standing right behind me.

"I thought you were asleep," he says.

"I just woke up." My voice sounds guilty to my ears, and I have to fight the urge to cringe.

His brow furrows a bit, and I know that he is worried that the nightmares came for me, prompted by Ethan's confession. "Are you okay?"

"I'm fine," I say. "No nightmares last night. You vanquished them all," I say truthfully. What Reed did—what my father did—will always haunt me. And my father's confession to Ethan about the whole sordid business only adds another layer of shadows to the nightmares I already fight. But Jackson has convinced me that I *can* fight them.

I lift a shoulder then, the motion minuscule. "It's just that I woke up without you. I didn't like it."

I don't know what he sees when he looks at my face, but

whatever it is, it's enough. He reaches for my hips, then tugs me to him, then presses his lips to mine. The kiss is soft, yet powerful. Deep, yet tender. I melt against him, all of my fears, my doubts, my angst swept away in a sensual fog, no match for the power that is Jackson.

The kiss is long and lingering, and with each passing second, my passion rises, my senses firing. My breasts rub against him, the sensation sending curls of pleasure swirling through me.

"It's morning," he murmurs as he pulls away. "We need to get to the boat and head to the island."

"Not just yet. Please," I say, that one word holding all my fears and insecurities. "Please, at least for a little while, just hold me."

He searches my face, then silently leads me to bed. He strips off his jeans and shirt, then slides under the covers beside me, tucking me in against him so that my ass is snug against his semi-erect cock.

I want more—hell, I need more. I need his touch to soothe and center me. But as far as I know, Jackson has been up all night and I don't want to demand when he's tired. More than that, I want to be able to stand on my own, because I'm terribly afraid that there will come a time when Jackson won't be beside me to battle away my fears.

So I close my eyes, trying to be strong. Trying to simply enjoy the feel of his arms around me.

Jackson, thank god, has other plans.

Lightly, so that I almost do not even recognize the contact, he begins to stroke my thigh, making me squirm.

A thread of sensual heat curls through me, and I shift, parting my legs slightly so that he has better access. As I'd hoped, he takes full advantage, his hand easing down along the juncture of my thigh and torso, then to my pelvis, and then finding the nub of my clit. I gasp, drawing in a stuttering breath as he makes his fingers into a V and slides along my now-slick labia but avoids the touch that I am desperately craving.

"Jackson," I murmur. My hips are moving in their own rhythm now, trying to direct his hand, his touch. But Jackson foils me, and the release that my now-primed body seeks is just out of reach.

Frustrated, I press my rear back against his cock, then close my eyes in satisfaction at his low, masculine groan of pleasure. Then his mouth brushes my shoulder, and his low, sultry words are sending ripples through me. "I need to fuck you, baby. Like this. Right now."

"Yes."

"Touch yourself," he demands even as he takes my thigh and pushes it forward. Now we are still spooning, but my legs are scissored as his fingers thrust inside me, making me wild with need. And only when I'm so damn wet that I'm sure the sheets must be damp, does he ease his cock into me and fill me with long, slow strokes that make me moan.

Slowly at first, and then harder, so that with each thrust we scoot a bit up the mattress. But I want it harder, deeper, and instead of teasing my clit, I lift my hand over my head and press against the headboard to provide some resistance as he pounds into me, harder and harder, until he finally explodes inside me, and then falls limp against me, his body draped over mine.

I sigh and stretch with pleasure. I'm close, and I know if I touch myself, I will go over, but I do not want that. Not now, when I have the pleasure of being so close that even the touch of the air is a sensual caress. And so when Jackson reaches lazily over me, then starts to ease his fingers down to play with my clit, I close my hand over his and shake my head, just a little.

"I want to stay here," I say. "I want to stay here on the edge."

"Why?" he asks.

How can I answer when I don't really understand myself? All I know is that I want to stay here for a little while, balanced precariously before I fall.

And so I give him the only answer I know. "Because you're the one who took me there."

Less than an hour has passed when I slide out of bed and start to get dressed. It feels like an eternity, though. Like I have slept and healed and come out fresh on the other side, renewed and brave.

That fades, though, when I pull a long-sleeved T-shirt over my head, and see the way that Jackson is looking at me, propped up on the bed on one elbow.

"What's wrong?"

"I spoke with Amy this morning."

I concentrate on stepping into my shorts—I'm dressing for the island, not the Tower—then look at him again. "Your attorney?" I ask, as if this is all news to me.

"I'm tired of leaving my little girl in limbo. I've asked Amy to get a court date. I want to bring Ronnie home."

I zip up the shorts, then go to sit on the bed. "Good," I say. "You're her dad."

I see the relief on his face, and know that I've said the right thing. "There's more. Do you remember what we talked about at the airport?"

"Sure." I'm proud of how normal my voice sounds.

"Did you mean what you said? Because I want to make it official."

"Official?"

He nods. "If something happens to me, I want guardianship of Ronnie to go to you. I want Amy to amend the guardianship papers. You, not Megan, if something happens to me."

"I—" I swallow, wanting to kick myself for hesitating for even an instant.

He notices, of course. "Yesterday, when I was being an ass about the paparazzi, what you said about believing I'd killed Reed. About staying with me no matter what."

His words are choppy, and I take his hand.

"That drove it home for me," he continues, more smoothly, and the knowledge that I've given him strength swells inside me. "How much I want you to be the one protecting her. Sticking with her. But I know it's selfish of me, too, and if you don't want that—"

"You were an ass about the paparazzi?" The question, voiced as a tease, slips out of me. I regret it immediately, but I'm latching on to anything but the real issue. Anything but the possibility that I will be raising a child alone.

"I was," he says. "I was pissed and acting stupid and you were right. I need to avoid them, not taunt them. And when we do encounter them, I need to play Evelyn's game and be polite and friendly. I hate it, but I'll do it because I know it increases the odds that I won't end up behind bars. That I'll stay here with you. With Ronnie."

Relief flutters through me. That, at least, is one thing I can stop worrying about.

"I'll call Amy this morning and tell her not to change anything," he says gently. "It's too much to ask. I wasn't thinking. I wasn't—"

"*No*," I blurt, gripping his hand tighter. "No, I'm sure. Of course I'm sure."

And I am.

Despite my fears, I am absolutely certain.

Because what other choice do I have?

In Jackson's world, there is him, there is his daughter, and there is me.

He loves me, I know that he does.

But if he ever has to make a choice, it is Ronnie that he will choose. Because unlike Jeremiah or my parents, Jackson is a good father. And for him, Ronnie's welfare will always come first.

And as for me?

All I can do is make certain that is never a choice that he will have to make.

All I can do is take a tentative step toward the role of Mommy, and hope that I never have to play that role alone.

But am I taking that step because I love Jackson?

Or am I doing it because I'm afraid of losing him if I don't?

fifteen

The enticing aroma of yeast and cinnamon wafts through the boat, making my stomach growl. "That smells amazing," I say, as Jackson opens the oven in the galley-style kitchen and pulls out a tray of cinnamon rolls.

We'd come to the marina before dawn, and had been lucky not to meet many paparazzi hanging around the gate. Presumably they knew Jackson wasn't on the boat and had gone home to sleep—or to the Tower to camp out.

Now we're getting close to the island, and making up for skipping breakfast in order to get under way quicker.

Jackson picks up a plastic bag full of gooey white stuff that I assume is a sugary icing for the rolls. I ease up beside him and take it, figuring I ought to contribute at least a little something to our breakfast. He snags the first one I ice, holding it on a paper towel as he nods generally toward the front of the boat. "I'm going to go check our position. I'll be right back."

I nod, then focus on my culinary task until he returns.

"Getting close," he says. "Ten more minutes and I'll take her off autopilot. But it's a gorgeous day. Let's take these up to the deck."

Since that's a brilliant idea, I don't argue. He takes the rolls and I grab some orange juice, plates, and cups, then follow him up.

He's right. It is a gorgeous day, and I silently decree that today there will be no talk of murder or jail. There will be no worries about Ronnie. No fear that I will be raising that little girl alone.

There will be only work and the island and Jackson and me.

Today, I'm holding tight to normalcy, and these moments at sea are a damn fine start.

The sky is a crystalline blue, and there isn't a cloud to be seen. The ocean ahead is smooth, the surface only rippled by a soft wind. We're close enough to both Catalina Island and Santa Cortez for seagulls to be flying overhead, and I watch as a few dive-bomb the water for their breakfast. I toss out a piece of my cinnamon roll and watch the closest one rocket toward it.

"Hey," Jackson says. "I slaved over those. Took them out of a box and everything."

"You picked a good box. They're great."

We're sitting on the main deck on a bench on the port side just over from the captain's chair. It's cushioned and the back of the bench is also the side of the boat. I've poured us both juice and we have the cups tucked into built-in holders. The pitcher is jammed into the center of a life preserver to keep it steady.

I've put the rolls between us, and Jackson makes a grab for his third. He takes a bite and grins at me, a tiny bit of white icing stuck to the corner of his mouth. I reach over and wipe it off with my thumb, then put my thumb in my mouth and suck it clean.

And all the while my eyes never leave his.

"Very naughty, Ms. Brooks."

"I have absolutely no idea what you're talking about, Mr. Steele."

He stands, then pulls me up as well. "I'm talking about the fact that your island is right over there." He points to Santa Cortez, growing larger by the minute. "And the fact that I need to take the boat off autopilot." He traces his fingertip over my lips, and I draw him in, then suck and tease his finger with my tongue.

He groans. "I'm talking," he says as he tugs his finger free, "about the fact that we don't have time for me to fuck you the way I want to fuck you right now. But soon," he adds as he slides his hand down to cup my crotch through my shorts. He slides lower to my thigh, then back up the inside of the leg. And then his brow lifts as his fingers find me not only bare, but hot and slick and very, very wet.

I bite my lower lip in response to his low groan of masculine satisfaction.

"Good girl," he says.

I look up, innocently meeting his eyes. "What were you saying about fucking me?"

He slips two fingers inside me, making me gasp. "Soon," he promises. "Very soon."

I sigh with disappointment when he steps away, leaving me longing and so sensitive that every brush of the canvas against my cunt is like a sensual torment.

For just a moment, his gaze lingers on me, hot and heavy, and then he turns and heads for the captain's chair to guide the boat in. And I'm left to my fantasies of what's still to come.

While he does his captain thing, I take our breakfast stuff

back downstairs. I'm covering the leftover rolls with plastic wrap when Jackson calls me, his voice hard and sharp. "*Syl.* Get up here!"

I abandon what I'm doing and hurry back on deck. I'm asking, "What's going on?" as I move, but as soon as I'm outside, I can see for myself.

And what I see is that my wonderful day has just gone straight to hell.

The moorings on one side of the dock have been smashed in, so that it tilts at an odd angle and isn't even close to being safe.

"But how will we get on the island?" I say, and then realize that is the least of our problems. Because when I follow his finger, I see that this entire area has been vandalized. From this perspective, I should be able to see the fuel tanks. For that matter, there are portable toilets, and I can't see the tops of them, and I really don't want to think about what it means if those blue boxes have been toppled over.

"Binoculars," I say. "Do you have some?"

"Dammit, yes." He hurries to the bench on which we'd just had breakfast and pulls off the cushion, then grabs a pair from the hidden storage area. He puts the bench back together, then steps up before raising the lenses to his eyes. "It's bad," he says, then passes the binocs to me.

I look, too, and see that he's right. Fuel tanks are spilled. The helipad is covered with debris. There are wires and cords everywhere, along with bits of broken machinery. About the only thing that hasn't been knocked over is the pole upon which the security camera is mounted.

A horrible greasy feeling swirls in my stomach, because this is bad—really bad. This isn't leaked emails or embarrassing photos or foolish rumors about government weapons. This is vandalism. This is real, honest-to-goodness sabotage.

And I'm taking it very, very personally.

"We need to see the extent of the damage," I say. "Can we still use the dock in that condition? Or can you get close enough to anchor and we can wade in?"

"No." Jackson's voice is firm. "We need to get Ryan and a team here. I don't want to run the risk of contaminating the scene. And there's fuel everywhere. I don't want you out there until we know it's safe."

I start to argue that I'm perfectly capable of taking care of myself, but he's right and so I say nothing. There's no cell service on the island yet, but the boat has a complete satellite communication system, and the phone starts to ring even as I am running below deck to get it.

I hurry to answer it, not surprised to find that the caller is Ryan.

"You saw the security feed?" I demand. "Could you see who did it?"

"Not exactly," he says, which makes very little sense. Clearly he knows what I'm talking about, but how would he without seeing the feed?

"I'll explain when we get there," he says, anticipating my question. "Damien and I will be there in forty-five minutes, tops. We're coming by boat with a full team following about twenty minutes behind. And, Syl," he adds, "stay off the island."

I hurry back to the deck, mentally running through the to-do list that is now growing in my head. The clean-up, the investigation, and—oh, hell—the press.

My mind is swimming with details as I relay Ryan's call to Jackson, who doesn't have any better idea than I do as to how Ryan could know about the island.

From what I can tell, he's been pacing the deck the entire time I was gone, but he'd stopped the moment I returned. Now he reaches for me, holding me firmly by the shoulders as he studies my face. "Are you okay?"

I understand what he's asking, and I nod. "I'm fine. Pissed, but fine." I offer him a smile. "It's work," I say, and with Jackson I know I don't have to say any more, because it's the same for him, and always has been. Work is our escape. Our safe place. The thing that drives us and centers us. Trouble at work is an irritation, and it might piss the hell out of me, but it won't cripple me.

It's the personal shit that can destroy me. Moments like last night that can conjure the nightmares and the fears and the need to just dig deep and hide inside myself somewhere.

At least, it used to have the power to destroy me. Now, I have Jackson and the strength he's helped me find.

My lover, my friend, my protector.

I slide into his arms, then tilt my head back for a kiss. "Come on," I say. "Let's go make a list of everything we need to check once Ryan clears us to go on the island."

In his office, he works at his computer and I pace behind him as I try to cover every contingency.

I'm mentally calculating what the cost of overtime for a cleanup crew is going to do to my budget when the phone rings again. I grab it up. "What's your ETA?"

"Sylvia?" It's not Ryan, it's a woman. And it takes me a moment to realize it's Harriet Frederick.

"Ms. Frederick." My throat has closed up, and it's hard for me to push her name out. "I . . ."

I give up. I have no idea what to say.

"May I speak to Jackson?" Her words are soft, as if she understands that a normal tone might actually hurt me.

He's already at my side, having risen at the sound of her name. I hand him the phone, feeling a little numb, then immediately hug myself.

Jackson stays at my side. "I'm here, Harriet. What's going on?"

I struggle to hear the conversation, wishing that Jackson

would put it on speaker but knowing that he can't because that could mess up the attorney-client privilege. So I try to interpret Jackson's facial expressions.

Considering he's standing as still as a statue, I'm not having much luck.

After a moment, he says, "I see. And worst case, when are we looking at?"

Worst case.

Oh, fuck. Oh, shit.

I don't bother with a chair. I just drop down and sit on the floor.

"All right," he says. "Thanks for calling." He laughs. "No, I won't. It's tempting. But no."

Then he ends the call and bends toward me, his hand held out to help me up.

I shake my head. "Until I know what that was about, I'd rather stay down here."

His small smile doesn't quite reach his eyes. "Apparently the police know that I was at Reed's house."

"Oh." I suddenly wish I'd gone for the small couch. At least it has a blanket that could ward off my sudden chill. "How?"

"A witness. Halloween night, remember? Reed's porch light was off because he wasn't doing candy, but a mother saw me under a streetlamp. She noticed a man walking alone."

"You? She identified you?"

"They showed her a photo line-up. She picked me out."

I close my eyes, and when I open them again, Jackson is crouched in front of me. "Syl, there's more. She heard Reed and me arguing."

"Oh, god." I tremble, then grab hold of his hand. "You said worst case. You were talking about an arrest?"

He nods.

"So?" I demand. "When?"

"She doesn't know. This may be the pivotal piece of information and they arrest tomorrow. Or they may try for more."

"You didn't do it." My throat is thick. "They can't take you away from me if you didn't do it."

"Hey." He takes my hands in his. "This isn't the problem we need to deal with right now. That's not why we're on this boat. It's not why we're at the island. We work now, okay? We work now, and we worry later."

I nod. Because he's right. And because worrying won't solve anything, and neither will fear.

And because I meant what I said earlier—work is my solace, just as it is his. And right now, we both need it.

"Okay," I say, forcing myself to think again. "Okay. We need—" My breath hitches as I say the words. "We need to prepare for the worst. The resort, I mean. We need a plan." I push myself up to my feet. "If you do . . ." I trail off, hating even having to say it out loud.

"If I end up in cell block A?"

"Don't," I snap. "I can function, okay? But I can't joke about it."

"I know," he says. "I'm sorry." He pulls me into his arms and kisses my forehead. "Finish what you were saying."

"I was just thinking that maybe we should hire someone who can step in and make sure your plans get executed the way you envisioned them."

Jackson nods. "You're right. I should have already thought of that." He drags his fingers through his hair. "I would suggest Chester," he continues, referring to one of his interns who has joined him in Los Angeles from the New York office. "But he's not licensed yet, and I don't think that would go over well with the investors."

"And to be honest, I'd like someone I've worked with before."

Jackson nods. "Are you thinking Nathan Dean?"

"Actually, yeah." Dean was the architect for Damien's Malibu house, and I'd worked closely with him during design and construction. Jackson met him briefly at a cocktail party not long ago at that very house, and they'd bonded over arches and trusses.

He's a nice guy and a solid architect, though he's not anywhere close to Jackson's level. I know that Aiden thought Damien would veto Dean as the primary architect for the resort—apparently he'd committed to designing a bungalow for Damien and then backed out about the time we were getting started with Cortez—but this isn't about Dean being the main guy. It's about having someone on the team who's capable of bringing Jackson's vision to life if the worst happens.

"He seemed like a decent guy," Jackson says. "If he's got the time and Damien gives the okay, I think bringing him on board is a great idea."

I nod. "I'll feel him out about his schedule first, and if it sounds like he'd be free, I'll run the idea past Damien and then we'll go from there."

I turn my attention back to the tentative list I'm making for cleaning up the island, and Jackson goes back to his drafting table.

By the time we hear the speedboat approaching, my list has gotten long, and I know it will get even longer once I see the damage up close and walk the island's perimeter.

"How did you know?" I ask Ryan as he and Damien board Jackson's yacht.

"Our saboteur is a bit of a show-off," Damien says wryly. He passes me his phone, on which he's saved a photograph of the destruction. It was taken at night, so only the parts illuminated by the flash are clear, and those bits are overly bright. It gives the image a haunting quality, as if we're looking at some sort of futuristic mechanical graveyard. "That arrived by email this morning."

"You've traced the email?" Jackson asks.

"Of course," Ryan answers. "One of my guys just got back to me, actually. Sent from a burner smart phone. A dummy email account to a fake ID. All we know is that it was sent from the LA area, but that doesn't do us much good. I've been assuming all along that the son of a bitch we're chasing is local. And most likely in-house."

"At least you're no longer looking at me," Jackson says, a wry edge to his voice.

"You said it yourself," Damien says. "You have too much pride in your work. You wouldn't fuck it over for a vendetta. Especially not one against me. I don't mean that much to you."

Damien glances at me. "There was a time you might have thrown your work under the bus if it meant getting back at Ms. Brooks. But I think that time has passed."

"It has." Jackson's voice is as stiff as his posture. "And you're right—you didn't mean that much to me. Or if you did, I wouldn't have wanted you to realize it."

Damien chuckles. "And now I can?"

Jackson looks as confused as I feel.

"You said I 'didn't' mean that much to you. Do I detect your growing respect and admiration?"

His voice is light, almost teasing, but Jackson answers seriously. "Yeah. I guess you do." He locks eyes with Damien, then smiles thinly. "But don't let it go to your head."

The corner of Damien's mouth twitches. "I'll do my best."

"Any leads?" I ask Ryan. So far, the investigation has hit dead ends and rabbit trails. "Surely the security team caught something today? They can't possibly have done all this damage and stayed out of range. That area's the whole reason we have the security cam."

Ryan glances at Damien and frowns. "They looped the feed."

"What?" I heard his words. I even know what he means. But somehow I just can't process what he's saying.

"How long?" Jackson asks.

Ryan shakes his head. "It's a thirty-minute loop. Looks like it was recorded about two A.M., and they started the repeat at two-thirty. There was no moon last night, so it's only the infrared, and nobody at the monitoring station noticed."

"So how did you find out?"

"Once Damien got the email, we knew what to look for."

I glance at Jackson, who is doing a valiant job of holding in his temper. I can see it though, pushing at the edges, building toward release.

He turns to me, the tension in his body palpable. "I may end up in prison after all, because I swear I will kill whoever is fucking with us."

"You'll have to fight me for the privilege," Damien says.

I look between them. "Don't even joke about that, you two."

They look at each other, and despite everything, I see a hint of amusement in their eyes.

I can't help it—I have to smile. They're brothers, all right.

sixteen

I spent most of Tuesday and all of Wednesday on the island with Jackson organizing cleanup and wading through the vile remnants of that horrible, massive act of vandalism. My stomach started hurting the moment I stepped onto the island and saw the destruction—machinery destroyed, storage sheds toppled. And that was only the tip of the iceberg.

It was horrible and vengeful, and all I want now are two things: to find the bastard and to fix the damage. Because fixing it will be like lifting my middle finger and telling the fucker he lost.

Thursday morning I'm back in the office, but I can't say that the day is shaping up to be much better. Damien has back-to-back international calls all day, which means that I arrived at my desk by four A.M. The only good thing about Damien's early calls is that I have no time to brood about the sabotage or worry that a detective is going to show up to arrest Jackson. Both Tuesday evening and all of Wednesday were blissfully arrest-free, but I'm still on edge.

The morning has been a blur of calls and emails and minor crises, both professional and personal. The professional all center around Damien's schedule and the resort. We're trying to get him ready for the China trip. He's spending only a week in Beijing, but with all the preparations we're making, you'd think he was staying a month. He's leaving Sunday night, and everything in the office is crazy.

The personal is entirely centered on me. We'd returned to the marina late last night, and as soon as we were back in range, my phone pinged with a dozen messages from Ethan asking if I was okay and telling me that he loves me.

As for Cass, as far as I can tell, she spent all of yesterday and Wednesday repeatedly texting me.

You there?
Hello?
Why did Ethan go racing out after you?

Do you want to come by?
Should I come there?
Jackson's not in custody is he?

Why aren't you answering me?

Dammit, Syl, you're pissing me off.

Sorry. Sorry. (Not that sorry, but dammit, call me or text back!)
WTF?
Hello?
Called work. You're not in.

Where. The. Fuck. Are. You.

As soon as Damien is squared away on his eight A.M. call,
I answer the ones from Cass:

Sorry! Sorry!
Was at the island. No service.
Everything is a mess with the island and with Jackson. But
not scary. Not much. Not yet.
Gotta go. Work insane.

Her answer is almost instantaneous. Clearly, she's been
waiting for me to reply.

You sure?
Don't go yet: Ethan. What was that all about?

I scowl as I remember that my dad dragged Ethan into my
personal horror, a little fact that had gotten buried in the hell
of sabotage and pending arrests.

Dad told him everything—really NOT happy.

Her answer is short and to the point.

Holy fuck.
U okay?

I hesitate, then answer honestly.

I am now. Mostly. Wasn't before.
Seriously—gotta go.
Don't worry about me. No new tats needed.
Promise.

Her reply—*XXOO*—makes me smile.

For Ethan, though, I can't just send a text. But I also know that I can't call him before ten. The company he works for—an online company that books travel packages—gave him a week off with pay and two weeks without so that he could get settled back in the States. For my brother, that means sleeping in.

To be honest, I'm okay with not talking to Ethan right now. My dad is the last person I want to be thinking of, and so I dive back into work with a vengeance. At nine, Damien gets on a conference call that is scheduled to last an hour, and Mila arrives at my desk.

She's one of the floating secretaries, and I'd asked for her to be assigned to me today since I'm doing double duty as Damien's assistant and as the Cortez project manager. I would have preferred leaving it all to Rachel, but she's off until Saturday and is up in Monterey with her sister.

But even with Mila, I still can't squeeze in a break because the press has gotten wind of the island sabotage and I'm fielding call after call, making statements about how we have everything under control, and that the leaked photo of the destruction entirely exaggerates the damage, and that the cleanup will in no way impact our projected opening date. And every time I say those words I want to strangle whoever the asshole is who caused that damage, took that photo, and fucked with my life.

But it's not just the press. No, the investors are calling, too, and while I've been able to assuage most of them, another one has dropped out. And although my contact didn't specifically say that he was shifting his dollars to Lost Tides, I can't shake the feeling that's the case. And that without planning it or wanting it, I'm now in a duel to the death with that damn resort in Santa Barbara.

And in the midst of all of that, I'm trying to actually do

what I've been saying is already in progress—organize and oversee the cleanup of the island, which is scheduled to begin as soon as Ryan says that his team is finished investigating and documenting.

In other words, I'm both exhausted and frustrated. And, frankly, I'm still pissed off that someone is screwing with me.

Well, technically they're screwing with the resort. But I'm taking everything related to Cortez pretty damn personally.

By eleven, Damien is on yet another conference call, this one scheduled for half an hour. Miraculously, it's calm enough that I can hand the reins to Mila and run to the break room for coffee.

I pass Trent on the way in, and seeing him reminds me of the conversation I'd had with Jackson about Nathan Dean. I know that Dean is working on Trent's new house, but if he doesn't have any other projects going on, he might be interested in being Jackson's second in case Jackson gets arrested. And, worse, convicted.

Just thinking about it makes me jumpy. Then again, I'm already jumpy. Every time the elevator opens I turn that way, expecting to see two detectives with handcuffs.

But I can't just push it out of my head. I need to get this wrapped up. I need to know there is someone in place if the worst happens. I consider waiting to run it past Damien, but the bottom line is that I'm the project manager, and this is the kind of call the manager makes.

So as soon as I'm back at Damien's desk, I pick up the phone. "Can you grab Damien's line? I need to make a call about the resort."

"Sure." Mila is smart and competent and in another month or two she could work Damien's desk alone. With any luck, it will be Rachel's job to train her because I'll be in my new office in the real estate division. Right now, though, she's my shadow.

Dean answers on the first ring, sounding a little out of breath. "Ah, Nathan Dean."

"Nathan, good morning. It's Sylvia. How are you?"

"Oh." He clears his throat. "Sorry. I was—I was just in the middle of something. I thought you were Damien. Is he—"

"He's fine, but I'm not calling on his behalf." As a rule, Nathan's quiet and pretty easy to intimidate. Hopefully if he knows Damien's not about to jump on the call, he'll chill. "I was hoping to set up a meeting. I've got a potential project coming up, and if you have time to add it in, we should talk. You know I'm working in the real estate department now, right?"

"Of course, of course. I—well, I'm flattered you'd think of me, but the truth is that my schedule is jam-packed through the spring at least."

"That's wonderful." I'm genuinely pleased for him. Since I hadn't read anything about him in the trade papers, I'd feared he didn't have many projects. "I know about Trent's house, of course, but what else have you got on your plate?"

"Well, there's another with Trent and—"

"With Trent?" I know it's not for Stark Real Estate Development. "Is he building a vacation house in Santa Barbara?"

I'd asked the question lightly, just as a toss-away because of Trent's recent trip up there. So I'm surprised when Nathan stumbles over the answer, saying, "Santa Barbara? No. No. I mean, he's not—actually, you know, I'm running late for a meeting."

"Sure. No problem." We end the call, and now I'm wondering what's up with Trent. I can't think of any reason why he'd want to keep a project secret. Unless he's relocating and doesn't want anyone at work to know yet? I frown, because that's actually a real possibility. He was genuinely pissed off when I got Cortez and he didn't. But I hadn't thought that he was pissed enough to go shopping for a new job.

I'd hate to see him go, but I can't silence the selfish little voice that points out that without Trent in the real estate division, there will be more opportunity once I shift permanently into that department.

I'm making a mental note to ask Rachel if she has any gossip when Mila glances up from the phone by the couch, where she'd just ended a call that had come in for Damien. "Everything okay?"

"Yeah." I frown. "Except that the one guy I'd hoped to entice with the promise of steady work is all booked up."

"But that's good, right?"

"It is for him." I puff out my cheeks as I take a breath, then blow it out, feeling edgy and frustrated and slightly off. "Not so great for me." I press my fingertip to my temple. "I need another coffee. Want one?"

"No, thanks. But I can get you one if you want."

I wave off the offer. "I need to move anyway."

I'm standing as my cell rings. It's Ethan, and I answer as I'm stepping away from my desk. "I'm so glad you called. I was on the boat and didn't get your texts, and I'm—"

"Sylvia, honey, it's Dad."

I reach out one hand to grab the side of the desk. "Why are you calling on Ethan's phone?"

"You know why." His voice is somehow both gruff and soft. As if he's frustrated, but trying hard not to show it.

"I can't talk to you right now. You had no right to tell him."

"Honey, you—"

"You need to stop calling me that."

"Please, let me talk to you. I love you."

I cringe, those words sounding harsh and horrible from

this man. "You have a funny way of showing it. And you need to stop calling me. I'll talk to you when I'm ready."

"When will that be?"

"Never," I whisper as a chill snakes up my spine. "That will be never."

I end the call, then start to slide my phone back onto my desk, but my fingers aren't working very well, and it tumbles from my hand and onto the ground. I spit out a curse, and I see Mila's forehead pucker. "Are you okay?"

I smile. "I'm fine. I'm just—not enough sleep, you know. I'm going to take a walk. Ten minutes. Okay."

I don't wait for her to answer. I hurry to the stairwell, shove through the door, and lean back against the cool metal. I want to cry. I want to scream.

But I don't do either.

Instead, I remind myself that I'm strong.

I hear Jackson's voice telling me that I can get through this.

In my mind, I clutch hard to his hand.

And then—because I know that he is right—I close my eyes, tilt back my head, and breathe.

seventeen

When I finally get down to twenty-six, I see Jackson's assistant, Lauren, huddled with the two guys from Jackson's New York staff, Chester and Doug, who have flown here ahead of the others. I nod as I pass, but otherwise don't divert from my path.

I enter his glass-enclosed office and pause in the doorway to take in the sight of Jackson. He is standing at an elevated drafting table, his shirt sleeves rolled up and his posture relaxed—completely in his element. He's wearing headphones, and from the way that his hand is moving with controlled fluidity, I imagine that he is listening to classical music. Something bold. Something sweeping.

I step further inside, my attention drawn next to the corkboard that Jackson has installed on the one solid wall of the office. It is covered now with sketches of the work in progress, as well as photographs of the island from every possible angle and location.

"Bastards," I whisper. "Fucking bastards."

Frustrated, I run my fingers through my short hair. I'm not sure if I came down here because I wanted to walk off the lingering irritation from my dad's call, or if I came because I wanted to tell Jackson that I survived it. That it was horrible talking to him, but I got through it, and I didn't melt down, and I didn't even shed a tear.

I'm not certain, but it doesn't matter. Because seeing those pictures has reminded me that my priority today is the resort, not my dad. I need to get it back on track, cleaned up and ready. Because Jackson is doing amazing work, and there is no way that I'm letting some invisible asshole beat us.

I'm almost out the door when a single word from Jackson stops me. "Hey."

I turn to see him looking at me, his expression filled with a combination of heat and tenderness that warms me all the way to my toes.

"Hey yourself," I reply, grinning.

"You come, you leave, you don't say hi?"

I cock my head, amused. "You're in a good mood."

"And why wouldn't I be? The design is coming along well. My girlfriend came down to see me. My office is finally finished. And so far, nobody has come to arrest me."

I laugh. "I guess you're right. You do have reason to be chipper."

He hits a button on a box mounted above the table, and blinds descend from the ceiling along the interior of each of the glass walls, turning the room from fishbowl to private in the time it takes for him to reach me.

"They finished the installation while we were on the island," he says, though I hadn't asked the question. "I thought a little privacy could be a good thing."

I see the heat in his eyes as he says the latter, and I understand what he means by "good."

He walks past me to close the door, and I hear the firm *snick* of the bolt turning.

I cross my arms as he returns to me, then lift an eyebrow. "What exactly are you doing, Mr. Steele?"

"Exploring the functionality of my new office space."

"Oh, really?" I'm amused. I'm also turned on. "Should I remind you that it's working hours? That you owe me a design? That there are people right outside these doors?"

"Are there?" he asks as he inches the front of my skirt up until I am completely exposed and actually whimpering. He slides his hands between my legs and thrusts two fingers inside me. I cry out, both startled and excited by his touch. "Careful, Ms. Brooks. You wouldn't want to attract attention, would you?"

I close my eyes, losing myself in the wild swirl of sensation that is cutting through me. "Jackson, please."

"Please what?"

I have no idea. Please stop? Please touch me? Please fuck me?

I know I should protest. I should back away. But how can I when every nerve in my body is firing for him? How can I think when I'm drunk on lust and desire? When the temptation to simply let go—to submit—is so close I have no choice but to go with it. To give in. To fly.

And because this is Jackson—because we both need and want this—that is exactly what I do.

He teases me with one finger, playing with my clit and generally keeping me on edge. "Christ, you're beautiful when you're aroused. You're lit from the inside, as bright as a candle. I want to make you burn, Sylvia," he whispers as he raises my skirt all the way, and then reaches around and slips his hand between my legs from behind, then teases the rim of my anus. "I want to reduce you to ashes, to discover all your secrets."

"I don't have any," I say. "Not from you. Not anymore." My body is thrumming with desire, and I am craving the sweet intensity of release.

He brushes his lips over my ear and the soft touch of his tongue and breath drive me just a little crazy. And when he speaks, his words almost melt me. "I'm so tempted to fuck you in the ass right now. To take you in the most intimate way possible right here in the middle of the day, twenty-six stories above this city. Tell me, baby. Does that excite you?"

I can hardly deny it. "Yes."

"I've never taken you like that. Tell me you want it."

"I do."

"Why?"

Why? Because I think it will feel good. Because I want to surrender to his every whim, every pleasure. Anything he could want to do to or with me. I have no shame where Jackson is concerned. Only pleasure and need.

I don't say that, though. I say only, "Because I want you. Because I trust you and need you."

He makes a soft sound of approval, then carefully slides my skirt back into place.

I turn in his arms, flustered. "But—"

I cut myself off, confused. Not only has he not done what he promised, he hasn't even made me come. All he's done is arouse me. Very, very thoroughly.

His smile holds a hint of mischief. "Soon," he says.

I raise a brow. "Bastard," I counter, making him laugh.

"I believe it's a workday, Ms. Brooks." He looks me up and down. "I certainly hope you're able to concentrate."

I'm trying to think of an appropriate insult to fling at him when his intercom buzzes. It's Lauren, letting him know that both Evelyn Dodge and Arthur Pratt are outside waiting to see him.

I glance at Jackson, who's grinning. "Perfect timing," he says.

I roll my eyes and adjust my clothes, and hope that I don't look as flushed and horny as I feel. "Let's go see what they need."

"Wait," he says, then pulls me back and kisses me—the kind of kiss that is a substitute for sex, and fills me all the way to my core. "A promise of things to come."

I sigh with pleasure. "I'll hold you to it, mister."

"I hope that you do."

We find Evelyn and Arthur next to a table that has an in-progress model of the resort. Jackson uses it to work through spacial issues, and while he swears that it is neither final nor to scale, I think it looks amazing, showing the private bungalows, the hotel-style buildings, the recreation areas, and more.

I want to tell him how incredible it looks. How every stone and angle complements the earth. How every brick and line seems to burst forth from the backdrop of the bright blue sky.

Architecture has always been a passion of mine, and I am a bit awed that this man I love can so spectacularly mesh form and function.

But I am looking at him. At the line of his jaw and hard angles of his face. He stands erect and proud, and right now it is so easy to see the strength and force of will that had the power to create such magnificence. Watching him, my fear dims a little. Because a man who can accomplish what Jackson can is not a man to be restrained.

Maybe we really will get through this.

Evelyn nods in greeting as she turns, then hooks her thumb back to indicate the model. "Nice work. Can't wait to kick back there for a long weekend."

"You'll be comped, of course," I say.

"In that case, make it a long week." She turns to Pratt. "Look who I found in the elevator. And since I'm as curious as you are to find out what our intrepid investigator knows, I'm going to ignore the ladies first rule and let him talk."

"So you've learned something?" Jackson asks.

"Learning," he corrects. "It's a process. But the pieces are coming together."

Jackson leads us all to the newly built-out conference room, and Pratt remains standing while the rest of us take a seat around the table.

"So a couple of things. We got some security footage from a neighbor a few doors down. Range of vision isn't stellar, but at least five people approached Reed's door the night of the murder."

"I was one of them," Jackson says. His mouth curves down into a frown. "Apparently a witness says so."

"I know, honey," Evelyn says, then reaches over to pat his hand. "Charles told me. But we'll get you through this."

"And now we know you weren't the only one," Pratt says. "So that'll give Harriet some ammunition."

"That's good," I say.

"Hell, yeah, it's good," Pratt says. "But it was also Halloween, and Reed had his porch and sidewalk lights off to discourage the kids. The images are terrible. We're trying to get some work done, but there's only so much you can do to video footage if the information isn't there to work with. With luck, someone else in the neighborhood will have a cam with a higher definition that also picks up Reed's sidewalk. My guys are on it. But the really interesting thing is that I confirmed that your dad had some one-on-one time with Reed recently."

"Halloween?" I ask.

Pratt shakes his head. "No. About a week before. But I thought that was just odd enough to mention. Apparently, so did the cops. They talked to him, I talked to my buddy at the PD. Stark says he was shooting the shit with Reed about architecture. Trying to get him to pump money into some foundation he's part of."

I nod, remembering that Evelyn told me once that Jeremiah is on the board of the National Historic and Architectural Conservation Project, which was one of the major backers of *Stone and Steele,* the recently released documentary that featured Jackson.

Jackson frowns. "Why exactly does that matter?"

"It may turn out to be nothing," Pratt admits. "But it has potential. Because I don't believe a word of it."

Jackson kicks back in his chair and extends his legs. "I'm listening."

Pratt cracks his knuckles as he paces. "The thing is, Reed was a player. Had an assistant and his assistant had an assistant. You know the type. Full entourage. Needs them to take a dump, because he's just that important and wants the world to know, right?"

I say nothing, but that sure as hell doesn't surprise me.

"Go on," Jackson says.

"He's not the type to take a meeting alone. I talked to three former assistants and they all say the same thing. So either he made an exception for Stark—"

"Or Stark is lying," I conclude.

"You got it. The question is why. And was that reason a motive for murder?"

"It's good work," Jackson says. "Thank you."

"Hey, you're writing the checks. And since you are, I'll get out of your hair. No sense paying me to hear Evelyn talk, as fascinating as that might be." He shakes Jackson's hand, promises to check in again soon, then heads out.

"I want to revisit the idea of putting out press about Ronnie," Evelyn says.

"Absolutely not," Jackson says.

Evelyn is unperturbed. "It's a good angle. A father trying to do right by his daughter amidst controversy. The public will eat it up, and we need to get ahead of this thing."

"I've already said no, Evelyn."

She holds up her hands. "And it's my job to keep trying to convince you. Moving on," she says when he starts to interrupt. "I've had some attention from magazines. All of them want to talk about the murder, not about your buildings."

"I presume you told them all no."

She looks at me. "The boy doesn't know me that well yet."

"You told them to fuck off," I say.

"You see? Sylvia knows me."

Jackson laughs. "So that's handled."

"Yes, but I don't like that mainstream media's looking at you that way. That's another thing we need to get ahead of. And a possibility to do that may have dropped in our lap. *Architecture in View*. This reporter wants to do a profile, but wants the focus to be the resort, not the murder. I think you should do that interview."

"You really think it's worth my time?"

Evelyn's mouth turns down into a small frown. "I think we can be assured they'll treat you favorably. It's a small magazine, just starting out. So far, the architects they've been able to line up for profiles are more along the lines of Nathan Dean. So you'll be a coup for them."

"He's been profiled in it?" He never did tell me about his other projects, and now I'm more curious than ever.

"That's what my contact said," Evelyn tells us. "At any rate, the magazine's doing a series on dueling resorts. This month it's mountain resorts, your month it'll be island resorts."

"Dueling?" I say. "In that case, they should be focusing

on Cortez and Lost Tides, because—" I cut myself off, because everything is kicking into place.

"What?" Jackson asks.

"Come on," I say. "I'll tell you on the way."

I share my theory with Jackson and Evelyn as we hurry up the stairs to twenty-seven on our way to Trent's office, and as soon as we reach the landing, Jackson bursts ahead of us.

"*Shit,*" I say, hurrying to keep up.

Karen, the receptionist, stands as we pass by, her eyes wide. "What—"

"Call Damien," I snap. "Tell him to get down here. And Aiden, too."

I glance at Evelyn as we both pick up our pace. I want to hear what Trent has to say for himself. More than that, though, I'm a little afraid that Jackson is going to pummel him into dust before I get there.

The truth is, my theory is only a theory, sparked by the idea that the resorts really are dueling—fighting it out, and playing dirty. I'm betting that whoever is developing Lost Tides has a chip on their shoulder against Stark International—and that they recruited insiders to do their dirty work. Trent, who was pissed off he lost out on managing Cortez. And Nathan Dean, who wanted a shot at designing the resort and wasn't even in the running.

Part of me hopes that I'm wrong, even though that would mean that we're left with a mystery.

But most of me knows that I'm not.

"You *son of a bitch.*" Jackson's snarl fills the hall, followed by a loud crash. I burst into the room to see that Jackson has Trent up against a bookshelf that obviously got rattled during the impact, sending books and knickknacks tumbling. Jackson's arm is tight against Trent's throat, and Trent looks as if he's about to piss himself from fear.

"Jackson!" His name is ripped from me. Not because I'm afraid he's going to hurt Trent, but because I'm so damned on edge about the murder investigation, and any flash of temper could bite him in the ass.

Aiden Ward, the vice president in charge of the real estate division and both my and Trent's immediate supervisor, hurries into the room. "Let him go." The words are clipped, Aiden's British accent more pronounced in anger.

Jackson ignores him. "Is it true?" he asks, getting right in Trent's face. "Are you fucking with my resort?"

Aiden looks at me. "What the hell?"

But I don't have to answer. Trent's doing that for us. "It got out of control. I never meant for it—and the vandalism on the island—I swear that wasn't me."

"Bloody hell," Aiden says. Apparently all the pieces have fallen in place for him, too.

"Let him go," I say to Jackson, only my voice is softer than Aiden's was. A little sad, even.

Jackson hesitates, but he complies. Even so, he's taut as a wire and practically vibrating with energy. He wants to beat the shit out of Trent—that much is obvious. Honestly, I understand the feeling.

"You're a fucking lunatic," Trent snaps, rubbing his throat. "I bet you did kill that asshole. Christ, you practically killed me."

"Don't make me regret that I didn't." Jackson's voice is low and very dangerous.

Behind us, pretty much the entire department has gathered in the doorway. Beside me, Evelyn shifts, and I know that she's thinking what has already crossed my mind—if anyone who's witnessed this scene tells the police, it's not going to look good for Jackson.

I tell myself they won't. They're loyal to Stark. To the project.

And I tell myself there's not a damn thing I can do about it right now, anyway. Right now, I just need to focus on this.

I draw a breath. "Are you the developer? Is Lost Tides yours?"

He shakes his head. "No—no, they came to me. They knew I got passed over, and—well, they came to me."

"Who?" Aiden asks.

"The development team. But Roger Calloway's the main guy."

"I know that name," Jackson says, looking at me. But I just shake my head. There's something familiar about that name for me, too, but I can't place it at all. I look at Trent. "Who's Roger Calloway?"

But it's not Trent who answers. It's Damien, who has arrived and is striding into the room. "Calloway was one of the players in the Brighton Consortium," he says, and another piece clicks into place.

The Brighton Consortium was an Atlanta land development deal that I was actually working on through my old boss back when Jackson and I first met. It was also the deal that went completely south after Damien snatched up a huge amount of acreage, ensuring that the project couldn't be completed. Jackson had been pissed as hell at his half-brother, and had only recently learned that the consortium's investors were about to be buried in all sorts of fraud and racketeering allegations. Damien's Hail Mary ploy had saved Jackson's ass—not to mention all the others who were about to get burned.

But now I can't help wonder if maybe Calloway didn't know that, either. And maybe he's been thinking of Lost Tides as a way to get back at Damien. And the sabotage as a way to ensure that Cortez floundered.

Honestly, though, I don't give a fuck about Calloway's motive. All I want is for the sabotage against Cortez to stop.

"Talk," Damien says.

"I—He got Nathan on board, first. And that's above-board, honest. Nathan learned what I was doing, but never did anything himself. Nothing but work on the plans."

"But you did," Damien says.

Trent nods. "Calloway wanted details on design, vendors, marketing plans."

"He wanted you to spy for them," I say.

He nods.

"They had you hack the security feed. Leak emails. All of that?" Aiden's voice is harsh. Demanding.

"Most of it. But I told them a few weeks ago that I'd had enough. And the vandalism on the island—I didn't have anything to do with that. I swear. They must have hired someone to go in and—"

"That's enough," Damien says. He turns to face me and Aiden and Jackson, as well as everyone who stands behind us, still lingering in the doorway. "Go on. I'm going to speak to Mr. Leiter alone."

Trent looks a little sick, but he doesn't protest.

I look at Jackson, and he nods. He looks exhausted, but I can't help but think that he also looks relieved.

When we're out in the hallway, with the door to Trent's office shut behind me, he confirms that assessment. "It's fucked up," he says. "But at least we have an answer now." He drags his fingers through his hair. "It's more closure than I have in my life, that's for damn sure." He looks at me. "I'll see you later. I'm going to go back to work."

He brushes a kiss over my cheek, but before he can walk away, Evelyn stops him. "I hate to be the bearer of more bad news, but I didn't get to finish telling you everything before our dramatic interruption."

I catch Jackson's eye, and I can see that he looks just as uneasy as I feel.

"Bad news?" he asks.

"Well, it's not good. I don't have confirmation, but rumor is that another production company is courting Graham Elliott, and he's still keen on making the movie. I'm sorry."

"Wait. What?" Jackson asks, as if he can't quite make sense of her words.

"The movie," Evelyn repeats. "Reed may be dead, but I'm afraid the movie isn't."

eighteen

"I can't believe it," Cass says Friday morning. She's come downtown because Siobhan has a job interview at the Museum of Contemporary Art, which is just a stone's throw from Stark Tower. Now we're sitting outside by Java B's coffee cart, sipping lattes and eating chocolate-filled croissants. "I met him once, didn't I? At some work party you dragged me to?"

I've just finished telling her about all the drama with Trent, and I nod. "Last year's Christmas party. He hit on you."

"Oh, right. I let him down easy. Told him it wasn't personal. He just had the wrong equipment."

I hide my grin by taking a huge bite of my croissant. "I actually liked the guy. Maybe if I hadn't, I would have seen it sooner."

"Don't kick yourself. It's hard to see the worst in people. Has Damien strung him up?"

"Fired him. No references. And he called Calloway, too."

"The one who owns Lost Tides and dragged Trent into the whole mess? Would I have loved to be a fly on the wall during that conversation?"

"I know, right?"

"Is Damien making him shut down Lost Tides?"

I shake my head. "Nope. He said he'd let the market decide—which is fine by me, because Cortez is going to kick serious butt. But he also said that if he catches even a whiff of more dirty tricks, he'll string Calloway up by his balls. And that's pretty much a direct quote."

"And Damien could manage it, too," Cass says. "Calloway must be pissing himself."

"I hope so. The one I feel bad for is Rachel. She really liked Trent, and now she's pretty much destroyed. I called and told her everything last night. I didn't want her to come in and get slammed with gossip unprepared." I make a face. "She's taking the day off."

"So your good deed landed you more extra work?"

I nod. "But that's okay. The busier I am, the less time I have for worrying."

"And Jackson?"

I crumple the bag from my croissant, then hold my coffee in both hands, wanting the warmth. "He's worrying enough for the both of us."

"About what Evelyn told you about the movie?"

"About everything," I say. "But the movie's got the big neon sign over it at the moment. It's like he's having to deal with all of the hell of being a suspect, but the upside was that at least the blackmail threat was gone and the movie was a bust."

"And now he's still a suspect and the movie may actually happen, so it's like fate just kicked him in the balls?"

"That's about it," I admit. On the whole, I think he handled the news pretty well. We'd actually gone to my apartment last night, then spent the evening walking the Third Street Promenade and then all the way down to the pier. After that, we'd watched late night television in bed and fallen asleep in each other's arms. On the one hand, it had felt nice to just be together. But that niceness was colored by worry and frustration.

"I just want a reality that isn't full of drama and uncertainty." I sound whiney and mopey, but since I'm only talking to Cass, I don't need to try and put on a good face.

Cass puts her arm around me, and I lean against her. "I know you do. You'll get it."

She says the words firmly, but I don't believe her. Every day, I'm getting more and more scared. Because every day seems to prove the adage that the good never lasts. It just gets swept away with the drama.

Hell, wasn't that the story of my life? My childhood destroyed by my father.

My romance with Jackson interrupted by my own horrible nightmares.

And now every time we take a step forward in our relationship, we're slapped back. Sabotage. Murder. Even the little victories get ruined. Like yesterday. We solved the riddle of the sabotage, only to learn that the damn movie was barreling down on us all over again.

And what really scares me is the pattern. Because if the good is always followed by the bad, then doesn't that mean that I'll inevitably lose Jackson? Either because he ends up behind bars? Or, god forbid, because we just can't make it work?

I pick at the label on my coffee, frowning. "There's more," I say. "About Ronnie, I mean."

Cass, who knows me well enough to understand that I've

got something major on my mind, turns to face me directly. "I'm listening."

I lick my lips. "Jackson wants me to be Ronnie's guardian if he goes to jail."

"Whoa," Cass says. "I'm not surprised, though. I mean, he loves you. Who else would he want his daughter to be with?"

"I know. Believe me, I get that. But—"

"But you're scared."

"Fucking terrified," I admit.

"Don't be. He's not going to jail."

I make a face. Considering everything that's happened recently, that kind of optimism is nothing more than a platitude.

"And if he does, I think it's great that she'll be with you. You'll do awesome, Syl. I know you, remember? And I know what you're capable of."

Her words are encouraging, and I cling to them like a lifeline. Cass had a great relationship with her dad, and I know that she believes that I can do this, and her faith warms me up from the inside. But that warmth doesn't burn away my doubt.

Cass is watching me closely. "You don't have to be someone else, you know."

I frown. "I don't know what you mean."

"You don't have to be Mommy, or Aunt Sylvia, or whatever it is that she might call you. Just be Sylvia. Just be yourself. You'll be fine."

I lift a shoulder. "Maybe. I don't know. It scares the crap out of me."

"I know it does." She puts an arm around me and squeezes. "But it's going to be fine. Is he bringing her out here now?"

I shake my head. "He's thinking about it. He told me last

night that he considered bringing her out this weekend, figuring that way he could spend time with her in case—well, in case he's arrested and there's no more time to spend. But then this thing with the movie ramping up happened and he's worried about dumping her into the spotlight."

"Makes sense. Poor Jackson, though."

I nod, because I agree. But my horrible, guilty secret is that I'm relieved. And I hate myself for it, because I don't want to deprive Jackson of his daughter. But I'm so damn nervous about playing a role in raising her, this fragile little life that I may end up being responsible for.

And while I'm almost convinced that I can do it, I'm still selfishly happy for the reprieve.

Beside me, Cass's phone beeps, and she glances at the screen. "Siobhan's almost done. Wanna walk with me to the museum?"

I'm tempted, but I shake my head. "I should get back to it." As we start to rise, I remember what I keep forgetting. "Ollie told me on Monday to tell you hello. And no rush, but he's wondering what you're thinking about the franchise."

"Oh." She's already on her feet, but now she sits back down.

My eyes widen. "Trouble?"

"No. I don't think so. But I've been talking with Siobhan and I'm going to put it on hold."

"Really?" I'm both surprised and concerned. This is her passion project, and one of the huge problems with her previous girlfriend, Zee, was that she wasn't supportive at all. I hadn't expected the same from Siobhan.

"Not permanently," Cass says, apparently reading my mind. "But Siobhan pointed out that right now, I'm the face of the company. But nobody outside the walls of my studio knows me. So I'm going to hire a publicist and start advertising. Really get my name out there. Create a logo. Brand myself. That kind of thing. Because I need that to lure franchisees, but also just to make my brand stronger, you know?"

"I think that's brilliant."

"It was Siobhan's idea," she says, and I'm certain she can see my relief on my face. "I know, right? Zee was such a slug. But Siobhan and I click." Her grin is wicked. "In more ways than one."

She stands again, then reaches down to give me a hand up before pulling me into a hug. "You and Jackson click, too," she says. "And that's important. It'll get you through a lot of shit."

"Maybe," I say, hugging her back.

"Trust me," she says. "It's all going to be fine."

I don't answer. I hope she's right, of course, but I can't quite bring myself to believe her.

Two hours later, I'm wishing I had taken that walk to the museum because my head is about to explode from juggling eight million projects at once. "I'll find room in the budget," I say to the recalcitrant supervisor on the other end of the phone line. "Work twenty-four hours if you have to, but the helipad and the entire area need to be cleared and repaired by Monday."

I hang up the phone and close my eyes, then press my fingertips to the bridge of my nose. Despite working nonstop since my coffee break, I've still only made a dent in the cleanup. Or in my to-do list, for that matter.

I'm about to dive into the next task when Ethan calls. At least, I think it's Ethan. Since I'm assuming my dad won't pull that horrible stunt again, I take the risk and answer it.

"I'm sorry," Ethan says. "I just found out. I can't believe he used my phone. I'm so, so, sorry."

"It's not your fault," I say. "He's the asshole." I take a breath. "I'm sorry I didn't call you back right away. Everything's been crazy at work."

"It's okay. I figured you were pissed about Dad telling me and needed to cool off."

"I wasn't," I say, even though I was. Hell, even though I am.

There is a long, uncomfortable silence, and then he says, "I shouldn't have told you."

Shit. I don't know what to say to that. Because part of me agrees. And yet another part of me hates the idea of more secrets between me and my brother.

"No," I finally say. "I was pissed at Dad, not at you. And even though I don't like you knowing, I hated us having secrets. And I swear that was the only one on my end."

I wait for him to tell me the same, but he says nothing.

I frown, not sure if his silence is relief that I'm not pissed or obfuscation.

"So, are we okay?" he asks after another long pause.

"We are." Because no matter my own issues and secrets, I'm not letting anything come between me and my brother. "I promise."

"Okay. Cool." He clears his throat. "Listen, about Jackson's little girl—"

"Jackson wants me to be her guardian if he ends up in jail."

"Oh, Syl. Shit."

"I'm doing it," I say. "And I'm only telling you because of the no-secrets thing. I don't want to talk about it right now." More, I don't want to talk about it with Ethan. I know what he'd say, and I've already freaked myself out enough about mommyhood for the day.

"I—fine. Okay. Whatever." He draws a breath. "Are we cool?"

"We are," I assure him. "And I have to go. I'm not the one still lazing around on vacation."

He laughs. "Fair enough. I'll call you in a day or so. Might even make you come down here and help me buy furniture."

"You found a place?"

"Tiny, but on the beach."

"Of course I'll help." As I'm speaking, the elevator opens, and Jackson steps off.

"Cool. Love you."

"I love you, too," I say, and when I hang up the phone, I'm smiling.

"I hope that was Ethan or Cass," Jackson says as he crosses the reception area to my desk. "Otherwise you and I are going to have words."

"My secret lover," I say, grinning. "But if you work very hard, maybe you can make me forget all about him."

"I'll certainly do my best." He leans against the wall between Damien's door and my desk. His hands are in his pockets and he has the kind of smile that suggests he has things on his mind that aren't remotely related to work. The kinds of things that send a nice little tingle through me.

"To what do I owe the pleasure, Mr. Steele?"

"I've been thinking about tonight."

"What a coincidence. So have I." We're planning to go to the island tomorrow afternoon to check in with the cleanup crew and stay overnight. Tonight, though, we're staying at my apartment again. I had been looking forward to sipping wine on my balcony and relaxing, but looking at him now I'm thinking that a more active evening would be very, very welcome.

"How important to you is our night in?" he asks.

I cock my head. "You have another plan?"

"Remember the Dominion Gate concert I mentioned?"

"Yes." I lean back in my chair and cross my arms. "Why?"

"I forgot that the tickets were by lottery. I found out today that I scored four. I thought it would be a fun way to escape reality for a bit."

"I guess it would." I frown. "Wait. You're saying the concert is tonight?"

"At The Rafters," he says, naming a relatively new club in Burbank.

"All the way in the Valley?"

"That's where the music's happening. You want to go?"

"Of course," I lie. "I've been wearing the T-shirt. I ought to see the band."

He starts to push away from the wall to stand up straight, but doesn't. Instead, he remains still, his attention on my face.

"What?" I finally demand.

"You really don't want to go." It's not a question.

I hesitate, but then concede. "I really don't. But you do, and I really love you. And I know I'll have fun once we get there."

"You're sure?"

I stand up and go to him, then hook my arms around his waist. "I'd do a lot more than that for you. Yes, I'm sure." I brush a kiss over his lips. "And you're right—escaping reality sounds like a damn good plan."

He cups my chin, holding my head in place as he looks into my eyes, his irises moving slightly as he studies me. "Do you have any idea how much I love you?"

Pleasure sweeps through and around me, as soft and warm as a blanket, and I realize that I'm grinning so widely it hurts. "Yes," I say simply. "I do."

I press my head to his chest, breathing deep as he strokes my back, and in that moment, I think I know what heaven must be like. Safe and warm and wonderful.

I sigh with pleasure, then lean back after a moment. "Did you say you have four tickets?"

"I'd originally thought we could invite Nikki and Damien."

My brows rise. "Really?"

"Hey, I'm all about the brotherly bonding. But Damien's in Palm Springs tonight, and Nikki's already got plans."

"Spa weekend with Jamie," I say.

"You're very well informed."

"It's my job. Plus Nikki invited me. I told her I'd rather stay here with you." I rise up on my toes so that I can whisper in his ear. "I'm hoping you'll give me a very thorough massage. Since I'm not getting my spa visit, I mean."

"You can count on it," he says as his hand slides around to cup my ass. He squeezes, and I squeal, then laugh. "You're going to need one after standing for a few hours."

I take a step back, eyeing him dubiously. "Standing?"

"No seats at The Rafters," he says. "But lots of good beer and definitely a lot of good music."

He looks so excited that I can hardly deny him, especially considering the hell he's been living through. "All right," I say. "It's a date."

"Then we'll do it up right. I'll pick you up at seven. The show starts at ten. We'll have dinner and get there by nine-thirty. Sound good?"

"Sounds perfect."

"Should I invite Cass and Siobhan? I've got the two extra tickets."

The question—asked so simply and with complete sincerity—sends an unexpected wave of pleasure washing over me.

"Yeah," I say. "That would be great." And then I ease back into his arms and kiss him softly. "As a matter of fact, you're great, too."

nineteen

When we'd first arrived at The Rafters—a nondescript build-ing near the North Hollywood/Burbank border—I'd as-sumed that Edward had pulled up at the wrong location. It had the appearance of a shack that someone had put up in their backyard and then painted black. Albeit a very large shack.

Jackson assured us that this was the place, though, and when I took a closer look, that was clear enough. Not only was there a sandwich board sign in the parking lot announc-ing Dominion Gate, but there was also a line of concertgoers that snaked around the building.

I'd glanced at Jackson, dubious, but he'd only laughed and told me it would be fun.

Honestly, he was right.

Now that we're inside, I'm not certain how the place man-aged to pass all the various required inspections because I am absolutely certain that the reverb from the band's bass is going to make all the walls collapse on us. Even the concrete floor is moving, though that may be an illusion. Or it may be the result of hundreds of people dancing madly to the ear-splitting music.

But despite all that, I am having a great time—and considering we are jammed in like sardines in an under-air-conditioned building and standing way too close to the speakers, that says a lot. About the music, maybe. But it's more about Jackson. He's clearly having a great time—worry free, loose. Hell, almost boyish.

And I'll put up with a lot to see him happy.

The crowd is thick, and I'm smushed in between him and Cass, who leans over to say something to me. I have no idea what, though, because I can't hear a damn thing. I hold up my hands in question, and she rolls her eyes, then points to a girl who's dancing a few people away. At first I think Cass is checking out the girl—which seems very un-Cassidy-like considering Siobhan is jamming to the music at her opposite side.

Then I realize that the girl is taking pictures with her camera phone. Not of the band, but of Jackson.

I'd like to think that's because he looks so incredibly hot in faded, threadbare jeans and a short-sleeved Henley shirt that sticks to his sweat-slicked body in a way that makes me sigh.

Unfortunately, I know otherwise. Someone had recognized him as we were coming in—and I'd heard the rumble of gossip about "that architect who offed the producer" as it rolled through the crowd before the opening band took the stage.

No one has actually approached us, though, and so Jackson is taking it in stride.

I look back at Cass and shrug, silently letting her know we're not going to worry about it. Tonight is about the four of us having fun, and so long as nobody gets right in his face, they can take all the snaps they want.

By the time the concert ends, I'm practically deaf. I'm also covered in a thin layer of sweat and the sleeveless mock turtleneck that I'd paired with a thin leather jacket and matching mini skirt is clinging to my body. I'm also thinking that despite the cool November evening, the leather skirt was a mistake, as it's stuck to both my ass and thighs.

And as for my feet—well, I have no one to blame but myself. Jackson warned me we'd be standing. Apparently my favorite low black sandals aren't the all-purpose shoes I'd thought they were.

All in all, I can't wait for the blast of cool air when we get outside. So I'm thrilled that we're heading toward the door, even if we are part of a human wave, so up close and personal that I can smell at least seventeen different shampoos and deodorants.

Jackson has his arm tight around my waist, and I can feel Cass pressed up behind me so as to not lose us in the crowd. The entrance is a set of wide double doors that open straight onto the parking lot, so the wave is actually moving pretty fast, and as soon as we step past the doors I sigh with pleasure as the cool air washes over me. And then I immediately cringe as the cameras start flashing.

Jackson grabs my hand and Cass presses her palm to my shoulder even as I register that these are not camera phones. These are Nikons and Canons and Ricohs, and they're being held by photographers who stand next to reporters with microphones sporting logos like *TMZ* and *ET* and god only knows what else.

I turn to Jackson, confused and panicked, because this is a step up from the paparazzi we've been dodging. I hope desperately that there is a movie star inside. Surely this isn't all about Jackson.

Except it is. They're calling his name. They're mentioning Reed. They're talking about the movie. About Damien. The assault. The Fletcher house in Santa Fe. And I don't get it because Jackson hasn't been arrested and nothing has changed, and—

"Is it true that Arvin Fletcher's granddaughter is your daughter?"

"Why is she hidden away?"

"Is Veronica the reason you've been trying to block the movie?"

"Is it true the movie's been green-lit? Do you think Reed's death drummed up more interest?"

Behind me, Cass gasps, pulling me out of the weird tunnel vision funk I'd slipped into when the questions started flowing. I hear Siobhan mumble something, and then take off running, shoving her way past us and through the crowd.

I have no idea what she's doing, but it doesn't matter, because I can't seem to move. My hand aches, and I realize Jackson is squeezing it tight, and I think that's good. Because if he's grabbing on to me, he's not pummeling someone else.

When I look at him, though, I'm certain that is exactly what's going to happen. And when another question rings out—*"Did you kill Reed to keep your daughter a secret?"*— I know that the paparazzi have gone too far.

I feel him tense beside me. I see the anger held tight in his face.

And, god help me, I feel the cool, helpless sense of loss when he lets go of my hand and bursts forward, undoubtedly to pound the shit out of the idiot reporter who has no idea what door he's just opened.

I lunge for Jackson, then actually yank him back by the waistband of his jeans.

He turns to me, his face awash with anger, and I think, *Oh, shit. That picture will be all over the tabloids,* then he's bursting forward again, his fist flying out, and before I even have time to scream his name, the reporter is flat on his ass, his hand pressed to his jaw, and Jackson is about to swoop down for another punch.

"No!"

I scream the word so loudly it hurts my throat, but it works. Jackson turns to me, his face eerily white under the flash of so many cameras.

He's breathing hard, his eyes wild, and I'm really not sure how the hell to get us out of this mess. And then I hear someone calling for Cass, and then Cass is tugging at the back of my shirt.

It's Siobhan, and her head is poked up out of the limo's skylight.

"Go," I say to Jackson, and the word seems to pull him back to himself. We push through the crowd, both Cass and I sandwiching him, and then we tumble into the limo through the door that Siobhan now holds open for us.

"Go!" Siobhan yells, her palm flat over the intercom button. As the limo starts to move, she looks back at us. "I figured we needed an escape route."

"You're brilliant," I say, but she doesn't answer. How can she when Cass has caught her in a wild lip-lock?

Outside, the cameras are still snapping, but I'm starting to breathe a little easier. Jackson is still wound up, though, and as I move to sit beside him, he pulls out his phone. He's just about to dial when it rings. "Evelyn," he says to me as he taps the button to answer.

"Goddammit, young man. What exactly does 'mind your temper' mean to you, anyway?" Her voice is tinny through the speaker, but her frustration is loud and clear.

Jackson ignores her question. "How the *fuck* did they find out?"

"You filed a paternity action, sugar. We knew this was a risk. *You* knew this was a risk. Now we have to handle it. The leak, and your lovely reaction to it just now. They got that whole fiasco on tape, children. And they're already bombarding Damien. Wanting to know about his niece."

Jackson slams his hand down hard against the polished wood paneling, making me, Cass, and Siobhan jump.

"Goddamn motherfucking son of a *bitch*." He sucks in a breath, then another. I start to take his hand. But something holds me back. *Not yet*, I think. *Not just yet*.

"I blew it." He grinds out the words as if each and every one cuts a slice out of his heart. "I lost my temper. I made it worse."

"You may well have." Evelyn's voice is firm. "I can do the spin—you were looking out for your daughter, keeping her safe from scandal, the whole big push—but you just rammed your fist into a reporter's face, Jackson. And our detectives may want to take that little media clip out for a ride."

"You think they'll arrest him?" My voice sounds like a squeak.

"I think Harriet will have a better sense. But they know he was in Reed's house and that they argued. They know he assaulted Reed once before. They know he had motive. And now the whole world knows just how quick a temper he has. Honestly, kids, you need to be prepared."

I look at Jackson, who is dragging his fingers through his hair. He looks both angry and exhausted. "I know," he says, as the limo pulls to a stop in front of a house I don't recognize. "I get it."

"Try not to dwell on it. Let me worry about this for now. I'll get in touch with Charles and Harriet. All you need to do is stay away from the press and calm yourself down. Get tonight out of your system. Your daughter is going to be fine. Do you understand me?"

"Yes. Fine. Sure." He ends the call, cutting off whatever else Evelyn intended to say.

What I notice, though, is what she didn't say. She didn't say that Jackson would be fine.

I'm trying to ratchet back my fear when I realize that Siobhan is scooting toward the door. She opens it and steps out, and I look up curiously at Cass, who is crouched down to give me a hug. "Siobhan's house," she whispers. "She figured you two could use the time."

And before I can reply or say thank you or anything at all, she's following Siobhan's path out of the limo.

She slams the door shut, the limo pulls back out onto the street, and I am left beside Jackson who sits perfectly, dangerously still.

I swallow, my skin prickling from the rising heat.

I'm breathing hard, my breasts rising and falling. My skin is warm, and beads of perspiration have gathered at the nape of my neck.

He turns his head slowly, his eyes meeting mine, wild and feral and hard. There's a hungry glint to them, and for a moment I fear that he will tear me to pieces. That I will truly stand as proxy for the bastards who leaked the news about Ronnie. For the fear that I know must be consuming him, just as it is consuming me.

But haven't I repeatedly told him that I can handle it, no matter how bad it gets? That I will be his release valve, his safety net?

That I'll willingly take in his pain—and then we'll turn it around into passion.

I am still holding his gaze, and I feel locked in place simply from the force of his will. He has not touched me, and though we haven't spoken, I know that he will not until I acquiesce. Not tonight. Not when he needs to push. To go as far as he needs, and then some.

"Yes," I say.

A muscle twitches in his cheek, but he doesn't otherwise move, nor does he say a word to me. He simply watches me for one beat, then another. It is as if he is sizing me up, testing my resolve. I stay where I am, looking back at him. But slowly—very slowly—I part my thighs.

Jackson sucks in a breath through his nose. Then he twists at the waist so that he can reach the intercom button. He jams his finger down on it.

"Don't go home, Edward." His voice is hard. Tight with control. "Just drive. I don't care where. Just drive until I tell you to stop."

twenty

"More," he says, in a voice so full of desire that it would melt my panties if I'd been wearing any. "I want to see you. I want to see how wet you are."

I lick my lips, then raise my ass just enough so that I can get a grip on my skirt, then I shimmy it up over my hips before sitting down again, my legs spread even wider. The leather is warmer than I'd anticipated, and I know why—my entire body is hot, fired by my own desire.

"Oh, Christ, Syl." There is heat in his voice, and his eyes swoop over me, his attention focused on my sex, now very, very exposed. And, yes, very, very wet.

"Do you want—"

"*You.*" Just one word, but it holds everything. Passion. Pain. Fear. Longing.

This is an escape. A release. A way to push past the terror of an impending arrest. A way for him to forget what he just did—that he may have actually made it worse for himself.

"You have me." I meet his eyes, knowing he can see how completely I mean that. "Just tell me how you want me."

He shakes his head, pressing a fingertip to his lips as he does. Then he is on his knees in front of me, his hands on my bare thighs. He grabs me, and in one motion lifts my legs so that they are on his shoulders even as he slams his mouth against my cunt, the ferocity of his assault forcing me back against the seat and making me cry out in both surprise and pleasure.

His tongue torments me, and when he sucks on my clit, I whimper, shifting my hips as I try to squirm away from this wild, relentless assault. He's having none of it, though, and he holds me firm, refusing to let me escape even one iota of the pleasure that is battering me, raising me, taking me right to the brink.

And then—right as I am about to explode—he pulls away, leaving me gasping and frustrated and desperate for the heat of his mouth against my clit.

"Jackson," I begin, but he cuts me off with a stern look and I remember his order of silence.

He eases backward, replacing my feet on the floor of the limo. I'm sprawled against the seat, my legs wide, my cunt bare and wet and throbbing with need, and though he doesn't ask me to, I pull off my shirt and shimmy out of the skirt, leaving me clad only in a lacy black bra and the vibrator necklace that he told me to always wear. I start to reach behind me to unfasten my bra, but Jackson shakes his head, his mouth curved up in a hint of a smile, and I wonder what else he has in store for me.

He eases forward, then slowly pulls the necklace over my head. He presses the button to start the device vibrating, ramping it up to the maximum intensity. Then he hands it to me, his eyes dipping down to my spread legs.

I know what he wants, of course. He wants me to finish

what he has started. He wants to watch as I use the vibe on myself. And even though I have no boundaries where Jackson is concerned, I cannot deny that this feels wild. Decadent.

And, yes, pretty damn compelling. Because when you get right down to it, there's nothing that I won't do with him, and there's never a time when the knowledge that he is watching me doesn't set me on fire.

I keep my eyes on him, then hold the thin cylinder as I drag my teeth over my lower lip. Then I very, very lightly trail it over my belly, along my pubis, and down to tease the sensitive area around my clit.

I'm so close already that the maximum vibe he set it on borders on painful, but doesn't quite cross the line. Still, it's almost too much, and I close my eyes, making little sounds of pleasure and pain without even thinking about it. I'm trying to find that right place, that right touch. I'm close—I can feel the storm growing inside me, sparking through my veins to converge at my center.

As I am breathing hard—not even sure if I'm trying to make the sensation last or push me over the edge—I open my eyes and am struck by the naked, blatant hunger on his face. He's on his knees in front of me, his hand pressed over his cock through his jeans, and I know that he is fighting a primal need, forcing himself to sit still and watch instead of taking and claiming.

His desire is so palpable it fills the limo, sweeping over me like a current and electrifying the air between us. I want to match it—I want to go further. Make it hotter. I want to make him wild.

I want to break him. I want him to be unable to do anything but fuck me.

With sensual purpose, I keep the vibe at my center, teasing myself for his pleasure and my own. But with my other hand I reach up and yank down the cup of my bra to expose one breast. I stroke it, tracing little circles around my nipple, teasing it, tugging it.

Jackson says nothing. And other than a tightness in his features that I know means he is fighting for control, he doesn't react. At least not at first. But then he unbuttons his jeans and takes out his cock, then strokes it in long, quick movements. And as he does, I feel such a rush of heated victory that it's a wonder I don't come right then.

He meets my eyes, the heat burning a hole through me. And I not only whimper, but my cunt, open and exposed to him, tightens at the sight. I see Jackson's brow raise and I know that he has noticed.

I look him in the eye, and before I can stop myself, I mouth two words: *Fuck me.*

I don't expect that he will. This is his show, not mine.

So even though it had been my purpose to break him all along, I am not expecting the violence of the motion when he reaches across the space between us and pulls me to him, surprising me so that I drop the vibrator, which hums uselessly on the carpeted floor.

He moves from the floor to his own seat and settles me on his lap. And then, before I even have time to breathe, he turns me around so that my back is to him. Then he lifts me up until his cock is right at my core. "Go ahead," he says. "One thrust. I want you to take all of me."

It's a challenge I gladly accept, and I lower myself slowly, just because I want to torture us both. Then I rise up again and repeat the process because, dammit, it just feels too good.

"More," he demands, even as he slips his hands around to cup my breasts.

I arch back as he squeezes my nipples to the point of pain—and that coupled with the sensation of him so deep inside me is undeniably erotic.

"More," he demands again, and this time his voice is a

growl. "Harder," he insists and I press against the roof for resistance as I slam myself down on him over and over, his cock filling me and his fingers teasing me until I am lost, my body nothing but sensation. Pleasure. Pain. Need. Hunger. I am reduced to primal urges, wanting everything. Wanting release.

Wanting Jackson.

And when the limo, which has been smooth so far, hits a bump, and I bounce a bit, I am thrown finally over the edge, and I come in a wild, violent release that has me crying out even as my vagina clenches tight around him. He comes, too, his mouth closing over my shoulder as he bites back a groan, his hands clutching my breasts, his cock deep inside me as he fills me with the force of his release.

And when his body stops trembling—when he turns me around so that I can see his face and the raw passion looking back at me—I can only breathe. "Better?" I ask when the power of speech returns. "You should be, because I feel deliciously used. But if you're not, I'm more than happy to go again. You know, for the cause."

He laughs out loud, the sound reverberating through my body in a rather delightful way.

"How do you do it?" he asks.

"What?"

"Brush it all away for me. All the shit and craziness. All the anger. All the fear. You're as cathartic as punching some asshole in a ring," he says with a wicked grin. "And one hell of a lot more fun."

"I'm very glad to hear it."

He meets my eyes, and the humor in his face fades, his words now soft and full of meaning. "You're my miracle," he says, as he pulls me close to cuddle against his chest.

I sigh, because he is mine, too. And while I know that nothing is perfect, and our world is still scary, in this moment at least everything is all right.

twenty-one

Since we're leaving for the island in the morning, we decide to go ahead and brave the paparazzi at the marina. Remarkably, though, the herd is thin, and we pass easily through the gate and into the parking area.

"They've gotten used to me sleeping at your place," he says. "After tonight's show, they're probably there, wanting me to comment on that poor defenseless reporter I slugged."

"Don't even joke about that," I say, as he hooks an arm around my shoulder.

"You're right. I'm sorry." He stops long enough to brush his thumb over my cheek. He's calmer now. I know he's still worried, but for the moment, at least, we can relax. If any more horrors are going to come, they can damn well wait until the light of day. And he knows damn well he doesn't need to be reminding me of it now. "Join me for a shower?"

"I'll join you anywhere, Mr. Steele," I say, and am rewarded by his smile.

"Do you want wine?" he asks once we've reached the boat. He's a few steps ahead of me now, as I've paused to take off my shoes. "It's late, but I could use a glass."

I don't answer. Frankly, I've barely heard the question.

What I heard instead were footsteps, and when I turn to look back over my shoulder, I see Harriet standing on the dock, as if waiting permission to step onto the yacht. She's on the approved guest list at the gate, but I have hoped never to see her here.

And seeing her now really can't be good.

I reach out, managing to grab Jackson's shirt. He turns back to look at me, his mouth curved into a question. Then he sees Harriet, and I watch as he goes completely stiff.

"Are you here about the concert?" I ask. "Because Evelyn already read Jackson the riot act."

"No," Harriet says. She glances down at the deck. "May I?"

I glance at Jackson, who nods stiffly. "Of course."

She steps onto the deck, and I look around awkwardly. My nerves are raw, and I'm on edge. If someone were to sneeze, I'd probably leap all the way into orbit.

I know this must be bad. It's well past midnight, and that is not the usual time for lawyers to make house calls. Something has happened, and while I desperately want to know what, I also don't want to voice the question.

So instead, I say lamely, "Do you want to sit down?"

She shakes her head. "I'm sorry, Jackson. They want you to surrender yourself Monday at nine."

My chest is too tight. I can barely breathe. So I'm not sure how I even force out the question. "If he doesn't?"

"Either way, they're arresting him. If he doesn't, it will be a media circus. If he does, we can get him inside without the fanfare."

"Jackson," I whisper, and he takes my hand, then holds it

tight. And in that moment, I know that he's wrong about me. I'm not strong. I'm weak. Because he's comforting me, and I should be the one comforting him.

Oh, god. Oh, god, oh, god, oh, god.

Harriet is still talking and Jackson is answering. His voice sounds almost normal. Maybe tighter than usual, but it has an efficient clip. I'm not even listening to what they're saying. I think she's going over what will happen tomorrow. How he'll be processed. How she'll request bail, but with his temper he might be declined.

"And they want to interview you, Sylvia," she says, making my head jerk up. "I can postpone that for a day or so, I think. I'll explain to Detective Garrison that you're in shock."

"That's true," I say, and she nods with sympathy.

"You both need to understand that this isn't over."

She is looking at Jackson when she says that.

"Not over, but also not good," he says. "The time I assaulted him. The witness who saw me, who heard Reed and I arguing. The movie and Ronnie. All of it," he finishes. "All of it cuts against me."

"Yes," Harriet says. "But now is when we ramp up for the fight."

He says nothing.

"I know you're worried. I know you're overwhelmed. That's okay. That's why you have me. This is what I do, Jackson. This is what you're paying me for. So that I can take over the fight now. Trust me, okay? I'll get you through this."

"Getting through it might mean that we enter a plea. End up serving less time, but still years."

"It might," she agrees, as my stomach twists at the idea.

He meets her eyes. "I didn't kill him."

"I believe you," she says.

But all three of us know that doesn't really matter.

* * *

After Harriet leaves, I hold tight to Jackson as he practically vibrates with pent-up energy. The need for action. And, yes, the need to fight.

Right now, though, there is nothing and no one to fight.

He pulls me even closer, the motion wild and desperate, and for a moment I think that he wants me again. Wants to lose himself in sex. Wants to pummel his fear with passion.

But that isn't what he is looking for. Not now. Instead, he holds me to him for a few seconds of blinding solidarity, then he releases me and begins to pace. His long strides eat up the length of the boat, and though he says nothing, by watching his face I can discern his purpose. He is thinking. Planning.

He is making a mental list, making sure that everything that matters to him is either already handled or that it will be by morning.

"Chester," he says, looking hard at me. "Have him put together a list of architects I've worked with. You'll want someone to monitor the work, just like you'd planned for Dean to do."

"Jackson. Stop. I can handle it."

He meets my eyes, his haunted.

"I can handle it," I say again.

"Can you? Can you really? Because I'm not sure that I can."

I step to him, then gently brush his cheek. "Yes," I say. "You can. This is just a step. One step on the path, just like Harriet said. You're going to get past this. You're not going to prison."

"Do you really believe that?"

"Yes," I say, because I'll be damned if I'll tell him anything else tonight.

He rakes both of his hands through his hair. "I need to call Ronnie."

"It's past midnight in Santa Fe."

"I know. But I might not—"

He doesn't finish the sentence, but he doesn't have to. "Go on," I say. "She'll think talking to you in the middle of the night is a grand adventure."

He flashes a grateful smile, then disappears below deck. I hesitate, not sure what I want to do. I feel that same need for action. The need to move. To *do*.

But do what? There's not a goddamn thing I can do.

I know, because if there was, I would have done it a long time ago.

Finally, after standing there too long feeling impotent, I take one of the blankets out of the waterproof chest and curl up on the lounge chair. I pull out my phone and dial Cass, but I only get her voice mail. I don't bother leaving a message. She'll call me back simply from seeing that I called. But considering the hour, I don't expect to hear from her before morning.

I close my eyes, thinking that perhaps sleep will be a good refuge, but I don't want that, either. Not now. Not with Jackson being arrested. That's a surefire trigger for a nightmare, and I cannot afford a nightmare tonight.

Not because I couldn't survive it, but because I don't want Jackson to feel compelled to soothe it.

I pick my phone up again, and this time I dial Ethan. He answers on the first ring with a drunken, "It's my big sister! Dudes, it's Syl!"

I hear more drunken male voices behind him shouting things like, "Hey!" and "Yo, baby!" and despite the day I've had I can't help but smile.

"Where are you?" I ask, when the commotion dies down.

"Mexico," he says. *"Gracias, por favor. Arriba!"*

I laugh. "Your Spanish stinks. Are you really in Mexico?"

"Just for the weekend. I'm with Larry and Jim," he adds, mentioning two friends from college. "I figured if I'm going to go, I might as well do it while I have leave. No diving. Just snorkeling and drinking. And enjoying the buffet of female companionship."

I roll my eyes. "God. My brother the hound dog."

"And proud of it. What's up?"

"I just wanted to hear your voice," I say, to which my brother, who knows me well, says, "Bullshit."

"Fine. It's Jackson. He's being charged Monday. He's supposed to surrender himself at nine."

"Holy shit." His voice has lost the drunken happy tone. "Syl, I'm—that's just fucked up."

"I know."

"Are you okay?"

"No." My voice cracks a little, but I'm determined not to cry. "No, but I guess I'll have to be."

"Do you want me to come back?"

I hug the blanket close, completely in love with my brother. "Thanks, but no. I'll be okay." I'm not sure how, but I have to believe it is true. "But I love you for offering."

"Anything, Syl. You know that, right?"

"Yeah. I do."

"How's Jackson holding up?"

"Stoic. Scared. Pissed." I close my eyes and sigh. "Pretty much everything you'd expect."

"What about his little girl? Is she—I mean, are you going to take care of her?"

I lick my lips, because my mouth has gone suddenly dry. That possibility hadn't occurred to me. "I don't know," I admit. "She's in Santa Fe right now. I don't know what Jackson wants to do. He's talking to her right now. He wanted—" My voice breaks, and I have to try again. "He wanted to talk to her before he's taken into custody."

"Yeah." I hear him draw in a long breath. "Listen, I should let you go. It's late."

"Sure. I'm glad I caught you. Have fun. I'll talk—"

"Samantha was pregnant." He blurts out the words.

I replay that in my head, not entirely certain I heard right. "Say again?"

"That's why we broke up," he says. "Why I left London. She was pregnant. I didn't want a kid—didn't figure I could handle a kid. We fought. I left."

"Oh." I lick my lips. "I'm sorry."

"No, I'm the one who's sorry."

"Because you left?"

"No." He sounds suddenly tired. "No, I mean it when I say I'm not cut out to be a dad. But I'm sorry for ragging on you about the kid thing. I was talking at you through a curtain of my own shit."

"So you do think I can handle it?"

"Yes. No. I don't know." I can picture him tilting his head back with exasperation the way he does. "I really don't know. Look at our role models, you know? But then again, we turned out okay."

At that, I really do have to laugh. "I'm not entirely sure that's the best argument."

"I guess I'm saying that if you think you can, then you should trust that. Okay?"

"Okay," I say.

"Does that help?"

"Yes," I lie. Because the truth is, I don't know if I can at all.

And if that's the feeling I should trust, where does that leave me?

More important, where does that leave me and Jackson?

twenty-two

I wake to sunshine and the wonderful sight of Jackson's blue eyes looking down at me.

"Hey," I say, blinking a bit as I try to wake up. I'm still on the deck, but I'm under a blanket, and I realize with surprise that I've slept here all night, and apparently alone. "Did you stay up all night?"

He doesn't answer my question. Instead he sits on the edge of the chaise, his expression so serious that it scares me. "We need to talk."

I shake my head, because whatever he has to say, I don't want to hear it.

"I have been up all night," he admits. He leans forward, then presses his head into his hands.

I sit up, too, my fear now taking on the color of panic. I force it down. With everything else that has been going on, the last thing Jackson needs is to see me losing it, too.

With some effort, I pull myself together, then press my

hand to his thigh. "Hey," I say. "I know you're scared, but Harriet's right. This is why you hired her. It's not over, Jackson, and we both have to believe that."

His nod is perfunctory, as if I'm talking about some irrelevant topic at a cocktail party. "I've done a lot of thinking," he finally says. "I think it makes more sense if I ask Damien and Nikki to take guardianship of Ronnie."

"I—oh." This is not what I was expecting, and I'm scrambling a bit to mentally shift gears. "Okay." I swallow. I should be turning cartwheels. After all, the thought of being the parent figure in Ronnie's life has had me terrified. But instead of joy, I feel an overwhelming disappointment. "I guess that makes more sense," I add. "After all, Damien's her uncle."

"That's part of it," Jackson says. "It's not all of it."

A strange sort of prickling builds at the back of my neck, then starts to trickle down my spine. "You're scaring me, Jackson."

"I know," he says, and there is pain in his eyes. "I'm sorry. But there's something I need you to do for me. No arguments, Syl. No questions."

I don't answer. These words are too much like the words I said to him in Atlanta. And those words just about destroyed us both.

He takes my hand. His is cold. Even a little sweaty. And I feel suddenly ill.

"Don't," I whisper. "Don't say it."

"I have to." The words sound like nails sealing a coffin. He draws in a breath, and his voice when he speaks is heavy with pain. "I need you to walk away."

"No." I'm shaking my head, but I don't even realize it until I have to stop because the world is moving back and forth, and I am getting dizzy. "No," I repeat. "I don't know what kind of game you're playing, but you don't need it. You don't want it. And I'm sure as hell not doing it."

"I'm not playing a game." The pain is gone, replaced by a firm intensity. "I should have done this at the airport. I should have sent you back to LA the moment those detectives showed up in Santa Fe."

"That is such bullshit." I'm searching for words, for arguments, for understanding. But I'm finding none of those things. "Why are you doing this to me? To us?" Tears are streaming down my face, and I don't even care.

Jackson's fingers twitch, as if he wants to wipe them away, but he doesn't reach for me. On the contrary, it looks as though he's fighting hard to not touch me.

"Goddamn you, Jackson. You said you'd never do anything if the price was breaking me." My voice is cracking and it sounds far away, as if I'm standing at the end of a very long tunnel. "What the hell do you think you're doing now?"

"I am protecting you, baby. And I'm doing it the only way I know how."

"The hell you are."

"I once told you that where you are concerned I'm neither brave nor strong because the thought of losing you destroys me. And that's true. But, dammit, Syl, I've found that strength. And it's not you but the world that has destroyed me."

"Jackson—" My voice is full of pain. And, yes, of understanding. But he doesn't let me continue. Just shakes his head and pushes on.

"I'm strong enough for the both of us, baby. And this is over. It has to be. So as of this moment, we're done. Because I won't live like this, knowing that you are tied to a man who can't even touch you. You deserve a life, Syl. I won't have you thrown into a cage of our making just because I'm being tossed into one."

"That's not a decision you can make for me," I say.

"The hell it's not. You've handed me control, baby."

My brows rise. "Control? In bed, sure. But about this? No fucking way."

"Do you remember the photo I took of you?"

I know what he's talking about, of course. I'd asked him to take it after Reed had sent me the blackmail photos. I'd needed to grab back some of what Reed had stolen, and so I'd had Jackson take a photo of me, bound and naked.

So, yeah. Of course I remember the photo.

I say nothing, but he knows that I do. How could I not? "That photo was the ultimate submission," Jackson says.

"Bullshit. I asked you to take it."

"You did," he agrees. "But now it's mine. I hold it. I control it. That wasn't just about sex, Sylvia. The minute you asked me to take that photo you handed me control in your life, too. Because I could destroy you in a heartbeat."

"You wouldn't." Despite everything he's said tonight, I know that much is true.

His smile is a little sad. "No. Never. But that doesn't change the basic fact—you gave yourself to me. Trusted me fully with your reputation. Your privacy. And now, baby, you have to trust me on this."

"But I don't," I say.

He sighs. "Fair enough. But I know I'm right. And if you won't walk away, Syl," he says in a voice that breaks my heart, "then I will."

"Are you sure about this?" Damien asked Jackson. They were on the Malibu property, meandering down pathways that led from the house to the beach. Now, they paused beside the tennis courts, and Damien opened the gate.

Jackson followed him onto the green surface, and took a seat at a courtside table across from his brother. "Believe me," he said, "I've been thinking about little else."

For hours now, he'd felt lost. Hollow. *He'd really left her.*

He was really going to move forward without Sylvia at his side. He'd fought so damn hard for her, and now he was throwing it away.

No.

No, he couldn't look at it like that. He was fucking saving her. She deserved more than some sad life as a prison widow. And while he believed her when she said she would take care of Ronnie, how the hell could he put that on her? Only by being a selfish prick, that's how.

Yes, he wanted his daughter with the woman he loved.

But even more than that, he wanted Sylvia happy and free. Not trapped.

So, yeah. As much as he hated it, he was sure about this. Sure enough that he'd walked away from her. Sure enough that he'd cut her to the core.

"I'm sure," he said once more to his brother.

Damien didn't nod, didn't argue. He just looked at him, those dual-colored eyes seeing more than Jackson wanted to reveal.

"She loves you," Damien finally said. "Do you really think that walking away will make her love you any less?"

Jackson ran his fingers through his hair, the words hurting him more than he wanted them to. "I think it will make her live her life."

Damien lifted a brow, the expression almost smug. "Like you did after she left you in Atlanta?"

Jackson's gut twisted as he fought against the truth of Damien's words. This was different, dammit. He was going to fucking prison. "I just need to know if you'll stand as Ronnie's guardian, Damien. The rest isn't up for discussion."

For a moment, he thought his brother would argue. But then Damien nodded. "Of course I will. I need to talk it over with Nikki, but I'm certain she won't have a problem. Ronnie's my niece, after all."

Jackson nodded slowly, relieved. "Thank you," he said simply.

Everything around him was going to shit. But Ronnie, at least, was going to be okay.

"Damien told me what happened," Nikki says. She's arrived at my apartment with a bottle of wine. "It may only be lunch-time, but I figured you could use this."

"Thanks." I step back to let her in. I'm not entirely sure I want company, but I can't deny that I appreciate the thought. And I know that Nikki understands what I'm feeling. Damien walked away from her once, too. I'd been working his desk, and even I hadn't known where he was. And like Jackson, he'd done it supposedly to protect her.

So if I'm going to commiserate with someone, it makes sense that it's Nikki.

"How are you doing?" she asks as I open the wine and pour two glasses.

We've moved to the patio, me on the chaise and Nikki in the chair. But right now, I don't feel like sitting, so I stand up and walk to the rail, then look out at the neighboring build-ing and the ocean beyond.

"Like the world is falling down around my ears," I admit. "The resort is a mess. Just this morning, we lost two more investors because the word is out that Jackson is surrendering himself on Monday. And of course the press is all over that, calling Santa Cortez 'troubled.' How fucking annoying is that?"

"Very," she says gently. "But I meant about Jackson."

"I know you did." I sigh deeply and return to the chaise. "Honestly, I don't know if I'm angry or hurt or something else all together."

"All of the above, I'd imagine."

I nod. "The thing is, I know that I *can* be alone." And it's true—it's true because Jackson taught me how to let go of my security blanket. How to find the strength inside myself. "But I don't want to be alone. I want Jackson beside me."

"Even though he might not be beside you?" she asks. "He's right, you know. Damien talked with Charles and Harriet. With all the evidence against Jackson—especially the prior assault, his temper, the argument that witness overheard—Harriet's pretty certain the DA is going to play hardball. And she's even more certain that they'll be able to get in evidence of the underground fighting he does."

My eyes go to hers. "You know about that?"

"I do now. The court will soon."

"Fuck." She's right; a history of violent behavior is only going to make Jackson look like a hot-head who lost his temper and killed the man who refused to back off the movie.

"Maybe he's right." Her voice is soft. "Maybe you should walk away."

My answer, when it comes, is fierce. "Hell, no. I want Jackson. I want Ronnie. I want the man I love and everything that comes with him."

Something sparks in her eyes, and when she says, "I know you do," I sag a little with relief at this proof that she really does get it.

"So how do I get him back? How do I make this goddamn stubborn man change his mind?"

"I don't know," she admits.

"What did you do?" I ask, knowing that she will understand I'm talking about Damien.

She lifts a shoulder. "I cried a lot. And then I fought." She looks at me, then actually smiles. "Actually, with Jackson, fighting's probably a damn good way to go.

twenty-three

I wake to the sound of Jackson's voice.

A wave of relief washes over me, followed quickly by disappointment when I realize he's not in my condo. Instead, I'm hearing his voice on the television, and I realize I must have fallen asleep in bed with the television on.

Now, a morning news show is playing, and the image on screen is Jackson on the deck of his boat with Harriet beside him.

"You're surrendering yourself tomorrow?" a reporter asks.

"I am," he says.

"What about the Cortez Resort? Are you resigning?"

"I'm not. Assuming I get out on bail, I'll continue the work. If I'm incarcerated, then we'll either figure out a way for me to work while in custody or I'll support the project's efforts to find another architect."

"The project's efforts?" another reporter repeats. "You mean Sylvia Brooks? She's the project manager, right?"

"Correct."

"So where is she today? You two have a personal relationship as well. How does she feel about your arrest?"

His face tightens. "Ms. Brooks and I have only a professional relationship. We're not together anymore."

That sets off a new buzz from the crowd of reporters, but all it does for me is make my stomach hurt. *Goddamn Jackson.* I know what he's doing. He's making sure that our break-up is coming at me from all sides.

He's making sure that I understand it's real.

Well, fuck that.

Nikki's right. If I want him back, I have to fight.

And I think it's appropriate that Jackson is a fan of bare knuckles fighting. Because right now, the gloves are coming off.

It takes me no time to get dressed, but my problem is that I don't know where I'm going. I try the boat first, but he's not there. Then I try the office, because maybe he's trying to get as much done on the resort as possible before he surrenders himself.

But there's no Jackson there, either.

I drive by the lot in the Palisades, thinking that perhaps he's simply melancholy. Again, nothing.

I'm still baffled and stymied when I swing by Cass's house. She, at least, is at home.

"He's probably beating the shit out of someone," Cass says.

I make a face, because I'm afraid that Cass is right. "I hope not," I say. "If the press gets a picture of that, it's not exactly going to help his case."

"Have you called Harriet?"

I haven't, and it's a good idea. I call, but get only voice mail. I'm about to bitch to Cass some more, when the phone rings, and I can't help but be impressed by Harriet's promptness.

"Are you okay?" she says, and I'm touched that she's asking. I'm not the one who is her client, after all.

"Not really. I want to find him, Harriet. Do you know where he is?"

I'm afraid that she's going to tell me that she's not allowed to say. Or worse, that she's certain he's made the right decision and she thinks it would be better not to tell me.

But she surprises me by saying, "He's got a room at the Biltmore."

"Thank you." The words are thick with relief. My next, however, are tentative. "Is he—I mean, how is he doing?"

"Let's just say that I wouldn't have told you where he is if I didn't think that seeing you would do him good."

I release a breath I hadn't realized I was holding.

"Thank you," I say again, then end the call.

I look at Cass.

"Don't waste time talking to me," she says. "Go."

I do. And I'm pretty sure I break every speed record known to man getting from Venice Beach to downtown LA. I leave my car with the valet then burst into the hotel, only to lose steam when the front desk clerk absolutely refuses to tell me Jackson's number. Some bullshit song and dance about privacy. And he digs his heels in even more when I decline his suggestion that I call up to Jackson's room.

Damn.

It's not even three in the afternoon yet, but I figure I can stake out the lobby if I have to, and for as long as I have to. But before I do that, I step into the Gallery Bar, just because it's Jackson's favorite place and being in there will make me feel closer to him.

And the moment I do, I see him.

I wasn't expecting it, not this early. But he's at the bar, and Phil is in front of him, chatting as he refills Jackson's glass.

I straighten my shoulders, strengthen my resolve, and march in that direction.

He knows I am there before I say anything. I can tell from the tightening of his posture. The way his drink stills on the way to his mouth. "Sylvia," he says, then turns in his stool to face me.

I take the seat next to him. "Fancy meeting you here."

He looks at me, and the flicker of pleasure I see in his eyes gives me hope. "You shouldn't be here."

"Free country," I counter.

"Dammit, Syl." Frustration spikes his voice, and Phil slips quietly away, letting us talk.

"Don't. I saw it in your eyes. You were happy to see me."

"Always," he says. "That's why it was so hard to let you go."

"You shouldn't have."

He doesn't argue. "How did you find me?"

"I looked for you at the boat. At the office. I ended up calling Harriet. Don't be mad at her."

"I'm not," he says, and that flutter of hope inside me blooms wider.

I take the scotch that Jackson still holds, then drink deeply, my eyes never leaving his. Then I put the glass down defiantly on the bar. "I need you to hear me out. If nothing else, you owe me that much, okay?"

He's silent for a moment, then he nods, his acquiescence surprising me. "All right."

"You're an idiot," I begin. "An idiot if you think you can push me away so easily. You can't, and you and I both know it."

He doesn't say anything, and once again, I take that as encouragement.

"Do you remember when Damien made me fire you and I felt guilty for not quitting my job, too?"

"Of course."

"Do you remember what you told me?" I don't wait for his answer. Instead, I hurry on. "You said you'd never ask me to walk away from something I love. But dammit, Jackson, there's nothing in this world I love more than you."

"Syl—"

"No. This is my time to talk. You told me once I need to trust this thing between us. I did. And Jackson, you were right. I trust it now, too. And you need to as well. Jail or not, daughter or not, this is real. It's right. Dammit, Jackson, you have to believe in us."

He closes his eyes. "I do."

My heart stutters in my chest. "Do you? Because I'm not walking out of here without you. Without Ronnie. I don't give a fuck if Damien is her uncle. I want to be her guardian, Jackson. More than that, I want to be her mom."

He cocks his head, his expression wary. "What are you saying?"

"I'm saying I want to marry you, Jackson." The words spill out of me, feeling so right, so perfect. "I'm saying that I don't want to go another day without knowing that I will be your wife."

Marriage.

Jackson's heart felt like it was going to burst.

He'd thought he'd lost her. That he'd pushed her away. And now here she was, back and determined to be his wife.

What the hell had he ever done to deserve her? He didn't know, but he was damn sure he wasn't going to deny her.

He'd been brooding about how to get her back for too long now, ever since he talked to Damien. Ever since he realized that pushing her away was only a Band-Aid.

Now he knew that the only way to make things right between him and Sylvia was to be together. Because being apart wrecked them both.

"Jackson?" Her voice was soft, her expression tentative.

He turned to her, knowing that his smile said it all. "Damn right you're going to be my wife."

He watched as she closed her eyes, her face going soft with relief, and he wanted to kick himself all over again for the way he'd hurt her.

"I'm sorry," he said, though those words could hardly convey all of his emotions.

"I get it. I do." She lifted a shoulder. "You're scared."

"I'm fucking petrified," he admitted. "Of leaving you. Of prison. Of the way everything is about to shift."

"Me, too." Her voice was barely a whisper. "But we're in it together now, right?"

Instead of answering, he slid off his stool, then held out a hand to help her down. "I need you, Syl. I need you right now." He could feel the need growing in him. A hole that had to be filled. A demand that had to be satisfied.

"I need to burn the feel of you into me. I want the heat of you to singe me. To mark me. Because even in prison, I don't ever want to be without you. And Syl," he adds roughly, "I need to have all of you. My wife? You're so much more than that. You're my life, Syl. You're my blood. You're the only person who can break me, and the only one who can save me. And right now, I need you more than I need to breathe."

His mouth is on mine the moment the door to his room closes behind us, and the kiss is wild and passion-filled, as if we are both making up for lost time and marking our future.

"Off," he says, plucking at my shirt, and we are both naked in a heartbeat, stripping off our clothes so fast it's a wonder that we don't topple over in our hurry.

I move to press against him, wanting the feel of his skin against mine, but he surprises me by lifting me up, then carrying me to the bed. The maid's been in, and it's neatly made, and we tumble onto it together.

Jackson rolls onto his back and looks up at me. "Kiss me," he demands, and I don't hesitate. I straddle him, positioning myself so that the tip of his cock is at my core. And as I lean forward to crush my mouth hard against his, I lower myself. I'm already wet, my body fired with arousal, and I take him hard and deep.

He moans against my mouth, his fingers dipping low to tease my cunt before he withdraws and slides his hand around, then slips his fingertip in my ass, making me gasp, because the sensation of being filled like this is both incredible and undeniably erotic.

"Yes," I whisper. "God, yes." I meet his eyes. "You can have me like that."

"I'll have you however I want you," he says, and the potent heat combined with these words of possession—of power—make my mouth go dry and my cunt throb all over again. "But I need you to go get my wallet."

I raise a brow, but don't argue. Instead, I get off him carefully, then return with the wallet I fished from his back pocket. As I kneel on the bed, he removes a small packet that looks like a condom.

I raise my brows, because we are way past that, but he just grins. "Lube," he says. "I thought it might come in handy."

I swallow and nod, wanting this, and yet uncertain. We've never done this before, and though the sensation of his finger inside me was undeniable enticing, I can't help but be just a little nervous. But Jackson erases my worries, or at least buries them. Because he's pulling me close to take my breast in his mouth. He's teasing me, his teeth scraping my nipple, then biting. There is pain, but the kind that spreads out into heated threads of pleasure, and I straddle him again, then arch back and moan. And as I do, I feel the cool brush of the lube against my rear, teasing my entrance where his finger was just moments before as he readies me for an even deeper invasion.

With his other hand, he teases my clit, so that I am being sensually assaulted in all directions, my body opening to him, craving him.

"That's it, baby. Relax. Let me take you there. Let me show you how good you can feel."

"Yes," I say, because tonight I will give him whatever he wants, however he wants it. And, yes, I want it, too. My breath is coming in gasps and my cunt is throbbing. I need so desperately to be fucked, and as if he is bending to my will, he slips fingers into both my vagina and my ass. I rise up, then lower myself back down, wanting even more than he is giving me.

I keep my eyes on Jackson and I see the answering heat in his eyes—the pleasure my response gives him. I feel it, too, in the way his cock twitches against my thigh, as if waiting not-so-patiently for its turn.

"Now," I beg. "Please, Jackson, now."

Even as I speak, I'm moving to get off him so that I can bend over facedown on the bed, but he holds me still. "No," he says. "Like this. I want to look at you."

"But—but I mean, I've never—"

"I want to look at you," he repeats. "And," he adds as he brushes a kiss over my lips, "you have more control." He grins a bit, as if telling me that he's giving something up. But that's not true. I am completely under his spell, fallen to mercy, and he knows it.

"I want you now. Like this." There is heat and demand in his voice, and the sound just makes me wetter. "Come here."

I lean forward and let him capture me in a kiss, then moan when his tongue thrusts hard into my mouth even as his lubed fingers tease my rear, entering me, spreading me.

I hear Jackson's soft chuckle of understanding, and feel him add another finger, widening me, playing me.

"Now, baby. Because I really will just turn you over and take you if I can't have you right now."

I rise up and let him guide me over his cock, and he's right, I do have more control. I feel the press of his shaft against my rear, and I pivot my hips, rising and falling as he teases my clit, relaxing me, making me bolder. Making me needier.

Jackson closes his eyes and groans, the sound one of both pleasure and frustration, and that turns me on even more. I thrust down, taking the tip in, biting my lower lip against a burn that feels remarkably, wonderfully good. And when my throaty sound of pleasure merges with his whisper of my name, I know that I can't take it any longer, and I thrust down hard, swallowing the pain and welcoming the incredible, awesome pleasure of being filled by this man.

The burn fades, and I rise up, then lower myself, letting the sensations grow. Letting the pleasure fill me as my body adjusts to accommodate him.

"That's it," he says as he slips two fingers into my vagina, but keeps the pressure of his thumb against my clit. "Come on, baby. Fuck me hard."

"This isn't how I expected we'd do this," I admit, and when he laughs in response, I feel even closer to him.

"But you like it."

"Yes," I say earnestly. "I do."

As we speak, I'm doing what he'd said and riding him,

and I'm already so close that the pressure against my clit combined with the new, incredibly erotic sensation of being penetrated both ways sends me over the top far too quickly.

It doesn't matter, though, because Jackson is not ready to stop, and he takes control of my body. He grabs my hips and pistons me, thrusting deep inside, and I'm tight around him, my body clenching hard, wanting him deeper, wanting more.

And though he is no longer teasing my clit, the building pressure is enough that it leaves that first orgasm behind as a wilder, more powerful release rips through me even as Jackson explodes inside me.

I go limp against his chest, our bodies still entwined as he gently strokes my back while we both let the universe shift back to normal.

When we both have recovered, he presses his lips to my head. I know we should clean up, but I'm not ready to move yet. I like the sensation of my ass pressed up against his now-soft cock. We form a circle, I think, and there is something about the thought that soothes me. As if no matter where I am—no matter how far we might push away from each other—in the end we are connected. And I only have to go a little bit further in order to come around to Jackson again.

I'm awakened from a deep sleep by a hard rap at the hotel door. "What the—"

"It's okay," Jackson says. "I've got it."

I nod and am just drifting off again when he returns. I start to speak, but he presses a finger to my lips, then holds out a hand to help me up. "I know it's late, but we need to go somewhere. Will you come?"

"Of course." He already knows I wouldn't deny him anything tonight.

The valet pulls his car around, and once we are traveling

north on the Pacific Coast Highway, I'm pretty sure I know where we are going, and my suspicions are confirmed when he makes a right turn and heads up into the Pacific Palisades. A few minutes later, he's parking the car in front of a stunning double lot with an ocean view. It's a lot that he owns. That he bought years ago, and has yet to build on. But I know that he has been thinking about the house he wants to put here for almost as long as he has owned the property.

He hasn't said why he wanted to come here tonight, but I can guess. He'd wanted to build a house here. For himself. For his little girl.

And now he's come to say goodbye.

And that's not something that I want to hear even though I'm desperately afraid that it is true.

I grab his hand before he can step out of the car. "Don't," I say.

"Don't what?"

"Don't start believing you won't ever get it done."

His smile is so tender it almost hurts. "Come on."

He gets out of the car, and I do, too. He grabs a small bag from the trunk, then he starts walking across the property toward the darkness that lies in front of us. It is the ocean, I know, but on this night, it seems to be nothing more than a void in space into which we are about to disappear.

The property descends after a while, almost as if terraced, adding an extra level of privacy.

"Right there," he says, pointing to an indentation in the tree line that forms a natural semicircle. "That's where I want to put her playscape."

I glance at him, surprised. He said *want*. Not *wanted*. And a little thread of hope unfurls within me.

I don't comment on his word choice. All I say is, "That's the perfect spot."

He turns to look at the ocean that is spread out below us, flowing to the horizon just past the snake-like length of the coast highway that separates us on this hill from the pounding waves.

"I hesitated to start on the plans," he says, as much to the world as to me. "Because I was afraid it would all go to hell."

I say nothing; he is echoing my earlier thoughts and I want to hear where this is going.

"I hesitated bringing Ronnie here, too. Hesitated making it official that she is my daughter when I should have done it so long ago. I put my life on hold because somebody else killed a man. Me, Sylvia. Who has never once changed the direction of my life because of someone else's whim. But I did in this. I stopped moving forward in my life because I've been afraid that life will be taken from me."

"And you're not afraid anymore?"

"I'm scared to death," he says. "But that's a goddamn lousy reason."

I swallow, so many questions and emotions churning through me that I can't identify any of them. "What is this about, Jackson?"

He doesn't answer. Instead, he takes my hand and raises it to his lips. He presses a kiss to my fingers, and although the gesture is sweet, it is also sad. And I'm not sure if I should be scared or hopeful, and the not knowing is weighing on me so hard it is like a physical burden.

"Tell me about the photographs." His voice is gentle, and I have no clue where he's going with this. "The pictures of houses you take."

"I have told you." My hobby is photography, and for most of my life I have preferred to take pictures of buildings. And not just majestic skyscrapers and brilliantly designed commercial buildings. But homes. Some plain. Some incredible.

Some in suburbia. Some tucked away on acres of their own land.

"Tell me again," he insists.

I frown, feeling a little unsteady. I'm not at all sure where this is coming from, but I'm not going to ask. Not tonight. "I've done it all my life. I guess I wanted to imagine what went on in those houses. All the different buildings. Small and large, fancy and ramshackle. I couldn't help but wonder if they had a better life. A father who watched out for them. A mother who knew they were alive." I shrug. "So I collected them. Little bits of lives that I thought maybe someday I'd want."

"And if you were to look at this lot with a house, what would you see?"

"Well, a ranch style. The lot's big enough to support it. But with raised sections on either side. One side would be a media room. The other would be the master suite. And there's a balcony that connects both and looks out over the ocean."

"I like it. And where's the kitchen?"

"In the back with a wall of windows. So you can have breakfast outside if you want."

"And it opens to the pool," he says.

"Of course. For easy entertaining. And there are three—no four—bedrooms in addition to the master."

He nods. "Not bad. Pretty close to what I have in mind, actually. I'll have to make a few tweaks to incorporate your ideas."

He takes my hand and leads me toward the north edge of the property. "This is where the master will be—upstairs, now. That frees up the space below, which would be perfect for your home office."

I raise an eyebrow. "Would it? And where's yours?"

"Right next to yours, of course. With a connecting door."

"I like this game," I say. But when I look at his eyes, I'm confused. "Jackson? Is this a game?"

His eyes are warm, with a spark of humor. "I guess that depends. If at the end of a game someone wins, then maybe it is. I'm building this house for you, baby. Your house with a view of the ocean. Even if I have to design it in prison and farm out the construction, I will have a home for my wife and daughter."

"Oh." The word is soft. A breath. But despite everything, I feel the stirrings of joy inside me, and I can only nod my head. Because this is right—how could Ronnie and I live anywhere other than a house that Jackson built.

"Okay?"

"Yes. Of course." My voice is thick with emotion. So many I can't identify them. All I know is that I'm full up. So much so that my fear is almost—*almost*—overshadowed.

"I have something for you." He reaches into his pocket and pulls out a small ring box.

I open it almost tentatively and reveal a diamond solitaire, its fire so magnificent that it sparkles even in the dim light of the moon. The setting is clearly antique, with a pattern of vines etched into the white gold setting.

"It was my grandmother's. I called Lauren after you fell asleep," he says, referring to his assistant. "I had her go to the boat and get it out of my desk."

I nod, realizing that it was Lauren at the hotel door earlier.

He takes the ring from the box and slips it on my finger. Remarkably, it fits. "My mother never got married," Jackson continues, "so she never wore it. I'd like you to."

I swallow, my throat almost too full of emotion to speak. Because while we'd worked everything out between us, this symbol truly seals it. I'm Jackson's. He's mine. And it really is forever.

I look up, meeting his eyes again. "It's lovely."

"If it's not your style, my feelings won't be hurt."

I've been staring at the ring, lost in its fire. Now I look up at Jackson, my eyes filled with tears. "No," I say. "This is perfect."

twenty-four

Jackson and I spent the night wrapped in each other's arms in the bed at the Biltmore, swept into sleep by the tug of exhaustion that finally vanquished fear, at least for those few blissful hours.

I'm glad of the sleep. Glad to have had the chance to hold him close for what I dearly hope wasn't the last time. And now, as we drive from Santa Monica to Beverly Hills, I tell myself that I'm glad we have this moment to share, too.

It's all a lie, of course. I don't want just this moment. I want all the moments. I don't want to have held him close one last time. I want to hold him each and every night.

But my hopes are not running the show here, and so I sit quietly in the car, trying to be brave because right now I think he needs that. Lord knows that I do.

"Stella and Ronnie arrive at two," he says.

"I know. You told me last night." Once Damien had agreed to take care of Ronnie, Jackson had started the ball rolling to get her out here. Now, of course, his daughter's care will fall to me.

I lean over and press my hand on his thigh. "I'll handle it. I promise."

He nods, his expression managing to be equal parts sadness and gratitude.

"Jackson—" I stop myself, not certain that this is a conversational door I want to go through.

I should know better than to open my mouth at all. "What?"

I consider simply telling him that I'm scared. It's true, after all. But I owe him honesty, and so I dive in. "Are you sure you want to bring her here? Now that we know the movie might happen and the press knows all about her . . ."

I trail off, hating that I even have to remind him of all the scandal he's been so worried about.

"I know," he says. "And I hate even thinking about it. But we've thought about this before, and although it's not ideal, we can shield her." He glances sideways at me. "Except I'm not going to be around to help. Do you want me to keep the guardianship with Damien and Nikki? Do you think I should keep her in New Mexico with Betty?"

"No. I want her with me." The words come automatically even though I'm not at all certain that answer is the truth. But it's only a lie insofar as I'm scared of my own ability to take care of this little girl. As far as scandal is concerned, I think he's right. It can be managed. It won't be fun and it won't be easy, but it can be done. Celebrities do it every day, and as far as PR manipulation goes, I won't find better resources than in Los Angeles.

I nod, the motion centering me. "Seriously, it's fine. Scandal doesn't scare me."

He looks at me, then stays silent for just a beat too long before saying gently, "You're going to make a great mom."

I feel my cheeks burn with the rising blush. "You see too much when you look at me, Jackson."

He takes my hand. "I see competence. I see strength. I see you, Sylvia. Really. You're going to be fine."

I shake my head, not in protest of his words—although he really has *not* convinced me—but in astonishment that he is the one comforting me this morning.

Gently, I squeeze his hand. "You don't need to worry about me," I say. "I'm nine kinds of good. Really."

I think he's going to say something, but my phone pings, signaling an email, and when I check it, I also see that I missed a voice mail from last night. I check the log, then curse when I see who it's from—my dad.

Jackson glances at me. "Are you going to listen?"

"No. Whatever he has to say, I don't need to hear it." But even as I'm saying the words, I'm pressing the button to play the message on speaker. I have no idea why. I guess I figure that whatever my dad has to say can't be any worse than what Jackson and I are doing right now.

"Honey, it's Dad. I just wanted to say one last time that I love you, and that I'm sorry. I won't call you anymore. I just hope—well, I hope that someday we can talk again."

And then the call ends, and that's it.

I frown, because I heard genuine pain in my father's voice, and I do not want to feel pity for that man. Not now. Not ever.

Shit.

I turn so that I'm looking out of the passenger window, not wanting Jackson to see my face. Because, damn me, I don't want to reveal that something in my father's voice actually moved me.

After a moment, his hand brushes lightly across my back. "It's okay, you know."

"What is?"

"To not completely hate him. That's not the same as accepting, or even forgiving."

I close my eyes and say nothing.

"Selling you to save Ethan was horrible. And I swear to god I could kill him for what he did to you. But at the same time I can't help but wonder if he isn't already dead inside. If making the choice didn't kill him already."

I shake my head. It doesn't matter. I neither care nor want to care about that man. "Maybe it did kill him," I say, because I am determined to hold tight to my anger. "Because god knows he's dead to me already. And," I add as I turn in my seat to face Jackson once again, "right now the only thing I want in my head is you."

I reach for his hand. "We're both going to be fine." If I say it again, maybe it'll be true. Or, at the very least, maybe I'll start to believe it.

We reach the station and park where Harriet told us, then walk inside to the reception area. From there, we're led to a conference room, where we find Charles waiting, along with Damien and Nikki. Damien strides forward the moment we enter to shake Jackson's hand.

"You're supposed to be on your way to China," I say to him, a little panicked by the fact that the boss I'm responsible for getting everywhere he's supposed to be has completely blown his schedule. "You were scheduled to leave Los Angeles last night. Christ, Damien, they're going to be—"

He holds up a hand to quiet me. "I handled it. Rachel's taken care of everything. But my brother's being arrested and my niece is arriving soon. I'm staying here, at least through the arraignment and bail hearing. Just in case there's anything you need," he adds, now looking only at Jackson.

It's not money that Damien thinks Jackson needs—even if

the court grants an astronomical bail, Jackson has the resources to pay it—it's support. And I can tell by Jackson's face that he realizes that, too. And he gives his brother both a smile and a silent nod of acknowledgment.

"Where's Harriet?" Jackson asks.

"With Detective Garrison," Charles says. "They'll come get you from here."

At that, Jackson nods stoically. As for me, I can almost feel myself go pale.

"What can we do?" Nikki asks Jackson. "Whatever you need, just say the word."

"Can you go with Syl to the airport? Stella's bringing Ronnie in. Maybe help her get settled?"

"Of course," Nikki says, and I don't argue, even though I'm more than capable of doing those things on my own. The truth is, as much as I'd like to say I can handle this by myself, I don't think I'm going to be able to.

"I need to find someplace else to stay, too," I say. "The boat has a spare room, but it's no place for a little girl. And my condo is only one bedroom. Even if I give that room to Ronnie, that still puts me in a bind while Stella's here." Stella is a saint as far as I'm concerned. She's staying for at least a week to help Ronnie and me get to know each other better— and to teach me all the ins and outs of caring for a toddler.

Jackson had intended to look for a rental house, but he hadn't had much time, and the few places he'd viewed just weren't up to par.

I glance at Jackson. "I wish—" But I don't finish the thought. He knows what I'm going to say, because I've already said it at least five times this morning.

"I know," he says. "You wish they could have gotten here before. Believe me, so do I."

"Harriet will get you out on bail," Damien says firmly. "You'll see your daughter soon enough."

I catch Jackson's eye. We both hope he's right. We both fear that he's not.

"You should stay at Stark Tower," Nikki says, looking to Damien for confirmation.

"She's right," Damien says. "Stay at the Tower apartment. Nikki and I can stay at the Malibu house. We'll be fine. And Syl will be closer to Ronnie during the day. You will be, too, once you're back at your drafting table. And I'll need you pulling a lot of hours," he says wryly. "I want my resort finished on time."

"*Your* resort?" Jackson repeats, and Damien just grins.

For a moment, everything is light, and it feels almost as if we're just standing around talking. As opposed to standing around a police station talking while we wait for Jackson to surrender himself. To be incarcerated.

Jackson meets my eyes, and I nod in agreement. The apartment is completely tricked out. Best of all, it's right inside Stark Tower.

"All right," he says to Damien. He turns to Nikki. "Thank you both."

"Well," Damien says, "that's what family is for, right?"

"I guess it is," Jackson says. "I never really knew before."

The conversation lags, and I'm about to fill the awkward silence with a question about which guest room Nikki'd choose for a three-year-old when the conference room door opens. I clutch Jackson's hand as Harriet enters with Detective Garrison.

"Mr. Steele," the detective says. "Thank you for coming."

Jackson raises a brow. "I'm not sure I had a choice, but you're welcome." His shoulders rise and fall as he gathers himself. "Okay, let's do this."

"There's nothing to do, Jackson," Harriet says gently. Her face breaks into a wide smile. "You're free to go."

His hand tightens around mine, but otherwise, he doesn't

move a single muscle. As for me, I'm certain that I've lost my ability to process words, because what she just said makes no sense.

Slowly, Jackson asks, "What are you talking about?"

"We have a suspect in custody, Mr. Steele," Detective Garrison says. "He's made a full confession."

Jackson's other hand reaches out for the table, and he slowly lowers himself into one of the chairs. His mouth opens, but no words form. Instead, it's me who says, "Oh, my god, it's over? It's really over?"

I squeeze his hand as Harriet confirms what Detective Garrison has said, and Jackson looks up, his eyes searching mine, as if this is a joke and he's waiting for the punchline.

"It's over," I repeat, and for a moment we just look at each other, basking in this moment. And I wonder if maybe—just maybe—the universe has decided that it's had enough fun with us. That the joke is all done and we can go on with our lives instead of playing some sort of cosmic game of dodge-ball.

"Thank god," Jackson whispers. "Thank god."

"Who confessed?" Damien asks the question, and it's only then that I realize that Harriet's smile is not as broad as I would expect.

"What?" I ask, suddenly wary.

"I'm sorry," she says, and I think it's strange that she's looking right at me. "Sylvia, it's your father. He turned himself in."

twenty-five

"Here," Jackson says, handing me a glass of wine even though it's not yet noon. "Drink this."

We're in my apartment, ostensibly to pack a few things to take back to the Tower apartment after we pick up Ronnie. Right now, though, I'm doing little more than getting lost in my thoughts.

"I'm okay," I say, tucking my feet under me on the couch. "Really." But I take the wine anyway, because the truth is that I'm not okay. Honestly, I'm not sure what I am, other than numb.

I've been numb, I think, since the detectives met our plane in Santa Fe. First numb about Jackson being a suspect. Then his arrest. Then a pleasant numbness when we found out that he'd been cleared.

That should have been the end of it.

I shouldn't have to feel this—this deep twinge of some

emotion that I really do not want to identify. Not for him. Not for my father.

But it's there, inside me, twisting me up. And all I want to do is stop feeling. And the only way to do that is to embrace being numb for a little bit longer as I hope that maybe it will all just go away.

I haven't yet spoken to my father. I'm not sure I want to. According to Harriet, it will be a while before I can anyway because he has to be processed, and it's the weekend, and things in the criminal justice system just don't move that quickly. All I know is that he did it—all I know is that it's true. Apparently the police kept a few facts about the crime back. A quotation that had been carved into the ivory statue with which Reed had been bludgeoned.

My father recited it to Detective Garrison.

He told the detective that he did it to protect Jackson, the man his daughter loved.

But I don't believe him. Or, rather, I don't completely believe him.

I think my dad killed Reed after Jackson told him about the blackmail photos.

I think my dad killed Reed to protect me, so that those photos would never have to come out. I think my dad was trying to save me.

But this is my dad, the man I've hated for years. And, honestly, I'm not sure how I feel about being saved by him now. After all, he let it get down to the wire for Jackson. He sat back and watched as the paparazzi swarmed around us. He waited, standing back, letting Jackson and me both suffer when he had the key to stop it all along.

I shiver, not wanting to think about any of that right now. All I want to do is revel in the knowledge that Jackson is free. That he's safe.

That he's mine.

Jackson sits beside me, then pulls my feet into his lap. I've kicked off my shoes, but am still wearing the skirt I'd put on this morning, and I close my eyes, enjoying the feel of his fingers trailing gently over my calf.

"I'm so sorry," I say.

"About what?"

I open my eyes to find him smiling softly at me, his expression so gentle it just about breaks my heart. "About being melancholy. We should be out buying confetti and throwing it from rooftops."

"I'm pretty sure that's against some city ordinance. I'd hate to get arrested," he says, raising a brow mischievously.

I laugh.

"Seriously," he says. "You can be happy for me and sad for your dad. Or confused or whatever," he rushes to say, obviously seeing on my face that I'm conflicted about how I feel about my father.

"I'm so happy that you're clear now," I say. "And I'm grateful to my dad, because he's the reason. But at the same time . . ." I lift my shoulders, unsure and unsteady. "What he did—and then what he did to you by not coming forward sooner."

"I know, baby. But you don't have to think about it right now," Jackson says. "Just let it settle."

"I don't even know if I want to see him." The word is a whisper, shameful because he killed the man who tormented me. And even though it came late, his confession has saved the man I love.

And yet I don't want to be in debt to this man. Not when he owes me so much more than he can ever repay.

"You don't have to decide that right now, either." His fingers are still stroking me, easing gently along my skin. It is just a light touch, and I close my eyes and let myself go, surrendering to this need to be tended and soothed.

His fingers ease higher, teasing me. The touch is so soft that at times I'm not even certain I feel him. And yet how can I not? This is Jackson touching me. Jackson taking care of me.

Jackson, loving me.

I don't know how long he strokes me, but I do know that with each caress I feel it more and more. As if he is polishing me, making my body shine with a sensual light. So that by the time his fingers sneak beneath my skirt to tease the soft skin of my inner thighs, I am aching for him. And by the time he reaches the juncture of my thighs to find me bare and gloriously wet, my vagina clenches in anticipation of those fingers thrusting deep inside me.

I'm breathing hard, my body warm, my breasts aching, and I arch my back in a silent expression of longing.

But he doesn't penetrate me. Just the opposite, and I whimper because suddenly the contact disappears. I feel the shift of the couch cushions and open my eyes. He's standing above me, looking down with such longing and passion that it makes my whole body tingle.

He's changed out of his suit into one of the pairs of jeans he keeps at my apartment, and I can see the strain of his cock against the denim. It makes me smile. I like that he is bound. That he's going just a little crazy. I like it, because it will make the explosion when he is released that much more astounding.

"Come with me," he says, but he doesn't wait for me to stand. Instead he picks me up, cradling me to his chest as I wrap my arms around his neck. It's a position that suggests comfort and tenderness, but when puts me on the bed and steps back, I see a building heat in his eyes that suggests otherwise.

"Hook your ankles behind me. Now," he demands, as if I were going to protest. "No words. No questions."

I comply.

The position leaves my knees turned out so that the space from my feet to my cunt form a diamond, and there is just a tiny amount of space between his pelvis and mine. Just enough room for his hand to torment me sweetly.

And that is exactly what he does. That finger that was easing up my thigh does so again, trailing lazily up and down as I squirm, my hips undulating in a needful rhythm.

"I like that," Jackson says, his voice so low I can barely hear it. "I like watching you silently beg. Your cunt slick and hot for me."

I close my eyes and drag my teeth over my lower lip. "Jackson. Please."

"Please what? Please this?" His fingertip trails lightly over my clit, and the shock of that touch ricochets through me.

"Or this?" He slips two fingers inside me, then presses down on my clit with his thumb, making me arch back, wanting more.

He pumps his fingers inside me, his thumb continuing to tease, and as he does, I'm losing the ability to think.

"I'm going to make you come, baby. I think you should just sit back and enjoy it."

I try to answer, but he adds another finger and thrusts deep inside me, and I realize that I am incapable of forming words.

My cunt tightens around his fingers. I want it harder. Deeper.

"Close your eyes," he says. "Slide one hand up inside your shirt."

I do. My skin feels hot to the touch.

"All the way up and then squeeze your nipple. Harder, baby. I know you like it hard."

He's right, and I comply, biting my lower lip as I tease myself, and then gasping as he takes my other hand and slides it between my legs. "Tease your clit for me, baby," he says as he thrusts his fingers inside me, finger-fucking me as I do what he says. As my worries and anxieties fall away. As pleasure builds. A celebration of now. Of freedom. Of life.

Of us.

"Come for me, baby." His voice is low and steady and seems to roll over me, as sensual as his touch. "Come for me and tell me you're mine."

"I am," I whisper. "Oh, god, Jackson, I am." The words are ripped out of me as I explode, my muscles convulsing so hard around his fingers that I probably have bruised him.

I let the storm wash over me, then sigh as he whispers, "I'm going to marry you."

"Yes," I reply. "You damn sure are."

twenty-six

"Daddy! Stella! Sylvie! Someone else is here!"

Ronnie races through the apartment toward the foyer where the elevator has just binged.

I'm standing by the wet bar with Nikki and Stella, but it's Jackson's face that I'm watching, and it has such an expression of rapturous adoration that I'm determined to figure out how to submit Betty and Stella for sainthood.

Not only has Stella come armed with a notebook filled with every detail imaginable about Ronnie, but more important, ever since Jackson first decided to bring Ronnie out here, Betty has been telling the little girl that Uncle Jackson is her daddy, and that very soon a court will give them a piece of paper to make it official. In the meantime, Betty's said, Ronnie gets to go live in a city with a beach.

She made what could have been scary seem like an adventure, and I will be forever grateful.

We didn't want to overwhelm the little girl, but we did want to celebrate, and so we've laid out a spread of chicken strips and pizza and invited a few friends to come join. Charles and Harriet have already stopped by and left, and I'm guessing that this newest arrival is Cass and Siobhan.

I follow Ronnie to the entrance hall and see that I'm right.

"I'm Ronnie," the little girl announces to Cass. "And that's my daddy and my aunt Sylvia."

"I know," Cass says. "She's my best friend. I guess that makes us friends, too, huh?" She's looking down at Ronnie and speaking with such comfortable assurance that I'm both impressed and intimidated. I still feel a bit like I'm putting on an act when I talk with her. As if I'm only playing the role of aunt or mother, but not really living the part.

"I'm Cass, by the way. And this is Siobhan."

Ronnie contemplates Cass, her bow-like mouth puckering, then looks up at Siobhan. "Do you like dogs?"

"Are you kidding?" Siobhan says. "Dogs are awesome."

"Aunt Sylvia says you have a dog," Cass adds. "Can we meet him?"

Ronnie glances at me, and I nod, and she takes off running. "Come on!"

Cass shoots me an amused glance. "We'll be back," she says and they hurry to Ronnie's room. Fred's tucked away there in his crate, the king of Ronnie's newly redecorated princess-themed room, courtesy of Nikki and Damien, who managed the overhaul in just a few hours.

"You doing okay?" Jackson asks, sliding his arm around my waist as we walk back into the living room to join Nikki and Damien.

I'm not sure if he's talking about the situation with my dad or settling in to having a little girl around, but right now, either answer is the same.

"I'm great," I say, bending to snag a piece of pepperoni

pizza from the box on the coffee table. "You're free. Ronnie's here and she's happy. Fred's housebroken. And my resort is safe because my architect can get back to work." I flash a smile to Jackson and Damien in turn. "I'm not even worried about the investors who've pulled out because I am going to burn up the phone lines and find new investors on Monday."

"Actually, you're not." Damien glances at Jackson. "It's covered."

I look between the two of them, confused.

"I talked with Damien earlier," Jackson explains. "Why should I ask someone to gamble on a project that I'm not willing to gamble on myself? And, frankly, I don't consider it a risk. I think we'll end up filthy, stinking rich."

"You're already rich," I say. "But I know how much the shares cost, and, Jackson, that's a serious chunk of change. Are you that liquid?"

"We are now," he says, and I feel a nice warm flush from the way he pulls me into that equation. "I'm going to talk to Isaac Winn about selling him my thirty percent interest in the Winn Building—the portion that's not part of Ronnie's trust—and buying out the rest of the Cortez shares."

"Jackson! You're sure?" The Winn Building represents a landmark in his career. I can't believe he'd want to let go of it so completely.

He lifts a shoulder as if this had been nothing more than a casual decision. "I'm familiar with all the relevant players. I think it's a sound investment."

"It is," I say. "The resort is going to kick vacation and leisure ass and make us a huge profit. But, Jackson, that was the first building you kept an ownership interest in. You really want to get out altogether?"

"Sylvia has a point," Damien says. "And thirty percent is steep. Especially to sacrifice on a property like Winn that has the potential for serious growth."

Jackson's eyes are on me. "I think Cortez has a similar potential."

"I agree with you," Damien says. "And that's why I have a suggestion."

We both turn to him.

"Sell Isaac a fifteen percent interest in Winn. I'll cover the difference personally."

I gape, then realize my mouth is hanging open. "But you never do that." He's wildly protective of his personal assets. In fact, when the investors first made noises about pulling out after we lost our original architect, Damien had specifically declined to invest personally.

"Never's a very long time," Damien says as he looks straight at Jackson. "And this time, I think it's worth the risk."

"Honestly, so much has happened my head is spinning," Cass says. She and I are in the huge guest bedroom that Jackson and I will be sharing. We've snuck away from the festivities for a quick BFF catch-up session. "I'm surprised you're still clinging to sanity." She narrows her eyes. "You are still sane, aren't you?"

I roll my eyes, then perch on the edge of the bed. "As sane as I was before. But that's not saying much."

Cass only grins, then starts counting out on her fingers. "Engaged. Small child. Non-felonious fiancé. And a father who's confessed to committing murder. There's more, I'm sure, but that covers the high points. Seriously," she says more gently. "Are you doing okay?"

"I am," I say. "Jackson being free trumps everything."

"True that. But—" She scrunches up her face as if she's caught a whiff of something unpleasant. "I mean, your dad. It's kind of freaky. Have you talked with Ethan?"

I shake my head. "I left him a voice mail to call me. I

think he gets back from Mexico today. And since he can't go see Dad yet anyway, I didn't want to worry him."

"Are you going to go see your dad?"

"I don't know. And, honestly, I don't want to think about it. Or talk about it, for that matter. Not forever. Just not today. Because there's nothing I can do anyway, and tonight is about Jackson being free and getting Ronnie. Okay?"

"You'll call me if you need me?"

"Duh."

She laughs. "Fair enough. You're off the hook for now. But . . ." She trails off, making the face again.

I shake my head, and force myself not to smile. "What?"

"Ronnie's entirely precious. And you seem really good with her."

I frown. "I shouldn't have said anything to you. I completely adore her, and Jackson is floating." All of that is true. What I don't say is that I can't seem to shake the feeling that I'm a character in *Barney* or some other kids' show, just playing the part of the grown-up. And while I want to step out of the role, I can't. Because what's my fallback persona? The girl who grew up with my parents? Without a script, I'll be swinging without a net. Yet with a script, it doesn't seem quite real.

But I tell myself this is all new. And since I really love Jackson and I really love Ronnie, I can make it all work.

I tell myself that. But I'm not certain that I believe it.

"So when's the paternity hearing, anyway?" Cass stands up and starts for the door, and I follow, understanding that this is her way of changing the subject. And, yeah, I'm grateful.

"Next week," I say. "We'll have to pop out to Santa Fe, but we'll only be gone for a day or two."

"And the wedding?"

"That one has a longer fuse. Next summer. I want to get married at the resort."

"Hell, yeah, you do. I'll be best man?"

I laugh. "Definitely."

We've reached the living room, and I immediately see Nikki chatting in the corner with Stella and Siobhan, but it's not until I look toward the far side of the room that I see Jackson. He's standing hand in hand with Ronnie in front of the window, their backs to me. Night has fallen, and they are looking out over the lights of the city spread out in front of them.

"Wow," Ronnie says, and I hear Jackson's soft chuckle.

"Yes," he says. "Very wow."

Then she lets go of his hand and hugs his leg tight. "I love you, Daddy," she says.

And in that moment, I can actually believe that everything will be just fine.

That belief lasts approximately seven more hours.

That's when I'm the only one left awake in the apartment.

We'd put Ronnie to bed at seven, after she'd hugged everyone good night and distributed a few sloppy kisses to "my Cassy" and "Uncle Damien."

Stella had already retired to her room, complaining of a head cold.

Cass and Siobhan left about ten minutes after Nikki and Damien, and although I'd been looking forward to unwinding with Jackson, it quickly became clear that wasn't going to happen tonight. Or, at least, not if I wanted him conscious.

He'd told me he was going to go lay down, and suggested that I join him with a bottle of wine.

I did, but by the time I got there, he was sound asleep on top of the covers, still in his clothes but dead to the world.

I took his shoes off, but left him dressed, opting to cover him gently with a blanket. God knew he had to be exhausted, both physically and mentally, and I didn't want to risk waking him up when he so desperately needed sleep.

I tried to drift off, too, but couldn't seem to manage it. And I was just about to try to induce sleep with a glass of the wine I'd poured when the high-pitched screams of a little girl had me leaping out of bed and sprinting across the apartment.

That's where I am now, frantically trying to soothe her. I hold her in my arms, this small bundle who is half-in and half-out of sleep. Who is crying out, her body red from the effort of trying to breathe through the tears and the convulsions. Who is screaming for her Grammy, but Betty isn't here to help her, and I'm too flustered to know what to do. Me, who has lived with nightmares my whole life and still doesn't have the power to help this poor child.

I think that hours must have passed and my ears are splitting from her cries and Jackson hasn't come and my body aches with the effort of holding her. But still she is crying and now I'm crying too, and I'm about to start screaming myself, I'm so lost and afraid and impotent.

And that's when Stella rushes in, her bathrobe half-open over a long cotton nightgown, her hair that is usually pulled back into a sensible bun falling loose around her face.

"Oh, baby," she says, and I feel a sudden stab of self-loathing when I see that her words are directed at me. At the fact that I must look so rattled and so helpless. "Here, let me have her."

She takes Ronnie, then bounces her on her hip. "It's okay, precious. Stella's here. Did you have a bad dream?"

As Stella coos to her and bounces her, the little girl's sobs slow into hiccups, and then, miraculously, fade away. Her body softens with exhaustion, and her thumb goes to her mouth.

"I've got her, Miss Sylvia," Stella says, finally looking up at me. I realize I've been standing there, frozen, watching her work some sort of magic that I don't possess.

"Right," I say. "Thank you."

And then I head out of the room and back to my bedroom, feeling a little bit lost, a little bit useless, and a whole lot scared.

twenty-seven

"So what do you think?" I ask Ronnie, who's standing beside me as we peer into the refrigerator. Nikki stocked it for us with kid-friendly yogurt, milk, and juice boxes, and those refrigerated staples are supplemented in the pantry by blue boxes of macaroni and cheese, some cereal with cartoon animals on the box, and a huge bag of goldfish crackers.

There isn't, however, much in the way of grown-up food.

Apparently, I need to make a grocery store run.

It's mid-morning on Sunday, and Jackson, Ronnie, and I have been up for a few hours. We've watched morning television and snuggled on the couch, and had cereal for breakfast. As far as I can tell, Ronnie has no lingering effects from her nightmare last night.

The same can't be said of me. I feel a bit like I'm walking on glass, but I'm determined to put it behind me and write it off to simply being both surprised and unprepared. I haven't told Jackson about it, though, and neither has Stella, who has gone out to do some sightseeing at Jackson's urging.

"Apple juice," Ronnie demands, holding out her little hand for the box. I pass it to her, help her stab the straw through the hole, and frown at the refrigerator.

"Why don't we make a special dinner for Daddy? We can pick up something yummy when we go to the store."

"I heard my name," Jackson says, coming in from the other room where he's been working on his laptop.

"We're planning dinner," I say, accepting his kiss, and then moving in for another.

"Ice cream?" Ronnie suggests, her expression entirely serious.

"I think we might need something that's not dessert," Jackson says.

Her lips pucker as she thinks about it. "Why?"

I glance at Jackson. "She has you there." To Ronnie, I say, "How about meat loaf?" I can actually make meat loaf, and according to the notebook that I now consider my personal bible, Ronnie will eat it. Three-year-olds, it turns out, have a rather limited palate.

"With ice cream?" she asks, because she's clearly inherited her father's determination.

I glance at Jackson, who is fighting a grin. Then I turn back to the little girl. "Perfect," I say. "And maybe some green beans, too?"

She sticks her tongue out and wrinkles her nose. Jackson grabs up the dish towel and pretends to sneeze, but it's very clear to me that he's laughing.

"Fench fies!" Ronnie says. "Pease, Sylvie?" She makes prayer hands and looks up at me with eyes so blue and familiar it makes my heart squeeze. "Pretty pease?"

I crouch down so that we're eye to eye and put on my most serious negotiation face. The truth is, I have no idea what I'm doing. For all I know, I should be setting firmer boundaries. Making strict rules about ice cream. Watching out for ways to sing the praises of green vegetables.

But I can only do what I can do, so I tap her nose lightly. "I tell you what. If you promise to eat at least a few green beans, you can have french fries, too. Deal?"

"Deal." She thrusts out her hand, sticky from the chocolate her father snuck her earlier. We shake gravely, and then I turn to Jackson, waving my soiled palm. He shrugs sheepishly.

"Sooner or later you'll have to quit indulging her," I tease.

"I'm well aware. Ten or eleven more years and I'll be completely over it."

I laugh. Frankly, I think he's underestimating. I lean against the counter and watch as she holds her hands up, demanding he lift her. He does, and lets her hang on his hip like a little monkey. He looks happy and engaged. Not to mention competent and completely smitten, and I think it's about the sexiest I've ever seen him.

"Okay, you two. I need to go to the store to get everything for our celebration. I'll be back soon."

"Me, too! Me, too!"

I glance at Jackson. "What do you think? Can you come?"

He shakes his head. "I have a call. About your resort," he adds, his eyes crinkling with amusement. "But you two go on ahead." He grins. "Your first mommy/daughter outing."

The thought makes butterflies dance in my stomach, and I'm about to protest. But I look at the little girl, so clearly excited to go out into the world. "All right," I say after a moment. "Why not." After all, how hard could it be?

I'm pretty certain that every person in Los Angeles is at the Ralphs on West 9th today. At least that's how it feels as I try to maneuver through the crowd with one hand on the cart and one hand tight in Ronnie's little one.

"Come on, kiddo," I say. "Don't you want to ride?" I'd tried putting her in the cart when we'd first arrived, but she is absolutely determined to help me, and apparently helping me means walking beside me while I try to navigate the crowd and figure out what we need to buy.

She stubbornly shakes her head. "Wanna walk, Sylvie. Wanna push the cart."

"You can't reach the cart," I counter. "But okay. Walking it is."

I've already grabbed the ground beef, eggs, tomato sauce, and ice cream. So now I need to get some potatoes, onions, and the green beans that we negotiated during our ice cream and vegetable summit.

I know my way around this grocery store pretty well as it's a short walk from Stark Tower and I come here on occasion to grab something for lunch. So it's easy enough to get back to the produce section and load up on the vegetables we need for dinner. "That's all we need," I tell her. "I'm going to weigh these and put on those little price labels, and then we can go check out, okay?"

She's staring up at the produce scale, watching a woman in front of us type in a code and get rewarded with a white label.

"Me! Me!" she says as the woman in front of us leaves.

"Do you know your numbers?" I ask, and she dutifully counts to ten, albeit out of order after she passes six. I decide that's close enough. "Okay," I say, then put the bag of onions on the scale. I haul her up and balance her on my hip, then slowly tell her, "Three, four, one, two."

She almost messes up on the four, but I redirect her finger and we end up with a label for the onions, which she enthusiastically slaps on.

The process has taken only about eight times longer than it should.

"You did great," I say. "I'm going to do the other two myself, really really fast. Wanna watch?"

She bobs her head, her black curls bouncing, and I go back to the scale, saying the numbers out loud as I punch them in, like some real life skit on *Sesame Street*.

When I'm done, I hold on to my vegetables and turn around to lead her back to the cart.

She's gone.

A bolt of panic cuts through me, and I tamp it down. *She can't be gone.* She's just in the next aisle. She's just behind one of these people.

But she's not, and reality is smacking me in the face. I've lost her. I've lost Jackson's little girl.

My stomach lurches, and I swallow both bile and fear. I don't have time for that. All I have time for is finding her.

"Did you see her? The little girl who was beside me?" I practically shout the question at two women who are chatting in the aisle by the tomatoes. But both just look at me blankly. One as if I am nothing more than a nuisance, the other with an apologetic smile and an explanation of, "Sorry, I haven't seen a thing."

Oh dear god.

"Ronnie!" I am completely uninterested in the looks that people are shooting me as I scream her name at the top of my lungs even while I race along the back of the section so that I can look down each aisle that runs perpendicular to this wall. "Veronica!"

Nothing. And I have no idea what to do. I don't want to leave this part of the store, but I need a manager. I need help, and I'm just about to scream that someone needs to help me when a short woman with a friendly face taps my elbow and says, "Is that your little girl?"

I peer down to find Ronnie under a free-standing display of brussels sprouts and cauliflower.

"Oh my god," I say, my body going limp with relief. "Ronnie. Ronnie, come here, baby."

She scrambles out, then shows me the tiny red bouncy ball that she'd spied under the display.

"Can I keep it?" she asks, but I don't answer. I'm too busy clutching her to my chest as I try to get my breath back and calm the beating of my heart.

I turn around to search for the woman who had found her for me, because who knows what would have happened if she hadn't been there today. But the woman is nowhere in sight.

And with Ronnie held tight in my arms, I abandon our cart and rush toward the door.

I can't think about food or dinner or ice cream or meat loaf.

All I can think is that I screwed up.

All I can do is race toward home.

"Calm down," Jackson says as I pace the bedroom trying to hold back yet another flood of tears. "Baby, calm down. It's okay. She's safe. You didn't lose her. You didn't hurt her."

Ronnie is down for a nap, and I don't even think she's upset at all. She cried in the car, but I'm pretty sure that was because I was fighting back tears, my body tense as I kept two hands on the steering wheel.

"I *did* lose her," I snap. "Just because she was only a few feet away doesn't mean I didn't. It just means I got lucky. What if I'd raced to get the manager before that woman found her? She might have crawled out from under the display and wandered out of the store. The produce section is right by the automated doors and the parking lot is right there and have you seen how fast cars go through there even though they're not supposed to?"

I'm breathless, my words—my fears—tumbling out on top of each other. And I know that he's right. She *is* okay.

And I am not the first person to take their eyes off a child in a grocery story. But that isn't the point. That's just a catalyst, and it's sparked all of my fears and doubts into one big explosion.

I know what I have to do—and I hate it. Because it will be the hardest thing ever. But I have to. For Jackson. For Ronnie. And even for me.

Jackson halts me on my next pass across the room, then pulls me into his arms. "Sweetheart, you were scared. I get that. But you need to step back. Take a deep breath."

I rip myself out of his arms. "*Scared?* I wasn't scared, Jackson. I was fucking terrified. Just like I was last night. She had a nightmare, and—"

"I know," he says gently. "Stella told me. But, Sylvia, you're doing fine. The fact that you're struggling doesn't mean you're doing badly."

I recognize my words to him from our fight at the airport. "You want to throw my words back at me? Fine. I told you then that I loved you. That I'd give you whatever you need. And I mean it, Jackson. But what you need is a relationship with your daughter. A strong one. A solid one. And I'm going to get in the way of that. I never thought—when I came after you, I mean. I didn't—"

"You're scared," he says again. "But, sweetheart, that's okay. Do you think you become a parent and all your fears go away?"

"I don't know. That's the point." I drop down to sit on the edge of the bed. "I can't be a test case for that little girl's life. I mean, Christ, Jackson, I'm a mess. I don't even know how to soothe my own nightmares, much less Ronnie's."

"Yes, you do. With all this, your father. My arrest. Everything that came before. You haven't had one in a long time." He grips my shoulders tight. "You're stronger, and you know it."

"I am, yes. But not with this."

"Then let me help you."

But I just shake my head. "Don't you get it? That's the point. If I'm going to be your wife, then I should be a help, not an albatross."

"Syl—" I hear the fear in his voice, and I know that he sees where this is going just as clearly as I do.

"I told you once that there was no price I wouldn't pay to be with you. And I know that I came after you. That I fought for you. For her. And oh, Christ, I meant it. But I was wrong, Jackson. Because I won't risk that little girl. I don't know how to do this. I should never have said yes. It was wrong of me. Selfish, even. I was so overwhelmed by your faith in me and by my fears of losing you that I forgot that faith isn't enough, and that fear is a crappy jumping-off point for anything."

I stand up, because I have to move. More than that, I have to leave.

"Sweetheart, please. Wait."

"I can't. I—I'm sorry, Jackson. I need to go. I need—" But I leave the words hanging. What I need is him. But as I walk toward the door—as I leave my engagement ring on the top of the dresser—I no longer believe that I can have him.

twenty-eight

I spend the rest of Sunday in my apartment watching reruns of *How I Met Your Mother,* and I don't even laugh once. Honestly, I'm not sure I'm even watching the show; more likely, my mind is elsewhere.

Monday, Cass calls to check on me and I assure her that I'm fine, which we both know is a big, fat lie. After all, I was a wreck yesterday when I called and told her the whole story, from Ronnie's nightmare to losing her at the grocery store to me walking out. No way have I gone from complete mess to fine in less than a day.

"I'm coming over after work," she says. "We'll talk."

"No. Please. I just want to be alone. I want—I guess I want to work through it myself."

I can hear her hesitation over the phone line, and I understand it. Because Cass has been there for almost all the crises of my life. And if she wasn't there, then Jackson was.

And that, frankly, is why I want to be alone. I need to

prove to myself that I can handle this—this intertwining of fear and anger and confusion that is the big ball of emotion that fills my gut shining bright with labels like *father* and *Jackson* and *Ronnie* and *parents* and *choices*.

"You know I've got your back."

"I'm counting on it."

"Are you going to need ink?"

I understand that question, too. She's asking me if I'm going to need her to give me a tattoo—a reminder to give me strength. To help me hold on and get through. "I don't know," I say honestly.

"Okay." I hear her sigh. "Whatever you need."

"I know. I do. Seriously, I'll be fine." But then, before she hangs up, I blurt, "Cass!"

"Yeah?"

I start to ask if Jackson has called her, but I bite back the question. I don't want this reality where I'm not with him, even if I'm still certain that I made the right choice. And hearing that he is worried about me or that he misses me or even that he is pissed as hell at me would be too damn painful. "Never mind."

There is a long pause, and then, as if she is deliberately honoring my earlier request, she says, "Okay, then. I'll talk to you later."

I am not going in to work today. Not only am I not ready to see Jackson in the office, but my dad's attorney has arranged a visitation. That, however, isn't until four, which leaves me with a day to fill. And since I don't want to fill it with my thoughts, I turn again to television solace. Only, reruns of *Friends* don't make me laugh, either.

The phone rings and I start to snatch it up, then slow my hand when I realize the single word that is in my head—*Jackson*.

But it's not him who is calling. It's Ethan.

"Hey," he says. "Have you seen Dad yet?"

"Not yet," I say. "I'm going in about an hour. You're coming up tomorrow?"

"Yeah. I'm supposed to see him at noon. Let him know, okay?"

"Sure."

"Listen, has Mom called you?"

I frown. "No." To say that my mother and I have a strained relationship is like saying that black is a dark color. It's just a flat-out given. I've been a non-entity to her for years, and I don't even know if she's aware of what happened to me—of what her husband did to her daughter. She pretty much wrote me off, all of her attention going toward my brother, leaving me to basically fend for myself. But considering what I know of my parents, maybe that was best.

"Dammit, I told her she should. I mean, our dad's in jail. Isn't that what moms do?"

Not our mom, I think. But all I say is, "So what did she say?"

"She asked me why she should."

I sigh. I'm not entirely sure why he's telling me this. God knows nothing has changed.

"I just—she screwed up, Syl. They both have. But that doesn't mean you will."

I lick my lips, but I don't say anything. I don't want to talk about this, and I'm regretting even telling him in my message that I'd left Jackson and Ronnie.

"I know we've grown up saying that we're not going to have kids because it's just a goddamn vicious cycle, but it doesn't have to be. You can stop it."

"That's what I'm doing," I say.

"You know what I mean."

I do, but I don't want to talk about it. "Listen, I need to get dressed."

"Shit, I'm sorry. I shouldn't have—"

"It's okay," I say quickly.

"No," he says firmly, "it's not. Listen, I've been thinking. And the thing is that you love him."

"Ethan, please." My voice is cracking with my words.

"Dammit, Syl, hear me out. You think you can't be a mom. You think you don't have a role model. But you do. Don't you get it? *You're* your role model."

I run my fingers through my hair, feeling too ripped up inside to try and figure out what he's talking about. "Ethan—"

"You *are*. I mean, if parenting is about taking care of someone—about being willing to sacrifice for them and make really hard choices—well, then you already know how to do that. Don't you get it, Syl? You did that for me already."

I suck in a breath, his words surprising me and making tears spring to my eyes.

"You were as much a parent to me growing up as they ever were. Maybe more. I'm sorry if I've made it harder for you. Made you doubt. I shouldn't have. Because you can do it, Syl. I promise you—you already know how."

"I—" I can't talk through the tears. I sniff and try to breathe, and then manage to tell him that I have to go. Because I can't handle what he's saying right now. I can't process if it's true or not, because it's just too much. Too big. "I'm sorry," I add. "But I have a scheduled time to meet with him."

I hang up without waiting for him to say goodbye.

Could he be right? I want to believe it, but I'm still scared. And with a little girl's life at the heart of it, I can't run the risk of being wrong.

Two hours later, I'm sitting in the private visitors' room at the county jail where my dad is being held. It's stark and cold and as much as I hate my dad for what he did to me, I can't stand the thought of him living in a room like this for the rest of his life.

The door opens and my father is brought in, his hands in cuffs, his body dressed in an orange jumpsuit.

I rise and start to go to him.

"No touching," the uniformed guard says, and I realize that I'd been about to hug my father, something I haven't done since I was thirteen years old.

"Oh," I say. "Right."

"I'll be outside," he says. "I can't hear you, but if you need anything you signal me."

I nod, and then I take a seat at the table as my father sits opposite. The officer unfastens one handcuff, then refastens it to a bolt on the table. Then he turns, leaves the room, and shuts it with a final-sounding click behind him.

"You killed Reed," I say without preamble, and I realize as I say the words that it is the first time since I was a child that I've felt the protection of this man. "You really did it."

He looks straight at me, and I see genuine warmth. "I should have done it a long time ago."

I look down at the tabletop, not wanting him to see how much I agree. When I've gathered myself, I lift my head, and I know my eyes are accusatory. "You let Jackson just twist in the wind. All that time. He was almost arrested. Hell, he was almost convicted."

"I know. I'm sorry. I thought—oh, hell. I was scared. I thought it would blow over. I thought they'd quit looking at him because, hell, he didn't kill the man. And when it got bad, I was afraid of what would happen to me, and I just kept hoping it would go away."

I cringe a bit. I don't like what he did, but I understand it.

"Did you go there planning to kill him?"

"No. I went there to ask him about those blackmail photos. The ones of you that Jackson told me about. Bastard sneered at me. He even pulled one out to show me." He lifts a shoulder. "That's when I lost it. I picked up that damn statue, and I went after him."

"Did you tell your attorney?" I ask. "About seeing the photo? Because what we heard after you confessed was that you were basically killing him to make things easier on Jackson. But if he provoked you, then surely that will come into play when you're negotiating the plea."

"I'm not going to say a word about those photos. You think I want those things out in the world? As it stands, nobody else knows, right?"

I nod. Harriet knows about the blackmail, but she'd learned it in the course of representing her client, and wouldn't say a word. Not only that, but as far as she knows, Reed's copies of the photos are still missing.

"I'm staying silent," my dad says again. "I'm not going to make it worse for you than I already have."

"Daddy." I blink, realizing that my eyes have filled with tears.

He starts to reach for me, but has to stop because of the cuffs. "Oh, hell, honey. Did I screw up that bad? Did I destroy you?"

"I—" I close my mouth because I don't know what to say. Yes? No? Sometimes I feel ripped to pieces? Sometimes I'm okay?

I choose to stay silent, and he just sighs.

"I fucked up, Sylvia, I did. And I know I hurt you, but look at you. You're so damn strong. Look at everything you've done. At all you've become. You're smart and you're poised and you go after what you want. And I think that's the only reason I can stand my life right now. Because I know that despite what I did to you, that you were strong enough not to let me destroy you."

He draws in a deep breath. "Jackson's a good man. I wanted to hurt the fucker for rubbing my nose in the truth.

But I'm glad he did it. You deserve a man who'll protect you. God knows it wasn't your father. Least not until I killed that bastard."

It's only when a fat tear lands on the metal table that I realize I've been crying. "Daddy," I say, but then I have to stop, because I can't get any more words out. After I calm myself and breathe a little, I try again. "Daddy, you have to tell them about the blackmail. They need to know you acted in a moment of passion. That's got to be important."

"Hell, no."

"Then I'll release the pictures to the press and I'll tell the cops myself." Even as I say the words, I know that I mean them. For years, I've been scared of those damn photos. Of the past they represent. Of the shame. But I'm tired of giving them power. Hell, I'm tired of giving Reed power.

Jackson's right—I know how to fight my nightmares. And the way to do it is by ripping the last bit of control from Reed's hands.

"No, honey, no. I already worked out a nice deal. A good deal. We pleaded down. No premeditation. Three years at most."

He's right, I know. That is a good deal. But it could be better if I turn over the photos.

But when I suggest it, my dad steadfastly shakes his head. "No," he says firmly as he meets my eyes.

"Why not? I can handle it. And if we just turn them over to the prosecutor, they might even seal them."

"Maybe you can, and maybe they would, but I want to do that time."

I blink, confused. "What? Why?"

"I owe you, Elle," he says softly, calling me by the name I stopped using when Reed started touching me.

"Being in a cage doesn't change anything."

His smile is infinitely sad. "Maybe not. But it makes me feel better."

The guard raps on the window, signaling time.

"I don't know if I can truly forgive you, Daddy," I say as the guard opens the door and starts to walk toward my dad. "But I think maybe I want to try."

twenty-nine

The only reason Jackson got through the rest of Sunday was because he had Ronnie to take care of. And the only reason he survived Monday morning was because Stella took care of Ronnie, and Jackson buried himself in work.

But by mid-afternoon, even the pull of the resort wasn't keeping him on track. He was edgy. Lost. Angry.

He wanted to lash out, and more than once during the morning he'd considered calling Sutter and getting him to open the gym. Maybe even go a few rounds. But the idea of losing himself to the dance and weave, the sweat and pain, the screaming muscles and pumped up adrenaline wasn't doing it for him today.

No, he knew what the goddamn antidote for his misery was—and she'd up and left him.

Goddammit.

And for that matter, goddamn her. He wanted to be patient. He wanted to help. But at the same time he wanted to grab her by the shoulders and shake some sense into her. And it frustrated the hell out of him that while he could grab control from her in bed, in life, she had to make her own choices, her own decisions.

He only hoped she made the right one. Because he loved her, and he knew that she loved him. He wanted to make a family with her, a life. And he believed with all his heart that she wanted the same thing. But it was fear that had pushed her away. And all he could do was hope that her innate strength would bring her back. She had a lot of strength, after all. She'd pulled him back, hadn't she?

Hell.

He glanced at the clock, saw that it was Ronnie's snack time, and decided to go see if he could share a PB&J with his daughter and her nanny. He was almost to the elevator bank when his assistant, Lauren, called out to him. "Mr. Steele? Rachel just called down. She says there's someone to see you on thirty-five."

Sylvia? Surely not, but maybe she was being coy. He allowed himself the pleasure of the fantasy that she was waiting for him at her desk, but when he arrived, he was disappointed to see that it wasn't her—and confused that it was Graham Elliott instead.

"Mr. Steele," Graham said, walking to him and holding out his hand. "I'm sorry to bother you at the office. I've met Evelyn Dodge a time or two socially, and when I said I wanted to talk to you, she suggested I come by." He shot a Hollywood smile toward Rachel, who looked like she was going to float out of her chair. "Ms. Peters has been nice enough to entertain me."

"I, um, water? Would you like water? Or coffee? Or—"

Graham shook his head. "I'm fine. Thanks."

Jackson slid his hands into his trouser pockets. "What

can I do for you?" He tried to say it politely; he wasn't sure he succeeded. This was the man who wanted to play him in a movie about the Fletcher house, after all. This was the man willing to foment the kind of scandal that would throw slime all over Jackson's daughter.

"Two things, actually. I wanted to say congrats on getting your name cleared. And I wanted to tell you that I'm off the movie."

Jackson shifted his weight. Not relaxing—not yet—but interested. And dubious. "Is that so?"

Graham seemed to deflate a bit. "Look, I'm breaking a confidence, but you should know that your dad was in bed with Reed. He was keen on getting the movie made. Figured it would be one hell of a payday. Even dropped that bomb-shell about you and your brother when interest waned. Guess he figured it would pick back up."

Jackson stood perfectly still. "And you? Why were you involved?"

"The material rocks, man. And it's not defamation. All that shit that happened to you—to the Fletchers—it's a damn solid story and it would make one hell of a movie."

"And yet you're not going to make it."

Graham met his eyes. "I'm not," he said. "The material's good, but my perspective has changed. My girlfriend's preg-nant, and if anyone messed with my kid, I'd fuck them up one side and down the other. But I guess you'd know all about that, wouldn't you? That's why you were trying to kill the movie."

Jackson nodded. "Yes. It was."

"Was your dad the leak? About your daughter, I mean."

"I don't know, but I don't think so. I think the press just did their job and found the court papers in New Mexico."

Graham nodded. "Listen, I can't promise that no one else

will hop on, but I can promise they'll get no support from me. And with you no longer a suspect, the tabloids will back off. I predict they lose interest."

"Thank you," Jackson said, but the simple formality of his words couldn't convey the extent of his relief. "And congratulations."

Graham's face broke into the smile that made him a household name. "Thanks. It's pretty amazing, don't you think?"

"What?"

"Fatherhood. It changes fucking everything."

"Yeah," Jackson said softly. "It does."

A few minutes later, the elevator doors closed behind Graham, and Rachel let out a long sigh. "Wow."

Jackson smiled indulgently. Considering she'd recently been burned by Trent's deception, it was nice she'd gotten a celebrity treat. "Is Damien in?"

"Sorry, no. Do you want me to leave a message?"

Jackson shook his head. "No. I'll tell him later." He headed back to the elevator bank, fully intending to take the express to the apartment. Instead, he got into the regular car and descended to the parking garage. His mind was whirring as he strode to his Porsche. They were cut from the same cloth, Sylvia's father and Jeremiah Stark. But at least Sylvia's dad was trying to mend what he destroyed, even if murder was a rather dramatic way to apologize.

But not Jeremiah. He just kept hacking away at Jackson's and Damien's lives, as if they were gemstones and he was trying to mine a sliver, not caring that he was damaging the whole.

That was something Jackson was damn sure he wouldn't do as a father. He'd make mistakes as a parent, sure. But he wouldn't repeat his father's. Sylvia knew that—he was one hundred percent certain that she believed in his ability to raise his child.

So why the hell couldn't she see that in herself?

He was already out of the parking garage before he realized that his destination was Santa Monica. He'd been trying to give her space, but he was done. He wanted her. He needed her.

And he was damn sure she needed him.

Time to go bring back the woman he was going to marry. Time to convince her that she should stay. That this would work.

Because, dammit, he wasn't going to lose her again.

thirty

I don't actually know how I got here, but instead of going home after leaving my father, I went to Van Nuys and to the warehouse where Reed ran one of the studios where he so often photographed me.

Now I'm sitting in the parking lot in my Nissan, just staring at those nondescript, weathered walls that seem so dull. And I can't help but wonder what is going on behind them now. For that matter, who knows what's really going on behind any walls? Or inside anyone's head?

I don't know what my father was thinking back then, but I believe him now. His regret is real, his overture legitimate. I will never be as close to him as Jackson will be to Ronnie, but despite the fact that I never would have believed it before, I really do want to try and heal. To take his apology and his retreat and turn it around, box it up, and move past it.

I slide the car back into drive, not entirely certain why I came at all. Closure? Maybe. Or maybe I just wanted to prove to myself that this wasn't actually hell. That there was no fire and brimstone, and that any of the demons who live here are in my mind—and I can defeat them.

I get back on the highway and head toward Santa Monica, but I take a detour into Brentwood and the house we lived in when I was a kid. This was where I started my hobby of photographing houses, because I couldn't believe that a house with such a perfect exterior held such horrible secrets. It was nothing but a facade, and I wondered if the rest of the houses I saw around the city were as well.

The house Jackson will build in the Palisades won't be, though. There will be love—and honesty. And I think that's what's most important.

I think about waking up there with Jackson beside me. About Ronnie rushing in and bouncing on the bed. About sitting on a long balcony and sipping coffee in the morning and wine in the evening and watching the ocean that is spread out to infinity.

I think about a little girl and a puppy and the man that I love.

I want that. Oh, god, how I want it.

I'm still scared, but I'll learn what to do. I won't be like my mom who checks out when it gets tough. Or my dad who waits decades to try to remedy a mistake or to protect a child.

It won't be easy. I'll stumble.

But with Jackson to catch me it will be okay.

Jackson.

Suddenly, I can't wait even one more second to see him, and I turn the car around and head the opposite direction, back downtown to the Tower apartment.

Traffic is a mess, and every moment is like torture. But I finally careen into my parking place and race to the penthouse. I burst into the foyer and call for him, for Ronnie, for Stella.

But there is only silence that greets me. And in that moment I am certain that I destroyed everything. That I convinced him that I wasn't worth the risk. That my stumbling efforts would come between him and his daughter.

That it was best for Ronnie not to have me in their lives.

Oh, god, what the hell have I done?

I look blankly around the apartment, not understanding where everyone could be. I call his phone, but there is no answer, and I feel even more lost. Even more lonely.

In the back of my mind, I know that an empty apartment does not mean all those things. But I'm so tired. And I fought so hard to break away that I am having a difficult time believing that now that I've seen my mistake, things will turn out okay. In my experience, it's usually the opposite.

Right now, I tell myself not to think about it. I tell myself it's time to just sleep.

Going home, I don't even bother to get in the left lane. I drive slowly, like a drunk who shouldn't even be on the road but is trying desperately to focus. I sleepwalk up the stairs to my apartment. All I want to do is crawl into bed. Tomorrow, I will try again. And if Jackson is still gone I will go to Cass and get another tattoo, because this is a pain that I must both fight and remember.

My apartment is dark when I get in, and I curse myself for not leaving a light on the way that I usually do. I kick off my shoes, then stumble through the dark toward my bedroom, stripping off my T-shirt and bra as I go, then tossing my jeans over the back of the couch before I finish crossing the short distance to my bedroom doorway.

I'm still there when I hear his voice. Just one word—just my name—but it means everything.

"Sylvia."

I stop in the doorway, entirely naked, and though I have never felt vulnerable in front of Jackson, I do right now. My eyes adjust to the light, and I see him get off the bed and come to me. He stands just inches from me, and suddenly I am very aware of my breathing. Of every hair on my body. Of his proximity. And, yes, of my need.

I lick my lips. "I looked for you at the apartment."

"Funny," he says, his voice gentle. "I looked for you here."

He moves a few feet to the left to the chair that sits next to the door. My robe is there, and he picks it up and then hands it to me. And that simple gesture, so seemingly polite, terrifies me.

My breath hitches, and I make a little gasping sound. I hold the robe clutched to my body, but I don't put it on. "Jackson—I—I'm sorry." I try to read the expression on his face, but I can't. "Did I ruin everything by walking away? I don't want to lose you or Ronnie because I was afraid."

"Was? You're not afraid anymore?"

I look down. "No," I say. "I still am. But it's a fear of what-ifs, and I don't want to live like that. I'm still terrified of screwing up, but I'd rather risk screwing up with you than not even try." I lift my head and meet his eyes. "I love you, Jackson, and I'm so scared that I've lost you."

I see the break in his expression. The glow of tenderness and relief. And when he steps closer to me, I can't help but notice the way his jeans are tight over the bulge of his erection.

"Don't you know you can never lose me?" He reaches out and strokes my cheek. "Do you think I don't understand fear? Being a parent—hell, being in love—it's about making scary choices. But choosing you—choosing us? That one's not scary at all."

My heart twists with emotion at his words, and I can't wait any more. I need his touch to match his words. I need to know that we're truly back, that the world has righted itself.

I drop my robe and without warning, I pull him tight

against me, claiming him with my mouth, pressing my breasts hard against him.

I slide my hands down and cup the firm curve of his ass, pulling him toward me until I can feel him beneath the denim. He groans, the sound full of need, and it rolls through me, battering my senses. I'm naked, my skin on fire, and there's no denying the reaction of my body as his pelvis crushes against mine.

One of his hands is on my hips, and I reach for it, stepping back enough so that I can slide our joined hands between my thighs. I'm wet and slippery.

"I'm yours," I say huskily, my words stuttering as a small, unexpected orgasm sends electric sparks fluttering through me. "And you're mine."

"Hell, yes I am."

He holds my gaze long enough for me to see passion and promise. And, yes, understanding. Then he draws his hand away, the sensation making me melt a little more. He licks his fingers clean and my cunt clenches in response to that simple, erotic action.

He takes a single step backward and pulls his T-shirt over his head. Then he reaches for his jeans.

"No," I say, then go to him. I unbutton his jeans and ease them over his hips, taking his briefs with them. His cock hardens as I do, and I bite back a satisfied smile.

I slide down his body until I'm on my knees, and his cock is stiff and magnificent in front of me. I tilt my head back to look at him. I meet his eyes, and I can tell he knows exactly what this is. It's more than desire and need. It's my apology, my submission, my promise.

I tease him first, licking the length of his shaft and teasing the crown. But I want more than that. I want to get him off. I want to give him that moment when everything disappears and he is reduced to sweet sensation. I want to wash away the pain I caused.

I cup his balls with one hand and take his cock into my mouth, and the taste of him, so very male, so very *Jackson,* slices through me, making my nipples hard and my own body demand attention. But I keep my focus on Jackson. On the way he's thrust one arm out for balance. On the low moans he is making as passion builds.

And—oh yes—on the way he holds my head and guides me as he gets closer and closer and then finally explodes in my mouth.

He is holding me in place, and I have no choice but to swallow. And after I do, I stand up and kiss him, sharing the taste of him as he slides his hand between my legs to stroke my slick cunt. "Your turn now."

I squeal as he scoops me up, then lays me on the bed. Then slowly, he strokes his hands over me, his touch driving me wild because there is no part of me to which he doesn't minister. I squirm and writhe under his attention, my skin sensitive, my body needy. He doesn't relent. Not until every tiny nerve ending is tied to my core, and when he thrusts inside me—when he strokes my clit and sends me reeling—it is like the sun is rising inside me, illuminating my entire body, turning me brighter and brighter until I can't contain it any longer and I explode into golden rays of sunshine.

I come down slowly, trembling, then curl up in his arms. "Is it this way for everybody?" I ask. "This intensity. This feeling that I'll shrivel up if I can't touch you?" I tilt my head up to look at him. "You know what I mean, right?"

"You know I do."

"Is it because we're a little bit lost, you and I?"

He kisses the top of my head. "Lost? Oh, no, sweetheart. Not anymore. We're found."

After a moment, he eases us both up off the bed so that we can get under the covers. After we're settled again, he turns to get something off the bedside table. I recognize it immediately—it's his grandmother's ring. *My* ring. The one I'd left behind.

"You asked me to marry you once before. Now it's my turn."

He slides out of bed, and to my delight, drops to one knee as he holds out the ring. "Sylvia Brooks, will you marry me?"

I look at him, and cannot hide my smile.

Second chances. That seems to be the way it is with Jackson and me.

And there's no way am I screwing this one up.

"Yes," I say, and as I tug him back onto the bed and kiss him sweetly, only one thing goes through my head. *Wife,* I think.

And I really can't wait.

epilogue

I stand on the main beach at Santa Cortez with Jackson beside me and the world that we have built rising up behind us, fresh and clean and so intertwined with the landscape that it is hard to believe that the buildings didn't burst up with the formation of the island.

Everything is ready. The guest rooms are primped and polished and made up with fresh linens. The restaurants are stocked. The gift stores overflow with merchandise. The pools sparkle. Not a detail has been spared, and every magazine and newspaper and blog that has covered the resort has called it one of Stark Real Estate Development's crowning achievements.

The guest list is already overflowing, and we are booked up for the next two years.

The official opening is over a month away, but already the island is bustling with administration, maintenance, and service staff. Most have moved permanently to their quarters on the island, but today there are about a dozen more people on the island who do not live here full-time.

They've come for our wedding.

The judge who stands before us has already read most of the vows, but I've barely heard a word. It's hard to hear from up here where I'm floating above the earth.

But when he asks if we have the rings and Ronnie bounces and squeals, "I do! I do!" I know that it is real.

I take Jackson's ring from the little pillow that she holds out to me, then gently slide it onto his finger, his eyes never leaving mine.

He does the same, and I swear that I can feel the shock of this moment, this new reality, settle through me as the ring encircles my finger, just as Jackson has encircled my life.

"You may kiss the bride," the judge says, and Jackson wastes no time. He pulls me to him, leans me back, and kisses me thoroughly, all to the applause and catcalls of our small audience.

"Well, hello, wife," Jackson says, when he rights me.

"Hello, husband," I reply, then wrap my arms around him and sigh.

"We'll leave you two alone soon," Nikki promises as she and Damien approach. "But we have a little reception set up in the main restaurant."

I glance at Jackson, who just shakes his head. We'd not intended a reception. Just a quick wedding squeezed in before my work life got crazy with the opening.

And, of course, a long weekend for a honeymoon.

The resort was designed so that a dozen bungalows on the north side of the island are actually for sale. And Nikki and Damien—now otherwise known as my sister- and brother-in-law—gave us one for a wedding gift.

"Just a little something for the happy couple," Damien

had said to Jackson, obviously trying to hold back a smile. "I figured if you designed it, then it must be to your taste."

Jackson had laughed. And though I'd feared he'd turn down the gift as too extravagant, he'd only said, "Hell, yeah."

Now, he bends down so that Ronnie—now officially Veronica Amelia Steele—can ride piggyback as he and I hold hands on our walk to the reception.

He's barefoot in deference to the sand, but he'd told me that he wasn't going to get married if he wasn't wearing a suit. It's black and perfectly tailored, the gloss of the fine material gleaming in the sun. His only nod to the casual nature of our wedding is the fact that he's not wearing a tie. Instead, his collar is open, and when he turns to grin at me, wide and happy, I see the indentation at the base of his neck.

I'm struck with the overwhelming urge to kiss him there. To lick him and taste him. Because he is truly mine now. Every delicious inch of him.

I manage to control myself; after all, we now have all the time in the world.

Unlike my husband, I'd taken the beachside nature of our wedding into consideration. I'm wearing a white silk tank top embroidered with delicate silver threads and a flowing white skirt. It's not sheer, but gives the illusion that it is, and the layers of gauzy material flicker in the breeze as we walk.

One of the resort's bands is playing when we arrive at the restaurant, and there is a beautiful three-tiered wedding cake standing in the middle of the dance floor. Ronnie takes off running for it, and when she turns back, her eyes are big. "Mommy! Daddy! Cake!" She claps her hands, delighted, and everyone around begins to laugh. I, however, am about to cry.

Because today, finally, I really am Mommy. And next

month it will be even more official, because that's when my adoption of Ronnie will be finalized.

I know that I'm not a perfect mother, and there are times when I still look at Ronnie and wonder what the hell I'm doing, but at the same time, I know that I'm doing my best. And I know that Jackson has my back.

More than that, I'm not scared anymore because I know that Ronnie is growing up healthy and happy and loved, and that's what matters most.

I take Jackson's hand and squeeze. He looks down at me, then gently kisses my forehead. "I know," he said softly. "Me, too."

We dance, Jackson and me, then Jackson and Ronnie, then me and Ethan who has been grinning like a fool through the whole wedding. He passes me off to Cass, who whispers that I've given her ideas as she glances over at Siobhan who is sitting at one of the tables having what appears to be a very serious conversation with Ronnie. I even dance with Damien once, while Jackson spins Nikki on the floor.

Betty and Stella are here, too, along with Megan, who is looking happy and healthy in a flowing yellow sundress. Jackson takes both her and Ronnie onto the floor when the band starts playing "The Twist." It doesn't last long; the little girl keeps dissolving into giggles before shouting "Daddy! Meggie! I twisting!"

Of everyone in our lives, only our fathers and my mother are notably absent. My father, because he still has months to go on his negotiated sentence. My mom because that's who she is, and I have come to terms with that. And Jeremiah because he is not welcome.

Jackson told me about what happened with Graham Elliott, of course. And though Jeremiah had later sworn to Jackson that he would never have pursued the movie if he'd known about Ronnie, to Jackson that was too little, too late.

Because the betrayal that Jeremiah perpetrated wasn't about Ronnie. It wasn't even about the movie. It was about Jeremiah playing off Jackson's life for personal gain. And Jackson told his father firmly and finally to stay away from his life, and also away from his wedding.

But I am not thinking about Jeremiah Stark today. Not when it's my wedding day and all around us is food and laughter and fun. Most of all, there is love. And when the festivities end—when Damien and Nikki scoop Ronnie up to take her back to the Malibu house for a long weekend—I hold Jackson close as we say goodbye to our friends, then kiss our little girl goodbye.

"I realize a honeymoon is no place for a toddler," Jackson says as we stroll hand in hand toward our bungalow. "But I've gotten so used to having her around, that it's a little weird now that she's gone."

The sun has begun to set, and the sky is a brilliant glow of orange and purple. "Good," he adds. "But weird."

"Maybe I can make it a little less strange for you." I pull him to a stop beside me on the path. Then I take our joined hands and place them gently on my lower abdomen.

I hesitate only a moment, then tilt my head back to look at him. "There's still a child with us on the island, Jackson."

The look of surprise and wonder and—thank goodness—happiness that I see in his eyes almost knocks me off my feet.

"You're pregnant?" he asks, but I don't get to answer because my "yes" is swallowed up by my squeal when he scoops me into his arms and holds me close to his chest. "I love you," he says simply, and I feel a quiet glow spread through me. The warmth of anticipation and wonder and excitement. Because for Jackson and me—for our family—our life together is just beginning. And it will be spectacular.

J. Kenner kicks off a darkly sexy, intensely emotional new trilogy set in the beloved Stark world. Beautiful bad-boy heir Dallas Sykes may appear to have the world at his feet, but beneath the surface lies his

Dirtiest Secret

Coming soon from Bantam Books.

Continue reading for a sneak peek.

one

Even by Southampton standards, the party at the nine-thousand-square foot mansion on Meadow Lane reeked of extravagance.

Grammy Award–winning artists performed on an outdoor stage set up on the lush lawn that flowed from the main house to the tennis courts. Celebrities hobnobbed with models who flirted with Wall Street tycoons who discussed stock prices with tech gurus and old-money academics, all while sampling fine scotch and the season's chicest gin. Colored lights illuminated the grotto-style pool, in which nude models floated lazily on life rafts, their bodies used by artisan sushi chefs as presentation platters for epicurean delights.

Each female guest received a Hermès Birkin bag and each male received a limited-edition Hublot watch, and the exclamations of delight—from both the men and the women—rivaled the boom of the fireworks that exploded over Shinnecock Bay at precisely ten p.m., perfectly timed to distract the guests from the bustle of the staff switching out the dinner buffet for a spread of desserts, coffee, and liqueurs.

No expense had been spared, no desire or craving or indulgence overlooked. Nothing had been left to chance, and every person in attendance agreed that the party was the Must Attend event of the season, if not of the year. Hell, if not of the decade.

Everyone who was anyone was there, under the stars on the four-acre lot on Billionaires' Row.

Everyone, that is, except the billionaire who was actually hosting the party. And speculation as to where he was, what he was doing, and who he was doing it with ripped like wildfire in a windstorm through the well-liquored and gossip-hungry crowd.

"No idea where he could have disappeared off to, but I'd bet good money he's not pining away in solitude," said a reed-thin man with salt-and-pepper hair and a furrowed brow that suggested disapproval but was most likely envy.

"I swear I came five times," a perky blonde announced to her best friend in the kind of stage whisper designed to attract attention. "The man's a master in bed."

"He's got a shrewd head for business, that one," said a Wall Street trader, "but no sense of propriety where his cock is concerned."

"Oh, honey, no. He's not relationship material." A brunette celebrating a recently inked modeling contract shivered as if reliving a moment of ecstasy. "He's like fine chocolate. Meant to be savored in very limited quantities. But so damn good when you have it."

"More power to him if he can grab that much pussy." A hipster with beard stubble and a man-bun wiped his wire-rimmed glasses clean with his shirttail. "But why the fuck does he have to be so blatant about it?"

"All of my friends have had him." The petite redhead who

pulled in a six-figure wife bonus smiled slowly, her expression suggesting that she was the cat and he was the delicious cream. "But I'm the only one to enjoy a second helping."

"All your friends?"

"How much pussy?"

"At least half the women here tonight. Maybe more."

"Man, don't even ask that. Just trust me. Dallas Sykes is the King of Fuck. You and me? Mere mortals like us can't even compare."

Three floors above the partygoers, in a room with a window overlooking the Atlantic Ocean, Dallas Sykes sucked hard on the clit of the lithe blonde who sat on his face as she writhed with pre-orgasmic pleasure. The blonde's cries of *yes, yes!* mingled with the throaty moans of delight coming from the curvaceous redhead who straddled his waist while he finger-fucked her hard and deep.

They'd surrendered to him, these women, and the knowledge that they were his tonight—for tenderness, for torment—cut through him. A wicked aphrodisiac with an edge as sharp as steel, and at least as savage.

"Please." The redhead's muscles clenched tight around his fingers, and a tremor ran through his body, his need for release now so potent that it crossed the line into pain. "I'm so close, Dallas. I want you inside me. Now. Oh, god, please. Now."

He could barely understand her words, lost as they were in the wet sounds of his mouth on the blonde's sweet pussy. But he heard enough, and in one wild, rough movement, he rolled the girl above him to the side, so that she stretched and trembled on the bed, her nipples hard and her cunt slick and open and inviting.

Dallas felt his body tighten with need. With desire. But only for release. He didn't want either of these women. Not really. Their company, yes. The escape they offered, sure. But them?

Neither was the woman he craved. Neither was the girl who had both saved and destroyed him. The woman he wanted.

The woman he could never have.

And so instead he sought pleasure and passion in the violent rapture of hard, hot sex.

"Sit back," he said to the blonde as he pushed away his dark thoughts and regrets. "Back against the headboard. Legs spread wide."

She nodded, moving eagerly to obey as he urged the redhead off his waist. "Fuck me," the redhead begged. Her green eyes flashed, her expression pleading. Her lips were swollen, her skin flushed. She smelled of sex, and the scent—so familiar, so dangerous, so goddamned compelling—made him even harder. "I want you to fuck me." Her words were a pout—a plea—and Dallas almost smiled in response.

Almost, but not quite.

Instead he lifted a brow. "Want? Baby, this isn't about what you want. This is about what you need."

"Then I need you to fuck me."

His lips twitched. He liked a woman who knew her own mind, that was for damn sure. And the redhead truly amused him. He'd plucked her from the crowd downstairs because he'd liked the way she'd filled out the flirty black dress that was now crumpled in a heap on his bedroom floor. That, and the fact that he happened to know that she had a cousin who worked for a diplomat in Bogotá, and that connection might prove handy one day.

As for the blonde, Dallas had no particular agenda with her. But he appreciated her limber little body and quiet obedience. Right now, she was sitting exactly as he'd told her, her legs wide apart and wonderfully vulnerable. She wasn't mov-

ing a muscle, but the beat of her pulse in her throat tele-
graphed her excitement at least as much as her tight nipples
and hot, slick cunt.

He met the redhead's flashing green eyes, then nodded
toward the blonde. "You want to get fucked. I want to watch.
And I promise you, she wants to do whatever I say. Sounds
like a perfect recipe, don't you think?"

The redhead dragged her perfectly white teeth over her
lower lip. "I've never—"

"But you will. Tonight." He met her eyes. "For me."

She licked her lips as he slid off the bed and stood. She was
still sitting, her knees pressed into the mattress as she sat
back on her heels. He leaned forward, then took her in with
a long, slow kiss. She tasted of strawberries and innocence.
He wanted to devour the first; he wanted to erase the second.
"Hook your legs around her waist and kiss her deep. Suck
her tits. Touch her however you want to. But she's going to
fuck you with her fingers while you and I both imagine it's
my cock. And baby? You're going to come harder for me than
you've ever come for anyone."

"And you?"

He could hear the tremor of excitement in her voice and
knew he had her. "I'll be right here," he said, as he took her
hand and urged her toward the blonde, who was flushed pink
with anticipation. He moved behind the redhead, cupping her
breasts as she put her legs around the blonde's waist, then he
squeezed her nipples hard as the blonde's fingers slid into her
core.

Pressed against her back, he could feel every tremor of
pleasure, every quickening in her pulse. And as she started to
shake with a series of little convulsions, he slid his hand between her legs from behind, dipping his fingers into her wet
pussy. As he did, his hand brushed up against the blonde's,
whose sensual moan shot straight to his cock.

Next, he slid his now-slick finger up to tease the redhead's ass as she bucked against him, her body clearly on fire from this dual assault. "Dallas," she moaned as her body shook with release. "Oh, god, Dallas, this is so fucked up."

"That's the way I like it, baby," he said. "That's the only way I play."

It was true. He liked his sex dirty. Wild. He wanted to be reminded of who he was. What he'd become.

He was damaged goods. As broken as a man could be. But he'd turned that shit around. Claimed it. Made it his own.

Maybe he would never again have the woman he craved in his arms, but if that was his reality, he was going to damn sure make the most of it.

With his free hand he reached down to stroke his cock. The sensation of his sex-slicked palm moving rhythmically over the steel of his erection mingled with the wild, almost feral sounds of the two women. He closed his eyes, imagining another place. Another woman.

He thought of her. He thought of Jane.

But not like this. Not fucked up. Not like a goddamn evening's entertainment, as fungible as a night at the movies and at least as unimportant.

Except everything was fucked up. Him, most of all.

Goddammit. He needed to shut it down. These thoughts. These wishes.

All these damn regrets.

The sharp trill of his cellphone startled him from his thoughts, and he slid back, away from the redhead, who cried out in protest.

"Sorry, baby." His voice was tense, his chest tight. "That's the one ringtone I always answer." He grabbed his phone off the bedside table, lightly brushing both women's skin before turning his back to them and taking the call.

"Tell me," he demanded, expecting the worst. His best friend, Liam Foster, wasn't due to report in until the next morning. If he was calling now, it meant something had happened. Something bad.

"It's all good, man," Liam said, his voice as close to excited as his military training would allow.

"The child?" Dallas had sent his team to Shanghai to recover the eight-year-old son of a Chinese diplomat, who'd been kidnapped ten days prior.

"Fine," Liam assured him. "Dehydrated. Malnourished. Scared. But he's back with his family, and physically, he should make a full recovery."

Physically. The word turned like a worm in his head. Because that wasn't all of it, was it? Not even close.

He shoved the thoughts aside, forcing himself to focus. "Then why are you—"

"Calling? Because the asshole who grabbed him tried to trade intel for freedom. He knows, Dallas. He knows who the sixth kidnapper was."

The words were simple. Their impact on Dallas wasn't. His blood turned to fire. The room turned hot and red. He wanted to beat the shit out of the sixth man. He wanted to curl up into a ball and cry.

"Not only that," Liam continued, "but the asshole knows where we can find him." His voice broke, just a little, and it was that small reveal of emotion and solidarity that kicked Dallas back into himself. He wasn't fifteen anymore. He wasn't locked in the dark, tortured and hungry and helpless.

He might be damaged goods, but he had money and power and he knew how to wield them together like a goddamn medieval mace.

"Almost twenty years on the hunt, buddy," Liam said, "but we're getting damn close to ending this thing. We get the sixth, take him in. We interrogate him. Get him to tell us who hired him. It's the last puzzle piece, Dallas. We get that, and you can finally say that it's over."

Dallas closed his eyes and drew in a breath, soaking in the words. Liam was wrong, of course. It would never really be over. But he couldn't deny the anticipation that was building in him. The fantasy that he really could end this.

For himself.

For his sanity.

But most of all, for Jane.

PHOTO: KATHY WHITTAKER PHOTOGRAPY

J. KENNER loves wine, dark chocolate, and books. She lives in Texas with her husband and daughters. Visit her online to learn more about her and her other pen names, to get a peek at what she's working on, and to connect through social media.

kenner.com

Facebook.com/JKennerBooks

@juliekenner